BOOKS BY STAN R. MITCHELL

Sold Out (Nick Woods, No. 1)
Mexican Heat (Nick Woods, No. 2)
Afghan Storm (Nick Woods, No.3)
Nigerian Terror (Nick Woods, No.4)

Little Man, and the Dixon County War

Detective Danny Acuff, (Book 1)
Detective Danny Acuff, (Book 2)
Detective Danny Acuff, (Book 3)
Detective Danny Acuff, (Book 4)
Detective Danny Acuff, (Book 5)

Soldier On

Learn more about Stan R. Mitchell and his other works at
http://stanrmitchell.com

NIGERIAN TERROR

Nick Woods, No. 4

STAN R. MITCHELL

This book is a work of fiction. Names, characters, places, and incidents either are the product of the author's imagination or are used fictitiously. Any resemblance to actual events, locales, organizations, or persons living or dead, is entirely coincidental and beyond the intent of the author.

Third Edition

Edited by Danah Mitchell (Story Editor) and Emily Akin
Cover by Danah Mitchell

FOREWORD

I would like to dedicate this book to SGT Daniel Carson, USMC. Carson is one of the most incredible men that I've ever met or had the pleasure of truly getting to know. He personifies everything that a Marine, a man, and a husband and father should be.

Also, in memory of Toby. A warrior like none other.

PROLOGUE

Nick Woods crawled along a dusty, nasty attic. Insulation hung on his clothes, and he felt an overwhelming urge to sneeze. He dragged his rifle along the ground by the sling, keeping it above his arm but low: the classic low-crawl sniper technique.

It had taken five whole weeks of planning to get to this point. It had also taken five weeks of juggling those plans while also training up newly formed squads for his company Shield, Safeguard, and Shelter.

But finally, he was here; here being the attic of a derelict, foreclosed home. It hadn't been officially lived in or inhabited by humans for six years, according to Allen's research. Nick could attest, though, that bums, snakes, and rats had certainly called the place home since its abandonment. The smell of garbage, rot, feces, and dead animals was almost overpowering on the floor below, and the stench was definitely not any better in the attic. Nick refrained from gagging a few times, and he had about the strongest stomach of anyone he knew.

"In position. Setting up," he whispered into a lip mike.

Nick reached his firing point and peered through a hole left by the partial cut-out of two small boards in the side of the home. The six-inch spider hole had been prepared days before during the site prep and was impossible to see from the target's location. Well, maybe if they had a pair of twenty-power binoculars, but otherwise he couldn't be seen.

Nick looked through the hole, but was scarcely able to discern the people one thousand yards away. They were blurry, fuzzy silhouettes, about the size of his pinky. They were so far away that it seemed impossible that he'd be able to hit one. But that was always how he felt when he first focused in on a target.

Nick moved the rifle to his shoulder, inching it into position slower than a particularly frail sloth might move.

Texas Senator Ray Gooden lacked any counter snipers assigned to his protection detail, but Nick didn't want to take any chances. He moved slowly. Very slowly.

Gooden only had two visible Secret Service Agents flanking him, though Nick knew two-to-four additional agents were lurking in the press and multitude of people. There were also ten-to-twelve local police officers on hand, for crowd control.

This all seemed a bit *too* easy, but that's what happens when you gather loads of intel and scout a target for weeks on end.

Nick lined up the scope of his heavy .338 Lapua Magnum, bringing his body and mind into that relaxed, sniper world. Years of training were required to master relaxing to the level he sought.

Nick took a deep breath, telling himself that the range wasn't great at all. The world's longest combat sniper shot had been made with a rifle identical to this one, when British Sniper named Craig Harrison killed a man at 2,700 yards in Afghanistan.

One thousand yards was a piece of cake, Nick told himself. It wasn't, of course, but Nick needed his mind to believe it.

Senator Gooden was droning on behind a podium, speaking about a redevelopment project for this ghetto-like part of Dallas. The abandoned home Nick hid inside was just one of more than three hundred slated for demolition through some kind of federal grant, which the senator had helped acquire. As was his character, Gooden was reveling in the moment, emphasizing and repeating his righteous deeds in the mighty halls of Congress.

Gooden had brought home the bacon and was receiving his just due from local officials and residents, most of whom secretly despised him.

Nick centered his scope on Gooden's chest and relaxed still further. He knew the range, the bullet's trajectory, the elevation of his position, the wind velocity, and the Coriolis effect on his bullet, which determined how much the earth would rotate while the bullet soared through the air.

Nick's formulas had been calculated and double-checked, and he'd been practicing with this same rifle for weeks on a sniper range in Quantico while the scout snipers studied Senator Gooden's habits and protective detail.

Now, Nick just needed to hit his shot.

He began pulling his trigger finger back, staying relaxed and controlling his breathing. The curved trigger inched back microscopically and finally broke, the gun booming in the attic so loud that had Nick not been wearing professional shooting muffs, he'd probably have ruptured his eardrums. The .338 Lapua was a monstrous rifle and he'd never fired one in such a confined space. It was really more of a cannon than a rifle – its bullet nearly twice as large as an M-16 round.

"Hit," Nick heard over the radio. "No second shot needed," the man said.

Nick removed his muffs and felt relief that he hadn't missed. His spotter had been watching the target from an adjacent building, which wasn't typical but was required because of the confines of the attic.

Any hit even close to center mass would guarantee a kill since the bullet was so massive – 300 grains, in fact. To put that in perspective, most M-16 bullets were 55 grains, and they had killed plenty of men. Hell, most deer-hunting rounds were 150 or 180 grains.

Senator Gooden had just eaten a 300 grain bullet. That was almost like shooting a fly with a BB gun. Gooden probably had a double-fisted size hole through his chest.

You don't stop the bleeding on a wound like that. You don't re-inflate a lung that's been ripped in two. Or if the shot had been low, you don't survive half of your intestines and organs being blown out your back.

Nick didn't know where he'd hit – he'd ask about that later – but as long as he hit anywhere from the waist to the shoulders, then the senator was a dead man.

Now it was time for the escape. Nick controlled his actions, trying not to panic at the thought of officers scrambling into an organized search, looking for the man who had just killed the Chairman of the Senate Foreign Relations Committee. One of the top five most important people in America had been gunned down and there'd be hell to pay for the man or woman who killed him.

Nick pushed that thought from his mind and calmly collected his gear, placing his rifle in a hard rifle case and exiting the hot, dusty confines of the attic. He moved with as little panic or haste as he could manage. Even the experienced veteran that he was, he couldn't fully shake what a big deal this was or how likely it was he could be caught in mere moments.

He wore blue mechanic's overalls as cover and exited the house from its rear, opposite where Gooden lay and hundreds of people were darting about.

Sirens roared from all over the city, a swarm of hornets descending to find the perpetrator. Nick quietly packed the rifle case in the back of the white van, along with his other shooting gear, which he carried inside a metal toolbox to complete his cover as a mechanic.

Nick closed the back doors on the non-descript van, walked around to the driver's side door, and waited for his spotter to step into the passenger seat. Once that happened, he slowly drove off toward safety. He avoided speeding, and he kept on his hat, sunglasses, and fake beard in place.

Nick had six vehicle swaps to execute, all of which had been staged for weeks. Getting away wasn't the primary concern. Barring just terrible luck, they would drive away safely.

The larger concern was how effective the disguise and vehicle counter-measures would prove against the investigation that would follow. That was why they had positioned the vehicles in place weeks before. Any agents studying footage would have to be enormously diligent. Plus, with luck, many retailers copied over their footage after a week or ten days.

Ultimately, the FBI could solve the case. They were that good. And if they did, Nick would do the time. This shot, after all, was for Anne. And given the dangerous nature of the now-former Senator, it was for America.

CHAPTER ONE

—Five weeks earlier, Mexico City—

It was nearing six o'clock in the evening when the lock on the front door rattled and Nick Woods's heart skipped a beat. He recovered quickly and reached for a Glock 19 on the end table, slipping it silently under his leg as the door opened. Isabella saw him, smiled, and turned to close the door behind her.

"How you doing, love?" she asked.

"Good," Nick said, placing the Glock back on the end table while her back was turned.

Isabella carried her purse and several file folders, which Nick assumed to be case files. Isabella Cabrera worked as a detective in Mexico City, trying to manage a never-ending line of unsolvable murders. She walked into the living room toward him and bent down. Nick paused the remake of the movie *True Grit* and leaned up to accept her kiss. Their lips touched and a ripple of heat coursed through his body.

Her mind obviously occupied by other things, Isabella pulled back unaffected.

"I'm so screwed," she said, turning and placing the files on a dinner table. "Had three murders assigned to me today."

"They happen while you were off?"

Nick and Isabella had spent two weeks together at a secluded beach resort. Isabella had taken leave from the police department and the days had passed much too quickly.

But now they were back at her large condo and Isabella had returned for her first day back to work.

"I wish they had happened when we were away," she said, a tired sadness in her voice. "No, these happened today. Just another day in Mexico."

Isabella had told him Mexico City's murder rate for last year, but Nick couldn't recall it now. Bottom line: there were more than enough to keep her and the rest of the department's detectives busy.

"I'm really sorry," she said, "but I have to get back to the office in a few. And probably work until at least nine or ten."

Nick knew that really meant more like eleven or twelve, but it was her work ethic and dedication to fixing her country that he admired. Hell, he was wired the same way.

She walked back in the room carrying a handful of uncooked baby carrots. She bit one in half and chewed on it as she plopped down in the couch across from him.

"I'm going to shower, change clothes, and eat a quick dinner before heading back in."

She raised her eyebrows seductively before adding, "Want to wash my back?"

Damn, she was beautiful, Nick thought, so caught up in admiring her that he initially missed the question.

"Uh oh," she said. "Someone's had a rough day."

Nick nodded, knowing there was no point in trying to hide it. Isabella could easily read him or any other man, woman, and child. She was a detective, after all. And a damn good one at that.

Hell, it *had* been a rough day. The hours passed slowly, making the day feel more like a week than a mere nine hours. Nick had tried to distract himself, but with no luck.

"This is where the cowboy rides off again, isn't it?" she asked.

Nick chuckled. Nothing got past her.

He sighed. It didn't make sense. The past two weeks had been wonderful and now suddenly he was feeling restless and miserable. Nick knew he could stay with her the rest of his life if he wanted. But the creeping guilt would never allow it. Guilt that he had survived, when Marcus and seven others had died.

Guilt that he wasn't at his company office, helping the unit rebuild and train. Damn it, Nick even felt guilty that he was simply able-bodied enough to step into the shower with Isabella when so many others couldn't. Men still incapacitated or in rehab for injuries that would affect them the rest of their lives.

The recent mission to Afghanistan had cost Shield, Safeguard, and Shelter mightily. Eight deaths and more than a dozen moderate-to-light injuries, in fact. It would take months to rebuild S3 into a fighting force. On the bright side, at least he had someone back in the States already working on recruitment while he was away.

"Nick," she said.

Nick looked over at her. "Yeah?"

"I lost you there for a minute."

"Sorry," he said. "Just a lot on my mind."

"I can tell."

"I have been bored out of my mind all day. I went for a run, did tons of push-ups and pull-ups, been all over Netflix. Nothing has helped."

"You've been through a lot," she said.

Nick wondered if she was referring to the recent mission to Afghanistan or the showdown in Mexico involving a sword-wielding psychopath. Perhaps, it was more about his days hiding under a different name and running for his life in the United States.

Most likely, she was looking at the collectively unfortunate picture that was Nick Wood's life.

To be honest, Nick had been thankful that, except for today, he'd been able to relax at all. Nick didn't travel for pleasure much and taking it easy wasn't exactly in his wheelhouse. But with the idyllic setting, the sand, the drinks, and the sun, the past two weeks had kept his mind easily distracted. Well, all that and a very healthy dose of Isabella.

But with her return to work, the high he had been

riding had ended. It had come crashing down like a helicopter slamming into a rock cliff.

"I need to head back," Nick said.

She didn't argue. Somehow Nick had known she wouldn't. The two of them were very similar creatures. He knew that she was just as sad to see their time together end, but eventually the cases had begun to call out to her. Mexico had her heart, and her job was her life.

It was an all too familiar feeling for Nick. He could feel the summons of his own responsibilities in his bones, causing him to become restless.

She peered out the window and he tried to read her body language. What was she feeling? Was it sadness? Regret? Or a truth she knew she couldn't defeat?

After a deep settling breath, Isabella finally turned toward him. "Well, I certainly understand, but I will only agree to let you leave with the condition that you get up, right now, and join me in the shower."

There was a bit of sadness in her eyes, though she'd attempted to hide it with a coy smile.

Nick didn't want to linger on that sadness – his or her's – so he stood and eased his way over to her. He grabbed her hands and drew her close.

"I think that's a fine idea," he said.

Nick kissed her lightly and turned to lead the way to the shower. He held her hand every step of the way.

CHAPTER TWO

Nick's philosophy on dealing with emotional pain was to throw yourself into work. Just plain ignore it and work your ass off.

So, while he and Isabella *did* make love in the shower, it had been detached and perfunctory. The type of love one makes before a break-up takes place. Nick felt awkward afterward and left as she finished eating a quick, reheated dinner.

Nick said he had to catch his flight, but there actually wasn't a flight leaving that night for Washington, D.C.

He left Isabella's condo and walked until he found a cab two blocks away. Nick directed the driver to the Hilton Hotel near the airport. Once the cab arrived, he paid the fare and tipped the driver. He entered the hotel, reserved a room, and inquired about upcoming flights. After booking a flight back home, Nick ordered a pizza and tracked down a Mountain Dew from the vending machines.

The latter was a habit he needed to kick, but when you dodge bullets for a living, you tend to tolerate a few bad habits. Especially when you run hard and exercise obsessively every day.

As Nick wolfed down the pepperoni pizza, he flipped on the TV and half-watched CNN. He wasn't sure how, but it occurred to him that he was successfully making it out of Mexico again. The place had nearly cost him his neck on his first trip, when a katana-wielding madman almost got the best of him.

This time it had nearly taken his heart, he thought gloomily, missing Isabella already. Truthfully, he missed her much more than he wanted to admit.

It just wasn't easy to let Isabella go. They had both been there for each other, and under very critical circumstances. Nick, and his unit, had helped her save Mexico from the grips of an evil cartel leader named Hernan Flores. And Isabella, in turn, had helped him as he tried to move beyond the death of his wife Anne.

He had repaid her by staying by her side after she'd been wounded during S3's desperate push into a nasty slum.

It would probably take a few days to shake the nagging weight in his chest. While they had never been anything official or long-term, saying goodbye to Isabella this time felt like the slow and withering death of something that had been very special between the two of them. It felt like something that was just not meant to be, no matter how much both of them wanted it, or even with how much they had been through together.

Heartbreak seemed to loom over any future Nick imagined for Isabella and himself. Either a painful breakup or divorce, or the slow demise of something that had been special.

Nick suddenly found himself overcome with a burst of rage and viciously threw a half-eaten slice of pizza across the room. It slapped the wall, splashed grease, and fell limply to the floor.

Sure, Nick wasn't exactly the suburban, family-man type, but he couldn't help but feel a deep, burning bitterness at having such a chance swiped from him.

He went for another slice of pizza, tearing into it like a starved animal. But the food was flavorless in his mouth as memories of Anne flooded to the surface of his mind. Anne, his loving, beautiful and loyal wife. She had deserved better.

Nick thought about the man responsible for her death and had a nearly uncontrollable urge to crush the slice of pizza in his hand and slam his fist through the wall. But he swallowed it down and buried it for a little longer.

He'd be able to release his anger on that man soon enough. And Nick would be damn careful about ever returning to Mexico, for both his and Isabella's sake.

CHAPTER THREE

Twenty-four hours later, Nick arrived at the company headquarters of Shield, Safeguard, and Shelter. It was late Tuesday night and Nick had spent most of his time trying to shake Isabella from his thoughts.

Nick needed to get his head back in the game. He had a company to rebuild and some unfinished business to attend to.

The headquarters for S3 was located on an old farm up near Quantico, Virginia. After their success in Mexico nearly a year ago, the decision had been made to not only continue S3's contract, but to find it a more permanent home base.

Nick and his CIA babysitter, Mr. Smith, agreed the base should be close to Quantico. However, Mr. Smith argued S3 should be housed in an abandoned warehouse or a rundown office building.

But Nick, ever the paranoid country boy, wasn't having it, bucking and cursing at every suggested address Mr. Smith offered. Eventually, Nick persuaded Mr. Smith to agree to the rural, remote hideout that Nick preferred.

The farm was more than a hundred years old and required some major upgrades, but most of the improvements had been completed and the farm maintained its natural appearance from the road. This was a crucial point for Nick. A big part of the base's defense rested on the fact that no one would ever make it out as a target.

The acquisition of the farm and its immediate improvements began less than a month after S3's showdown with the Godesto Cartel in Neza-Chalco-Itza. In addition to nabbing a home base, Nick also rapidly expanded S3; completely funded by new government contracts, of course.

Nick brought in a former Marine staff sergeant, who had spent much of his career guarding U.S. embassies around the world. The man, Cormac, was installed as the head security man for S3. Cormac oversaw the unit's guard force and was always tightening the group's physical security.

Also brought in by Nick was a logistical expert named Dean, who had been trained by the Army to be an expert in logistics. The man lived for planning and seeking ways to provide everything from food to transport. Not only was he better at it than Nick or Marcus, he also lifted a huge load off their shoulders so they could focus more on tactical planning and individual training of the team members.

Cormac and Dean coordinated to turn the farm into a base most units would be envious of. Though it retained its look as a farm from the road, the entire property had been rigged with perimeter sensors, hidden cameras, and even thermal detection devices.

The only noticeable changes were a couple coats of paint to the old home and the addition of a new iron gate with a brick entryway. S3 also repainted the white horse fence that surrounded the perimeter.

While the outside remained quaint, the inside was converted into a high-tech command center. The interior now sported world-class communication networks, back-up generators, and numerous workstations and security monitors.

Nick smiled as he drove his 1997 red Jeep Grand Cherokee up to the entrance. Damn, he had missed this place. He used an electronic key to open the iron gates and drove up the farm's sole driveway.

Having a couple decades of experience in road construction during the years he spent hiding, Nick traversed the gravel drive slowly. Sticking his head out the window, he thoroughly inspected the gravel path, looking for any flaws.

The decision had been made to keep all the labor in house, avoiding contractors and the eyebrows that might be raised from their peculiar setup. Thus, Dean enlisted the aid of his own team, hauling gravel in their personal trucks and laying out the old road themselves. It wasn't a perfect job in Nick's eyes, but it was passable and certainly the best option for keeping their presence at the farm unknown.

A second gravel path had also been added, extending the main driveway from its ending at the farmhouse. The gravel road now went behind the home and down the backside of the hill, where it couldn't be seen from the main road.

Tucked behind the hill, and invisible from the road, sat two rows of four trailers. Seven of the units were quarters for his shooters, while the remaining trailer served as Nick's personal lodging and private office.

This last trailer was where Nick headed on this late Tuesday night. He drove his Jeep up the gravel road toward the farmhouse and circled behind it, waving at the simple-looking building. Doubtlessly, several of Cormac's guards were watching his entrance through cameras.

Cormac was fanatical about security, so there had probably been even more installed while Nick was in Mexico. But that's why the man had the job. Nick had bigger things to worry about and it helped him stay focused to know Cormac was over-the-top about security measures.

Nick continued down the gravel road between the two rows of identical, white trailers. Originally, this had been a field of grass, but, as instructed, Dean had extended the gravel road and added parking pads for the trailers.

Nick parked by his trailer, unlocked the thin door, which he could have probably punched through, and entered his new home. The place was empty, as he expected. It was after ten o'clock so he didn't expect Red to be on site. The man was with his family, where he should be. Especially since Nick hadn't warned him when he would be arriving.

Nick immediately felt a loneliness come over him. He hated when the farm felt so empty, but things would pick up when the rest of his shooters arrived in the coming days.

After the Afghanistan mission, except for Cormac's security men, the entire unit received three weeks off. Taking his promotion to second-in-command seriously, Red declined the three-week offer, informing Nick that one week was long enough for him. As such, Red returned last week to begin the vital recruiting process.

S3 desperately needed to refill its ranks. Eight dead and a dozen wounded was almost fifty percent of S3's active operators.

The unit had saved Afghanistan and taken down the venerable Taliban leader named Rasool Deraz, but it had paid dearly in its fight. Nick remembered the dozens of Taliban fighters closing and gaining ground on S3, shooting at them from apartment buildings that overlooked the palace.

He shuddered as he recalled the truck bombs racing toward them. Each coming closer and closer before S3 could destroy them.

And the tanks. He'd never forget the tanks arriving. The feeling of hope. The sight of Marcus disappearing in an explosion of fire and smoke.

Get ahold of yourself, he thought. Otherwise, you'll drown yourself in a bottle and wake up at noon tomorrow with Red looking down at you.

Nick shook Afghanistan from his thoughts and walked over to his office. It used to be the living room of his trailer until it was renovated.

He grabbed his cell phone off the top of the desk. He had left it with Red before he departed for Mexico. And once he arrived there, he had purchased a throw-away cell, giving only Red the number.

Nick had been that determined to make sure Mr. Smith didn't bother him. With anything.

Now he needed to get back into work mode. He dreaded how many alerts would be on the phone. How many texts, voicemails, and emails had he missed while he was with Isabella?

He tapped the button on the bottom, powering the phone on. But surprisingly, there were no alerts of any kind. That seemed odd. He laid the phone down and reached for a file folder on the desk. It hadn't been there when he had left.

He flipped it open, finding a note from Red. It read: "Nick, not sure when you're coming back, but on the off-chance you come in some night when I'm not here, let me give you a quick update.

"I've been dealing with all the messages you've been getting. So there won't be a ton of them waiting for you. And in this folder is a list of the top thirty candidates we need to test and evaluate for inclusion into our unit. I've taken the liberty of narrowing down a stack of two hundred, but if you want to see those candidates, as well, they're in our team file cabinet. See you soon. Red."

Nick smiled. Damn if Red wasn't already killing it as his second-in-command.

He hoped Red would continue to handle many of the administrative duties that a first-in-command should technically deal with. As bad as it sounded, Nick had already decided that regardless of how many emails, texts, or voicemails he had waiting on him, he would delete them all. Quickly. Without reading them.

Nick didn't have time for that kind of work. Besides, if it was important, they usually called back. That was his philosophy.

Nick's plan for getting caught up – after deleting all the incoming messages – was to call Mr. Smith, mostly ignore everything the man said, and then get to work on the tasks Nick felt were a priority.

What others needed from him wasn't very high on his list of things to do. In his world, he drove the agenda. The world did not arrange his agenda.

And right now, at the top of his agenda was taking down a son of a bitch by the name of Senator Ray Gooden.

CHAPTER FOUR

Ray Gooden was a battle-scarred Texas Senator and a warrior of the U.S. Senate. The man had served nearly forty years in the Senate, fighting his way up the ranks into a position of seniority and power.

Gooden chaired the Armed Forces Committee, a position he'd held for close to two decades.

From this position, he had coordinated with the CIA to create a top-secret group. It had started with the best of intentions, but soon veered off course.

By the time anyone realized how out of control things were, the group had crossed too many lines to count. Not the least of which was illegally seizing a reporter – Allen Green – and instigating an illegal, unlawful raid by the FBI on Nick Wood's home. At that time, Nick was living under deep cover, using the alias of Bobby Ferguson.

The hastily planned raid had cost Nick everything, including his wife Anne. A barely competent, paper-pushing FBI agent, who had been assigned to watch the rear of the house, had panicked and killed her as she ran from the home.

He had thought she carried a weapon, and later, even tried to plant one on her in order to cover up his mistake. Nick, in turn, killed the agent, using the man's death as a means to draw out his enemies. It wasn't exactly a move that Nick was proud of, but he also couldn't really say that he regretted it either.

The blood hadn't stopped there, of course. Senator Gooden's off-the-books group had hunted and hounded Nick and the reporter, Allen Green, for weeks, as hard as it could. The carnage and body count had been unbelievable.

Eventually, Nick, with the help of Allen, killed the leaders of the top-secret group, a couple of guys named Whitaker and Tank.

Nick believed it was over until a mysterious caller revealed a much higher hand at work. The caller offered Nick and Allen a deal: buzz off and take a ton of money; or accept death from a drone strike and some circling Special Forces troops.

Since then, Nick had been rabid and itching to uncover the identity of the true leader behind the top-secret group. *They* were the ones with blood on their hands.

Mr. Smith hadn't been willing to share the man's identity until Nick was just about to depart with S3 to

Afghanistan.

Senator Gooden had violated more laws than Nick could count and had set in motion the dominoes that led to Anne's death. But even if you accepted that Senator Gooden had good intentions when he created the group, and even if you accepted he wasn't directly responsible for Anne's death, it didn't take a rocket scientist to know he was a dangerous individual who needed to be put down for the good of the country.

Nick barely followed political news, but even he had heard whispers of how dirty and corrupt the Senator from Texas was. Gooden was always under investigation for something. Not to mention he had a serious black mark on his record following the mysterious death of a Democratic opponent.

The opponent had been more than twelve points ahead of Gooden in every poll, with the election just two days away. And that's when the Democratic front runner's plane crashed moments after takeoff. An investigation eventually found faulty wiring, which oddly had not been found in a preflight inspection conducted two hours prior to takeoff.

It was a shadowy death. One of those gray events that happen where no one is charged, but everyone, deep down, knows what really happened.

During that campaign, four major newspapers in Texas (two of them were conservative) had endorsed his Democratic opponent. Even conservatives wanted the vile man out of the Senate. Since then, the number of papers endorsing against him, regardless of the opponent, had continued to rise.

Senator Gooden was hated. By the press. By his opponents. By the majority of the people across the country, including most of the Republican voters in Texas.

And yet Gooden kept getting elected. Everyone knew how dirty he was. He had taken illegal campaign contributions. He had been investigated twice by the Senate Ethics Committee for conflict of interest and corruption allegations.

But, with every opponent since Democratic candidate Bob Kile, who died with his wife, four aides, and two pilots in the fiery crash just outside of Houston, Gooden had easily been re-elected.

Gooden's tactics were as brilliant as they were barbarous. Nude pictures of daughters or wives of rivals leaked to media outlets and bloggers. Strange investigations by the IRS were launched on his opponents. Unexplained endorsements would pop up for Gooden from Democrats who had spoken poorly of him just weeks before.

Gooden was the embodiment of old-school politics, and he believed a little dirt and leverage could win any political battle. To date, he'd been right.

But now, Nick knew Gooden had been the man who created the illegal CIA group, and Nick planned to put a 7.62 mm boat tail bullet right through his brain bucket.

Putting Senator Gooden in the ground for the good of the nation was Nick's number one priority. That was the bottom line.

He glanced at his watch and realized he had spent more than twenty minutes daydreaming over Gooden.

Nick directed his attention back to the file folder prepared by Red. He glanced over some of the potential new operatives S3 could bring on. But as he flipped through the pile, he found he couldn't concentrate past the thoughts of Senator Gooden.

He sighed and stood. He needed a drink. Or three. And probably some sleep.

Luckily for Nick, he didn't have to travel far for that drink. In fact, he was one of the only members of S3 who lived on "base," as he liked to call their farm.

S3 members could live wherever they wanted, as long as they could make it to base within 30 minutes if called in. Many of the single men rented apartments in nearby cities, while other members had families and lived in homes nearby.

But for Nick, work was home. S3 was his life, and he lived in this small trailer at the end of Paradise Row. That was the nickname the members of S3 had decided to call the mini-trailer park hidden on the backside of the hill.

Nick moved to the kitchen. He grabbed a glass, a bottle of Jack Daniels, and headed toward his bedroom. He was in the middle of a great Vince Flynn book, and a little whiskey and fiction would clear his mind up nicely from thinking about the corrupt Senator.

CHAPTER FIVE

Nick was up, showered, and working at his desk by 6 a.m.

It helped that he lived fifty feet from his office. It also helped that he wanted to get to Gooden so badly.

He had just popped open his email when he heard the sound of gravel churning under approaching footsteps. For a brief second, Nick held his breath, expecting, almost begging, to see Marcus walk through his door.

Dwayne Marcus had been Nick's second-in-command at S3, and by the end he had become a dear friend; a brother even.

But when the door to his trailer opened, in walked 5'5" of holy, amber-headed terror. Red stepped in and said, "About damn time you showed up for work."

Nick couldn't contain himself. He was grinning from ear-to-ear.

"How the hell are you, Red?" he said, standing. "I've missed your damn ass."

Red rushed at Nick, almost tackling him as he wrapped his arms around the older man, slapping him hard on the back a good five or six times.

Nick wasn't one for showing his emotions, but Red had always been the opposite. Whether it was anger and a desire to smash someone's face in or an almost giddy excitement and happiness to see a long lost friend, you always knew where Red stood.

It was a refreshing sight to see from a heavily experienced veteran. If the Marine Corps plus seven tours in Iraq or Afghanistan didn't dampen your spirit, then you were a special kind of badass. At least that's how Nick saw it.

"You doing ok?" Red asked, closing the door behind him.

Nick nodded.

"Isabella helped me get my bearings straight. I'm really glad you forced me to visit her."

"It's what you needed," Red said. "It hasn't been exactly easy for any of us. We were all so close to Marcus. But, getting back stateside and seeing the family helped."

Nick pushed down any thoughts of Marcus. He simply couldn't go there right now.

"How's Angel?" he asked, replacing the thought of Marcus with the image of Red's smiling wife. Angel was as real and down-to-earth as a woman could get.

"She's doing great. Wasn't real happy you had me away for so long, but probably ready to get me sent off somewhere again."

"Well, I'm getting the impression that Angel is very practiced in the art of patience," Nick said with a grin. "She did marry you, after all. And it's not like she didn't know what she was getting into as she'd been married to you before."

Just two years ago, the couple had rushed into a divorce only to find out that they were still in love. The two had remarried a few months back.

"What can I say," Red stated with a twinkle of mischief in his eyes as he gestured at himself. "No woman walks away from all of this that easily."

"No, I imagine it takes at least a crowbar to pry a woman from you," Nick replied with a grin of his own. "What are the girls into? How old are they now?"

"Aleena is nine now, and she's into horseback riding and running, if you can believe that. Loves competing in the mile run."

Nick laughed. "Well, she didn't take that from you."

"Hell no, she didn't."

Red's notorious hatred for running and heavy smoking habits assured he wouldn't be winning any races any time soon.

"And, Lilah?" Nick asked.

"Lilah's still big into soccer, and she's really been into 4-H projects lately."

"They still have their rabbits?"

Red chuckled. "Yeah, they love those damn rabbits, and they're multiplying like crazy. And not in the natural way. We just seem to keep adopting more."

Nick smiled, but felt a twinge of envy. Red's wife Angel was beautiful and kind, and the two of them certainly seemed to have the picture-perfect life: a cozy home on a small farm and two darling daughters.

Nick briefly tried to imagine having a family of his own and something other than work to throw himself into. But it was a fuzzy image at best, and something he just couldn't wrap his mind around.

Truthfully, Nick was afraid to open himself up like that again, seeing nothing but the possibility for pain and heartbreak. Losing Anne had nearly ripped his heart out, and watching Marcus disappear in the explosion reminded him of what happens when you develop more than professional relationships with others.

Nick didn't plan on that happening again. He immediately shut down the emotionally-fueled thoughts and self-pity.

"Well," Nick said, "let's get the hell to work. Uncle Sam doesn't pay us to stand around and we have a ton to do."

"You have no idea," Red grunted. "I have so much to update you on that I don't even know where to begin."

"If that's the case," Nick replied, "start anywhere."

CHAPTER SIX

Red walked toward the desk and sat in one of the two chairs in front of it. On the other side of the desk, Nick took a seat as well and pulled out a legal pad and pen.

"Let's begin by going over some of the administrative details that happened while you were in Mexico," Red said.

Nick knew this was mostly smaller stuff that barely merited a moment of his time, but he bit his tongue and decided to concentrate and take a few notes.

Much of what Red would share, Nick knew, was about the public and on-the-books element of Shield, Safeguard, and Shelter. Following the success of S3 in Mexico, it was decided by certain elements of the CIA leadership to keep the group going.

Given that S3 would continue to do off-the-books

work in hostile places under Nick's leadership, there had to be a legitimate part of the company. This would help with prying reporters and potential Congressional questions.

As such, Mr. Smith had hired an older CIA operative he had overseen to serve as the Chief Financial Officer of the public part of S3. The CFO supervised above-board, completely legal security work in foreign countries.

Nick had always struggled to care about the details regarding the public side of the company. That was the CFO's headache.

Yet he tried to listen as Red quickly discussed a couple of bid requests sent to S3 from foreign governments. S3's CFO had submitted bids on the work and won, beating several other military contractors. Nick nodded but didn't bother writing down the financial totals or number of guards required.

"Move it along," Nick said, waving his hand impatiently.

Red glanced down at his notes.

"Here's something. We've had a couple press inquiries that came in about our work in Afghanistan. Apparently, a couple of reporters heard that a security contractor, allegedly S3, helped save and reinstall the Afghan government after it fled in panic."

This got Nick's attention.

"What did you tell them?"

Red glanced up from his notepad and smiled.

"I told them that as a Marine who had probably done a few too many combat deployments, I really wish that had been the case. But the fact was our contractors, as well as myself, were in the southern part of the country – nowhere near the capital when all that fighting took place. And that unfortunately, we spent the entire three months bored out of our mind, training local police and soldiers in the district."

"Nice answer," Nick said.

"Yeah, they totally bought it. Even stated it must have been some other contractor who was operating in the country. They asked if I knew what other companies had been in country at the time, but I told them I had no clue. We had little communication with anyone while we were there."

Red smiled. "And since then," he said, "there hasn't been a peep from them or anyone else. And those recent bid wins by our CFO will help keep our cover strong. To the outside world, we're just another boring military contractor, who gets paid too much to provide security services."

"Did the CFO issue press releases on those recent bid wins?"

"Absolutely," Red said. "And if he keeps winning so many bids, we're going to have more than three-hundred contractors working under him in his division."

"I don't care how many bids he wins," Nick said, "or how many employees he hires. Just as long as it's not something I have to deal with."

To date, it hadn't been. S3's public headquarters where the CFO worked out of was in North Carolina. The company had a two-thousand-acre piece of property in the mountains where the men trained and deployed from. None of this mattered one iota to Nick.

The CFO told any reporter who asked to speak to S3's CEO, listed on the website as Nick Woods, that the former Scout Sniper was a reclusive vet who stayed below the radar and merely trained the men.

"He's not big on having a public presence," the CFO had said many times. "He specifically told me when he hired me that I'd be the public face of the company and the man who handled all the paperwork and administrative details. So, any further questions you have, I'd be more than glad to answer."

The lie had always held and probably always would. You didn't have to have money to get four or five military buddies together and start a military contractor company. That's how so many had started in the first place.

And any reporters who asked would conclude that S3 had skyrocketed in its growth because its owner Nick had been smart enough to bring in professional business assistance in the form of a CFO – something most military contractors resisted.

Nearly every start-up security company preferred the loosely-run style of employment among friends instead of the rigid, professional style necessary for serious growth. S3 appeared and acted as a legitimate company to anyone investigating. The company even went so far as to offer tours to members of the press who were willing to go trekking about the woods of their massive base.

None had taken them up on their offer yet, and the CFO and Mr. Smith felt confident none would in the future either.

"Anything else you need to tell me?" Nick asked. "You know I don't care about what the CFO is doing. That's for him and Mr. Smith to deal with.

"As far as our business goes," Red said, "we just need to screen that list of candidates to refill our ranks."

Nick instantly knew Red had shifted talking about the public part of the company to the off-the-books part of the company that he and Red commanded. He recalled the stack of thirty applicants and realized he didn't want to deal with that now.

"We'll get to those," Nick said, "but Senator Gooden goes down first."

"Roger that," Red said, a smile creeping across his face.

Red wanted to take the dirty, corrupt senator down almost as badly as Nick did.

"Thanks for the updates and taking care of everything while I was gone," Nick said, picking up his encrypted phone. "Let me call our buddy, Mr. Smith. I'm sure he's been waiting to hear from me."

Nick carried the brick-sized, massive phone with him and stepped out of the trailer. Mr. Smith was his CIA contact, and the man behind the formation of S3. But Nick preferred to walk and get some exercise while he dealt with the man. The exercise would keep Nick from exploding while he talked with Mr. Smith, since the man was as ornery and hard to deal with as an ex-wife with a bad attitude.

The phone made all kinds of clicking noises as it encrypted itself and dialed Mr. Smith's secure number. While it worked its magic, Nick eased away from his trailer toward the outer fence of their property.

Nick wore blue jeans, a T-shirt, and work boots, so even if a neighbor or hunter saw him, he fit in with the locals. He strolled along the white, wooden fence, taking his time. It reminded him of walking the fence of his grandfather's farm when he was a boy. He was enjoying the cool morning air when Mr. Smith finally picked up.

"Do you know what time it is?" Mr. Smith asked.

Nick glanced at his watch. It was 0620. Or, 6:20 a.m. for the civilians in the world.

"I don't work banker's hours," Nick said.

"Says the man who's been in Mexico completely out of contact for the past two weeks."

Nick swallowed down his anger and briefly allowed himself to think that Marcus would be proud of him for keeping his mouth shut.

"I'm here now," Nick said. "Do you want to get to work or whine like a little kid because you haven't been getting your way?"

Mr. Smith responded with silence, and Nick knew their conversation would be just like all their other ones: a shitstorm.

CHAPTER SEVEN

The first piece of news from Mr. Smith that upset Nick involved his friend Allen Green.

Mr. Smith wanted to assign Allen Green to S3. Allen was the former reporter at *The New Yorker* who had broken the original story of Nick and his sniper partner, Nolan Flynn. The two had operated in Afghanistan against the Soviets in a series of top-secret missions, back in the '80s before being sold out by an asshole by the name of Whitaker.

It wasn't that Nick disagreed with having Allen assigned to S3. It was more that Nick hated when Mr. Smith made a decision about S3 without consulting him or gaining his consent.

Nearly a year ago, when Mr. Smith had recruited Nick to lead S3 on an ambitious mission into Mexico, the agreement had been that Nick would have full and absolute control. But from the very beginning Mr. Smith had jerked Nick around, imposing changes, issuing new rules, and generally pissing Nick off.

First, Mr. Smith had changed the deal on the unit Nick would take with him to Mexico from a CIA/paramilitary task force to a private military contractor named Shield, Safeguard, and Shelter. This company would be "owned" by Nick.

Next, Mr. Smith pushed up the timetable by several weeks on the unit's deployment to Mexico. Doing so had greatly decreased their time to train and bond as a unit, which had certainly increased the risk of potential failure and high casualties.

Clearly, nothing had changed and Mr. Smith had yet again made a decision without Nick's input. Nick felt like throwing the phone and high-tailing it back to Montana again.

"I don't think I heard you right," Nick said.

"I said," Mr. Smith stated, "that Allen Green has agreed to come onboard with S3."

"Interesting," Nick growled. "And a bit odd because I don't remember us ever discussing him. But I do recall you telling me that I was in charge of S3 and that I have total operational control. Now that you've had your memory jogged on who handles all hiring and firing, what was it you said?"

"I said," Mr. Smith began, all good-humor drained from his voice, "that Allen Green has agreed to come onboard with S3."

"Oh, I heard what you said. But unless we're launching a newspaper as part of our deep cover strategy to hide what we really do, I'm not sure I see the reason."

"Of course you don't, Nick," Mr. Smith said, sounding frustrated. "I think you're a bit out of the loop here. Allen Green is not only aware of our secret organization, but he absolutely has a skill set that I'm not sure you understand."

Nick gritted his teeth, fighting the urge to smash the phone.

"Listen, I like Allen. I even consider the guy to be a close friend. But you'll have to forgive me if I don't exactly understand why you think we need him."

"Think about your last mission," Mr. Smith said. "You had to call Allen to have some crucial stories placed in the news, and you were lucky he was by his phone to answer when he did. If he hadn't been, we wouldn't be having this conversation and you'd be in a body bag."

"I wouldn't have needed him if you and the rest of the so-called leaders in D.C. hadn't turned into gutless pansies. I was improvising out of necessity when I called him."

"That might have been the case," Mr. Smith said, "but look at what happened in Egypt with their revolution. Twitter easily took down Egyptian President Hosni Mubarak in mere months, and this was a man who had fiercely ruled that country for thirty years."

"The internet didn't take him down," Nick said. "Brave, courageous people took him down. Same as it's been in every uprising since the beginning of time. The people stood up together."

"The people had stood up against him dozens of times before," Mr. Smith countered. "They failed each and every time. But this final time, the people had social media at their disposal, and they used it to communicate, sway public opinion, and broadcast their message internationally in the news."

"So, we need a person who knows Tweeter and Face-whatever?" Nick asked. "Shouldn't be hard to find someone who knows that, so I'll hire someone. I'm in charge of hiring and firing, in case it slipped your mind again."

"You don't even have a Twitter or Facebook account," Mr. Smith said, slowing down and over-pronouncing the websites' proper names. "That means even if you hired someone, you wouldn't have a clue on how to properly utilize them. You just don't understand the power of social media. That's why Allen is joining S3. Allen knows how to use social media, and also knows political messaging. As if all that isn't enough, Allen knows dozens of media contacts around the world. He's highly respected and even has insider contacts at the highest levels of our government. He can help protect S3 from above, while also assisting S3 on the ground while overseas."

Nick wanted to argue further, but he honestly couldn't think of any other valid complaints. Mr. Smith, for once, was probably right.

Besides, Nick was truthfully excited about the idea of having Allen along for the ride. He was, as Nick had said, a good friend. Despite how differently he and Allen saw the world, they had been through an ordeal together, living on the run and relying on each other for weeks. Nick just hated Mr. Smith interfering with his command of S3. That's what his objection really boiled down to.

Unfortunately, the conversation got even uglier after the Allen Green topic was resolved.

"When will S3 be operational?" Mr. Smith asked

"How the hell should I know?" Nick replied. "I just got back yesterday, and today's my first full day of work. Most of the shooters are still on leave. They don't return until next week. Three weeks off, remember? Not to mention we haven't recruited our new replacements. So, it's going to take some time."

"Well, as you so eloquently reminded me earlier, you are the leader of S3. You should know," said Mr. Smith, a brief hint of satisfaction in his tone. He rarely got to throw Nick's own words back in his face. "Listen," he continued, shifting back into business mode, "there are hotspots in the world where you guys are needed. Like yesterday. Bottom line, for my briefings and meetings, I have to be able to state when S3 will be up and operational again."

Nick sighed. This was the part of command he hated most. The Catch-22s that they put you in. They wanted an exact date on when a unit was "ready," but if you deployed and the operation was a flop, then they were covered because you had given them a date and confirmation of being fully prepared for operation.

To hell with it.

"Six weeks," he finally growled. "We'll be ready to

deploy in six weeks."

"I'm writing that down, so don't be surprised if you all are wheels up flying somewhere six weeks from now."

Nick glanced down at his watch, noted the date, and felt his heart pick up in pace. Six weeks would be a challenge, but he wanted S3 to remain relevant. As usual, leaders in Washington were all about now, now, now.

"It's been a good talk," Mr. Smith said, trying to wrap it up. "I've got to run."

"We didn't discuss Senator Gooden," Nick interrupted.

There was silence on the other end.

"You didn't think I forgot about him, did you?" Nick asked.

"Of course not, and I'm prepared to discuss him. But, I need to be very clear on this: this is not a sanctioned event. The Director of the CIA is not involved in this. The Deputy Director of the CIA is not involved in this. Neither is the President, the FBI, or any other law enforcement agency. Do you understand what I'm saying?"

"I think so," Nick replied, "but lay it out in clear language that a country boy can understand."

"What I'm saying is that this is on you. No one, and I mean no one, at my level or above is involved in this. Or even aware of it. After you take this shot, assuming you do, every agency in the country will hunt you as hard as they'd hunt a terrorist who had planted a bomb in a school full of children"

"Explain it fully," Nick said. "When I pull the trigger, what happens?"

"When you pull that trigger," Mr. Smith said, "the biggest manhunt in our country begins."

Mr. Smith exhaled loudly.

"Nick, it's been fifty years since we've had a U.S. Senator assassinated. The last one was Robert Kennedy, who was gunned down in 1968."

"And he was shot at close range with a pistol," Nick said. "They immediately knew who killed him."

"Exactly. Frankly, Nick, I have no idea what happens when you pull that trigger. Now granted, Senator Ray Gooden is probably the least popular official in a long time. The media and most of his elected peers aren't going to shed many tears. But his popularity won't affect the FBI. Their best agents will be assigned, and this isn't just the biggest manhunt in decades: it'll be the biggest manhunt since technology took over crime fighting. The FBI will review every camera, every piece of satellite footage, every cellphone tower, you name it. They'll track the shooter's movements back for hours and hours prior to the shooting. Probably even days. They'll find security footage from nearby businesses to discover what vehicles were swapped out, where the person stayed, where they came from, you name it. There will probably be two hundred FBI agents, with assistance from thousands of local law enforcement from around the country."

"I'll have a complete facial reconstruction done," Nick said. "Best makeup you can find. We'll swap vehicles with fake tags. Avoid public areas with cameras. You name it."

"Nick, it may not matter. The FBI will assign its very best agents to the case. They'll be hungry and eager to make a name for themselves. They'll run down every lead they can find, regardless of how big of a dead end it is."

"Why are you telling me all this?" Nick asked.

"You deserve to know. And since the day I told you that Senator Gooden was behind everything, I've been haunted by what could happen."

"Why, Mr. Smith," Nick asked sarcastically, "I didn't realize you cared about me."

"I don't. Not much anyway. But I'm concerned about what happens to S3 if this goes badly. I can't have agents tracking down leads that come back to the group. If you're going to do this, you need to, at a minimum, leave Red out of the operation, as well as most of the unit. As I said before, I need the unit ready to deploy in six weeks, whether you're able to lead it or not."

"We'll plan this perfectly," Nick said. "But let me assure you, Mr. Smith, that Senator Gooden will be meeting his maker soon. The man's a murderer who's trampled the Constitution. He'd be put to death if he could ever be dragged into a courtroom. But since that won't happen, you can rest assured that I'm going to take care of the situation."

"Don't say I didn't warn you," Mr. Smith said, before clicking off the phone.

CHAPTER EIGHT

Nick marched back to the trailer, attempting to take deep breaths and calm down from his conversation with Mr. Smith. But by the time he'd stepped through the door, it was obvious that he'd failed miserably.

"I'm gonna guess that didn't go so well," Red said, his eyebrows arched in curiosity.

Nick simply grunted in response. Then, after settling himself, he quickly informed Red that Allen would be coming on board, that the hit on Senator Gooden wasn't sanctioned, and that they needed to be ready to go wheels-up on a mission in only six weeks.

Red walked over to the kitchen counter and hopped up on it to sit down, hanging his head and grasping the edge of the counter. He'd only been at work thirty minutes and already looked exhausted.

"Damn," he said, his legs hanging, "Is it too early for a drink? Cause that's a lot to take in."

"Yeah, it is," Nick replied. "We need to set up our qualifications test immediately so we can get our candidates selected."

"Agreed," Red said. "Okay. How about a Thursday or Friday test, with them coming to work on Monday when all the regulars return?"

"That should work," Nick said. "And when our scout snipers return on Monday, we begin our surveillance and study of Gooden's habits. We'll locate the public events he'll be at and see if we can make something happen before we leave."

"You know where we're going?"

"No clue," Nick replied. "Either Mr. Smith doesn't know or he knows but isn't sharing until he's sure I'm not locked up in some jail cell."

"Probably the latter," Red replied.

"Probably."

"You better not end up in jail," Red said.

"Why? Would you miss me?"

"No. I just don't want to run S3 or have to deal with Mr. Smith on a daily basis."

"You little asshole," Nick said.

Red grinned, jumped down, and walked toward Nick's desk.

"Let's get this qualification test figured out," he said. "Then I can handle the logistics of planning it and alerting everyone that they need to get on the road and be ready for it."

And just like that, the Energizer Bunny was recharged and marching, Nick thought. It had taken just thirty seconds for Red to process the significance of the challenges they faced, and even less time to come up with a plan of attack. Damn, Red might be one crazy little shit, but he was steadier than Nick would have thought in the leadership department.

Nick felt his heart involuntarily swell with enough pride for two men, briefly thinking of his former second-in-command. Although he was almost a full foot shorter than Marcus, Red would be more than capable of handling the new position.

Nick and Red met the S3 candidates in a public park early Friday morning. It was an 0430 formation, which wasn't fun for anyone. It didn't matter how tough you were, early mornings were a bitch.

Red greeted the applicants, called off names from a roster to confirm everyone was present, and whistled loudly. Nick stepped out of the woods behind them, walked around the formation, and took his place by Red.

Nick didn't say anything, greet anyone, or provide the smallest hint of a warm welcome. He stood tall, arms hanging down and out wider than normal, chest fully pushed out, and eyes sizing up the group skeptically. His hands were balled into fists as he met each and every one of their eyes.

He wondered if any would have the nerve to break

formation and come at him. Most broke away when he met their eyes, but a couple held his stare. Yet even they shifted their weight or paused their breathing.

Nick stepped closer.

"We're here today," he finally said, speaking louder than necessary, "to separate the badasses from the rest of you. We know all of you are talented and tough. We've read your files, and we know you're all warriors of the highest degree. Otherwise, we wouldn't have called you here."

Nick scanned the faces and paced a bit, moving nice and slow. Screw 'em. Make 'em wait. See if anyone gets frustrated and shows it.

They were in a public park, though no one in their right mind was out jogging or walking at 4:30 a.m. Nick and Red had picked the park for the tryouts to avoid exposing the location of S3's headquarters. Even though every single candidate had Secret or Top Secret clearances, along with impeccable records of service with the SEALs, Rangers, Marines, or Pararescue, Nick and Red refused to give away S3's location.

These guys didn't even know what company they were applying for. Mr. Smith had sent word out to a few senior Sergeant Majors that a black-ops team needed to replace a few holes in its ranks. From there, the word had been quietly spread, strictly through word of mouth among the *very* small community of Spec Ops.

Nick continued.

"You guys need to know before you even start

that the unit you are joining is incredibly dangerous. Should you make the selection, the chances of you dying are very high. In our last mission, we lost eight men and suffered more than a dozen moderate-to-light injuries. Of the injured, many of the operatives will not be returning. This is precisely why we have twelve openings that you all are competing for.

"On the mission prior to the last one, we tangled with a hundred-plus fighters and damn near didn't make it out of a miserable slum in that nasty fight. So you need to know before you even try out how dangerous the work is."

Nick rubbed his rough hands together, flexing his arms. He wore jeans and work boots, and he knew his arms and chest stretched the USMC Scout Sniper shirt that he wore. A nearby light pole provided just enough illumination in the darkness for him to make out the men, and he knew they could see him as well. They were probably judging and measuring him as hard as he was judging them.

"I know," he continued, "that each of you has done some pretty dangerous stuff. But let's be clear: your work up to this point has been done with the full support of the U.S. military. I assure you that you will *not* have that on your side when you sign on with us.

"And it's for that reason that we must have the absolute best."

Nick paced a few minutes, slowly walking along the front ranks of the formation. He wanted to let the words sink in well. He walked back to the center of the formation and continued.

"In a perfect world, we'd screen you all for a couple weeks or longer. But it's not a perfect world. We already have our next mission coming down the pike and we're leaving in just five weeks. That's a mere five weeks for you all to get integrated into our squads, so it will be an aggressive training schedule. Let me assure you of that.

"With all this being said, here's how we're going to find the cream of the crop among you. It's pretty damn simple really. We're going to load you guys up on a school bus, haul your asses onto the Marine Base at Quantico, and test you in five different areas.

"Test one," Nick said, lifting his left hand and raising his index finger, "is a two-stage pistol competition, testing you for accuracy in the first phase and assessing your ability to shoot under duress in a timed event in the second phase."

Nick raised a second finger.

"Test two is a rifle evaluation. Same deal. Two stages. Accuracy, then shooting under duress."

Nick continued to raise an additional finger as he ticked off each test.

"Our third test is a thirty-mile ruck hump. There will be eighty pounds in the pack, which may be light for some of you, but thirty miles is no joke. We all know that. And you'll be timed. So, top twelve of you win that event.

"Test four is a land navigation test. That course is a bitch, let me assure you. It's six miles long, through some of the thickest woods in Quantico. At every location where your objective is found, there are three different ammo crates painted white. These boxes will have six digits written on them. Write the one that you believe to be the correct one. And believe me: your azimuth and pace count better be dead on or you *will* pick the wrong box."

Nick grinned.

"And the last test, after you have worked your asses off *all* day, will be a good ole' boxing match well after midnight. We're looking for toughness and grit, and I'm sure some of you are jujitsu nuts or some other MMA shit, but I can't have any of you getting arms dislocated or shoulders yanked out of socket just before we leave the country. So, drop the fancy shit and just bring your balls. We'll put gloves on you, hand you a mouthpiece, and see who's still hungry enough to fight their guts out after an absolutely brutal day."

Nick started to walk off but then turned back with a single finger held up.

"Oh, and I forgot to say. We'll be getting you all the water you can drink, but you won't be eating anything from this point forward."

A couple of groans came from the group, and several men shook their head. Nick knew the feeling. He hated missing meals, but he'd seen many of the biggest and toughest-looking gym rats in the world shut down the minute they weren't getting enough food.

This wasn't CrossFit. Nick needed guys who could push beyond the hunger and exhaustion and keep going.

He wrapped up his speech.

"I'm not going to lie, guys. Your next eighteen

hours or so are going to suck. As bad as they've sucked in some time. But we've got to sort you out, and this is the best we can do on such short notice."

A heavy diesel engine could be heard making its way toward them. A yellow school bus could just be seen, its lights cutting through the morning darkness and mist.

The bus pulled into the parking lot and opened its doors.

"Looks like it's time for the fun to begin," Nick said. "Load up."

CHAPTER NINE

—PRESENT DAY—

After Nick took his shot from the attic and made his getaway, the assassination of Senator Ray Gooden captivated the country. The media and the FBI flooded the area, in hordes not seen in years.

But after the initial shock died down, and the days passed, it soon became clear the media was squawking and jabbering 24/7 about an event that they lacked any new information about.

Time after time, they showed the footage of Gooden getting hit – blurred, of course – and the chaos that followed, but the media and public soon realized nothing new was emerging. Could it be that there was little-to-no progress in the investigation?

Publicly, the FBI offered the confidential requirements of an investigation as their excuse. It assured the country and media that it was making real headway.

Privately though, the FBI was scratching its head in frustration. It had finished the initial sprint that major investigations take on and had entered the slow, deliberate phase of tracking down small, possible leads.

The FBI had nothing. Two hundred agents had scoured, dug, and searched relentlessly across the scene for the big break, and there was nothing. Barely a clue.

A ghost had shot the Senator and slipped away silently, leaving the FBI feeling powerless. Everyone needed and wanted answers, but there were none to be found. And the pressure from the public, media, and even Congress was growing.

Sadly, agents were hoping for the lucky break at this point. The phone call in from someone with a crucial clue that might unveil a great lead that could be investigated and tracked down. So far, that hadn't happened and the world's greatest investigative service was looking like a third-rate police force in some impoverished country.

It hadn't started this way.

The FBI had discovered the sniper hideout quickly, but not a single clue was at the site. And while no site had ever been scoured so hard, there was nothing. No fingerprints. No fabric threads. No shoeprints.

They didn't even have a shell casing, much less a stashed rifle to track the history of.

Fingerprints had been found on the ground floor, but they all led to various homeless residents and vagrants in the Dallas area.

An unreliable witness had seen a Caucasian male drive off in a van from the home after the shooting. The shooter was white, bearded, and in mechanic's overalls.

"Did you not see more?" an agent asked.

"The shot echoed, and I thought it was several blocks over. I was barely paying attention. I just assumed he was a handyman or electrician working on the home. Besides, he wasn't even in any kind of hurry."

They learned the man had carried a hard case into the van, so it was probably the rifle. But the witness had been so disinterested that he hadn't even watched long enough to see the second man enter the van.

Worse, he admitted in a taped interview that he was homeless and drunk at the time. He wouldn't be worth a lick in court, but he did give them a decent starting point.

Using the vagrant's clue regarding the van, the FBI located surveillance footage of the van exiting the neighborhood but lost it several miles away from the shooting site. It had disappeared in heavy traffic in Dallas and agents were studying thousands of pieces of footage from various businesses.

They knew the van had pulled off one of thirty different exits, which they had narrowed it down to thanks to other footage and the time of the shot, but that's all they had for now.

What complicated the search most for the FBI was the slum Senator Gooden had been shot in. Most assassinations happened in crowded, populated cities. But this shooting site was littered with derelict, unoccupied homes. Almost no businesses existed in the area, except for the sparse pawn shop or occasional liquor store. And with so few businesses, they lacked the chance to find video footage of the shooter or his vehicle.

Making it worse, since it was a neighborhood with mostly unoccupied homes, they lost the opportunity to find witnesses. Without witnesses, they had no idea if the shooter had spent days or weeks prepping the site.

They checked area hotels, but had no idea what they were looking for. It was mostly agents staying busy, hoping for that needle-in-a-haystack kind of break. A man loading a rifle case into a van? A man wearing mechanics overalls? Anything.

Because for now, an invisible killer had shot one of the most powerful Senators in the country, and the FBI had nothing.

They had no idea, of course, that Nick, Red, and Allen were the brains behind the plan that had removed Gooden with barely a clue. Between the three of them, they had talked through what allowed the FBI to solve most shootings and assassinations.

Generally speaking, the FBI solved the shootings because of evidence left behind. A gun. A getaway vehicle. A bloodstained piece of clothing.

With this in mind, the three of them had planned from the beginning to ensure not a single shred of evidence remained from the crime. Nick's clothing – every single piece, from the fake beard to the glasses to the work overalls to his socks – had been taken to a safe location and burned. No leaving it in some getaway vehicle as an easy win for the agents pursuing them.

The rifle had been taken to a metal processing plant and melted down to nothing. They accomplished this feat after the night shift ended and only a single man remained at the place. Allen had personally supervised the melting of the rifle, and handed the man $2,000 cash. (He'd been wearing makeup and a wig, of course.)

The man on the night shift was smart enough to know it had been used in a crime, but failed to connect the dots to the assassination. That's partly why they paid so little. The man wouldn't shut up to Allen about an aluminum jon boat he planned to buy for fishing in the river.

"This money will go a long way," the man said, slapping the stack of cash against his palm.

"I'm sure it will," Allen replied. "Just tell your wife, and others, that you earned the money with a few lucky bets."

"That's a good idea," the man chuckled.

He didn't seem the brightest to Allen, so Allen reached in his pocket and handed the man a couple hundred dollar bills.

"Buy your wife a necklace, or she'll be bitching about you buying the boat."

"Hey," the man said, pointing at Allen, "that's a good idea, too!"

Allen confirmed the rifle was melted and walked

a half mile down the road to where his car was parked on the side of the road. They wouldn't be getting his license plate from this man. Or from some video camera that S3 might not have noticed at the plant.

The final part of the plan involved all six cars used in the getaway. Each and every one had been picked up by a different member of S3 within hours of Nick switching them out. Nick, Red, and Allen knew the FBI would eventually find where each had been dropped, so Nick didn't want them around when that happened.

The vehicles, each sporting a stolen license plate, had been driven to a shady scrapyard in South Texas, near the Mexican border, that often crushed cars in the middle of the night for $10,000 cash. The place was owned by a cartel, and there was *no* chance someone from there would be calling the FBI tip line.

But just to be safe, they'd removed the stolen license plates and hauled them to a crammed-full dumpster up in Oklahoma, which was slated to be emptied the next morning.

In each of these actions, every S3 member involved had donned fake beards and worn professional makeup – bigger noses, thicker eyebrows, wider jawlines, you name it. Despite earlier scouting revealing no cameras at any of the sites, no one was taking any chances.

Best of all, none of the S3 members had any idea why they were asked to perform their actions. Nick and Red had told them they were doing a test exercise of working undercover. They were not to be seen and were to report any suspicious people watching or following them.

Each member after the exercise had turned in a long list of possible "tails," during which Nick and Red had kept a straight face and congratulated them on their skill.

The bottom line was this: a week after the shooting, only four people in the world knew who the shooter was. That was Mr. Smith, Nick, Red, and Allen. And the FBI didn't have anything concrete to build their case on. The rifle didn't exist; the clothes didn't exist; all six cars were gone.

The FBI wanted to make headway – desperately wanted to make headway – but there was nothing to investigate. And less than one week after a .338 round tore through the chest of Senator Gooden, there was no case. There were no leads.

And time was up for the FBI because the covert, off-the-books division of Shield, Safeguard, and Shelter was in the air and flying to Nigeria. The African country was being ravished by the terrorist group Boko Haram, and Mr. Smith had made the case to his superiors that S3 could handle the problem. The CIA director had agreed, briefed the President, and earned approval to deploy the unit.

CHAPTER TEN

"Let's take five," Nick said before stepping out of his temporary office in Nigeria. Red, Allen, and the other squad leaders nodded in agreement and stood to stretch from their hour-long meeting.

Nick closed his eyes and took in a deep breath as he entered the courtyard, then opened them slowly with a steady exhale. Nearly 60 men and women of the "off-the-books" side of S3 were still rushing to unpack and prepare for their upcoming mission. The unit had been provided three unused barracks on the edge of a Nigerian Army base, and since their arrival two days ago, they had been moving at double time to get set up.

Cormac and his security team had been working hard to create an effective security barrier around their small base. By Cormac's over-reaching standards, the result was by his estimation: "half-assed." But looking over the work himself, Nick was uncharacteristically impressed. The small base now featured full-perimeter fencing topped with concertina wire, temporary guard posts at the corners, and even sandbagged bunkers at the front gate. Cormac had also brought in concrete vehicle barriers that the Nigerian Army had leased to S3.

Men patrolled the sixteen-foot-high fence, and Nick realized that the overall appearance made the base resemble more of a prison. Nick found himself really liking the effect. Who would have thought prison-chic makes for a great cover?

The Nigerian Army had been insulted that S3 didn't trust their own base security or fortifications, but Nick wasn't in the business of fretting over hurt feelings. He had lives to protect, and he'd already made his assessment of the Nigerian Army: they were pathetic. In fact, they were far worse than anything Mr. Smith had reported in his briefings.

There was a reason the terrorist group, Boko Haram, had been kicking the Nigerian Army's ass since 2002. In fact, the terrorist group controlled 20,000 square miles of land – half the size of the state of Ohio. Sorry. But, Nick wouldn't trust the Nigerian Army to provide security at an elementary school, much less try to provide S3 with adequate protection.

As a matter of fact, Nick didn't trust the Nigerian Army for anything. He had already refused to rely on their air force for air cover or even using their helicopters for transportation. Besides the poor maintenance of their aircraft and lackluster training of their pilots, Nick didn't want to risk the intelligence leak of alerting the Nigerian military on where S3 would be operating and when.

It was no secret that the Boko Haram had sympathizers and informers inside the Nigerian military's ranks, which is partly what gave them such an edge. Nick wouldn't give the terrorist group a similar edge against S3 by allowing for any breaches of security.

He'd operate his team solo and off the radar unless the Nigerian military operated nearby. That wouldn't be a problem from what he could see. Whether it was based out of fear, laziness, or any overall unpreparedness, the Nigerian Army seemed to stick to city limits and wait for Boko Haram to either hit them with suicide bombers or actual assaults with dozens – or even hundreds – of troops rushing in by vehicle, motorcycle, and on foot. These attacks were almost coordinated waves of vehicles and men.

Nick couldn't wait to give Boko Haram a taste of the new guys in town, but first there was still a lot to do. Nick glanced over at S3's logistic officer, Dean, who was inspecting several rows of up-armored Humvees.

For nearly 60 men, Nick needed a minimum of 15 vehicles. But to be safe, he'd ordered Dean to lease 25 of them. After the fiasco in Afghanistan's capital on the last mission, he wouldn't be limited on transport ever again.

Dean hollered at the men working on vehicles, already looking frazzled from the tight deadline they were under. Nick watched a moment, wanting to help, but kept his distance. He didn't like it when Mr. Smith interfered, so he'd be damned if he'd walk over there and hover like some kind of ass with an ego trip.

Nick knew it was easy for a commander to say he needed 25 up-armored Humvees. It was quite another thing to deal with getting machine guns and ammunition for each vehicle, plus checking everything from the engines to the tires to the axles and everything else, to make sure they were ready for the rigors of combat.

Dean's men were fitting some of the Humvees with M2 .50 caliber machine guns, while others were topped with M240s, the best medium machine gun on the market right now. Nick could imagine the logistical nightmares Dean was working through. He knew the man would be getting extra parts, tires, you name it. You didn't want to wait until you needed something to actually get it.

I'm just glad I outsourced all that, Nick thought.

Nick scanned their small base one more time to confirm all looked well. Watching everyone work, he experienced that proud, father-like feeling commanders so often experience.

He smiled, stuffed his hands in his pockets, and observed a while longer. This hellhole in Nigeria was his piece of heaven on earth. He had his mission, he had his command, and the only thing missing, Nick thought, was Marcus.

Don't even go there, he thought. His brief remorse was interrupted when Dean jumped on a Humvee and yelled, "No, it goes like this!"

Nick chuckled and turned to go back in the office. Everyone was doing their job and doing it well. Dean was handling the logistics. Cormac was overseeing the security. Now Nick needed to finish up his job: planning their mission.

CHAPTER ELEVEN

The five squads of S3 filtered into what would serve as the unit's briefing room until the mission in Nigeria ended. With luck, that would only be two or three months from now.

Outside the briefing room, the sound of hammering and power wrenches drifted through a few open windows. While the logistics and security teams continued to do their work, the other remainder of S3 had gathered for intel on their mission's target: Boko Haram.

"Everyone's here," Red said, confirming the headcount as the last man entered the room.

Nick walked in front of a covered map and reached for a pin in one of the corners. Red pulled the pin from the other side and carried the white sheet away. Nick waited while Red tossed the sheet on a chair and walked behind the assembled fighters. Red took a position next to Allen, crossing his arms and leaving Nick with the floor.

Allen smiled with genuine excitement on his face. Nick had been surprised by how much Allen was enjoying working at S3.

The former journalist stood out from the group for two reasons.

First, he was the only man sporting hair that had obvious streaks of gray in it. And as the unit's oldest man at 55, he'd earned the gray hairs.

Second, he stood out because he was wearing khakis and a polo shirt. Everyone else, Nick included, wore Nigerian local camouflage uniforms and black boots to fit in and appear as elements of the Nigerian Army.

This would help protect the knowledge of their presence in the country from Boko Haram, while also reducing the chance of any friendly fire incidents once they were operating out in the field.

Nick had debated with Allen, asking the man to wear a local uniform like the rest of them, but Allen resisted, saying he wanted to stick to the clothes he felt comfortable in.

"Nick, I'm not a soldier. It's not like I'm going to be leaving headquarters and going on missions with you all. Plus, I'll mostly be liasoning with reporters and civilians. My safest cover 'uniform' is civilian clothes."

Nick couldn't really disagree, and he certainly couldn't argue with the results, as Allen was already proving to be a great asset to the unit, despite his lack of a military background.

He had already connected with the most important media contacts in Nigeria, working on building a relationship with them in case S3 needed their help in an emergency. Allen had also called a couple of times to check in with the media watchdog organization he had founded back in the States, but the new chairman and executive director had things running nicely. And with that organization safely operating without his supervision, Allen had thrown himself completely into his work with S3.

He had proved surprisingly effective in helping Nick and Red with their planning. Since Allen didn't have a background in military operations, he had a great advantage: he thought completely outside the box, as only a civilian could.

Red had taken up nicely with Allen, while Nick had instantly reconnected and rebonded, as he had expected he would. Allen remained entirely focused on S3's task, and Nick had to admit it was nice. And for about the hundredth time, Nick cursed the fact that Mr. Smith had been right about adding Allen to S3.

In truth, the shadowy CIA leader had been right about so many other things, as well, but Nick didn't plan on admitting that, since it might give the man a big head.

Nick scanned the eager, expectant faces before him.

"You guys ready to hunt?" he asked.

Nick watched as smiles, both male and female, spread around the room. A few began clapping in anticipation, and a couple of "ooh-rahs" came out.

"Our mission is pretty simple," Nick said. "We're here to break the neck of Boko Haram. The group was founded in 2002 with the goal of creating an Islamic state here. Clearly, they've been successful, and they have the second largest caliphate in the world – right behind ISIS in Syria and Iraq. But their days are about to be numbered, because trouble has rolled into town."

Several people roared with delight. Nick grinned and proceeded to lay out the mission plans.

CHAPTER TWELVE

Dawn broke and a line of armored Humvees spilled out of the Nigerian Army base, carrying S3 members on their first assault against Boko Haram. The Humvees cruised along paved streets of a small city that had so far remained safe from the terrorist organization.

A few residents stopped what they were doing and watched the column stream by. Their faces showed a look of gratitude toward the troops venturing out against the savages of Boko Haram. A few waves were shared by the column and the onlookers as the column made its way north-east toward danger and the bastards who had been terrorizing the country for over a decade.

Two police cruisers led the column with flashing lights, escorting them until they exited the city proper. As the Humvees passed safely out of the city, Nick watched a few of the police escorts waving grimly with looks of pure dread. He could almost feel their expectations of a shot-up column returning soon, driven by ghosts and bearing the weight of many wounded passengers.

It was a look Nick had seen on the faces of many men before. Both policemen and soldiers. Places like Mexico just the year before, and Afghanistan a few months ago. The look was one of something deeper than fear.

The look was defeat.

Nick knew the Nigerian Army had some good units, but most were underpaid, undertrained, and underappreciated.

Half a mile beyond the city outskirts, the column of Humvees moved through a Nigerian Army checkpoint. Twelve sweaty, exhausted-looking soldiers manned a sandbagged road block, fortified with Toyota trucks topped with machine guns on them.

Damn, Nick thought, couldn't they get these men some armored vehicles up here instead of thin-skinned, light trucks? Nick was stunned they didn't have any armored Humvees or tanks of some kind. Hell, the troops were no better equipped than Boko Haram.

These men, too, waved, but with looks of astonishment as the column of massive, armored vehicles weaved and worked its way through concrete vehicle barriers and concertina wire.

Nick and Red were in the lead Humvee, with Nick

in the front passenger seat and Red sitting behind the driver. Red leaned forward and yelled to Nick.

"You know damn well that no military patrols have gone up these roads in weeks. Just look at how they were gawking at us, not to mention how long it took them to figure out how to move all the concertina wire out of the way."

"I'll bet it's been months," Nick replied, "since any unit has come out of that checkpoint. Or any checkpoint period. The generals just lie about patrols and battles half the time."

"Given what they're paid, can you blame them?" Red said.

"Not really," Nick said. "Though I would like to think I would behave differently."

"Terrible leadership spawns terrible troops," Red said.

Sitting behind Nick was a bulldozer of a man who went by the nickname "Truck." Under normal circumstances, "Truck" drove the lead vehicle. He had driven the lead vehicle in Mexico and the lead vehicle in Afghanistan.

Truck was a prior Special Forces man with a neurotic penchant for driving. While it wasn't exactly clear where Truck's automotive impulses came from, his resume certainly revealed a proficiency in the art. After getting himself kicked out of the Army, Truck had worked for a military contractor hauling anything and everything across war-torn lands in vehicles of all shapes and sizes. And even once that job had fallen through, with the "volatile" man being officially blacklisted from further contract work, he'd reverted to driving big rigs as a civilian.

As such, his present moniker seemed to make perfect sense. Still Nick had asked the man about the nickname when he'd first interviewed to join S3. The brawny man had simply replied "I've driven a lot of trucks."

So Truck had most likely earned his name due to his extensive experience and vehicular precision behind the wheel. But, Nick would bet big money that it was Truck's matching rough-and-tumble personality and big 'n broad physique that made the name really stick.

And today had required that Nick and Red spend over an hour convincing the red-faced and rampaging man to consent to taking a backseat on this mission.

S3 was trying something new this time. Instead of having squad members drive and man the machine guns on the Humvees, S3 was using support troops from the logistics and security element to drive and crew the guns. This greatly increased the number of men S3 could field, and there was little point in leaving men behind at their hidden base when most of the unit was out on raids.

In fact, Nick and Red had left just four men back at their mini-base to guard it. Allen had stayed back, as well, waiting by the radio to serve as a liaison to either Mr. Smith or the Nigerian Army, if necessary.

One lesson Nick had learned painfully in Afghanistan was that he would never get surrounded and overwhelmed again by a larger, better-armed force.

Nick had desperately needed additional men while defending the capital in Afghanistan, but his support troops had been stuck at Bagram Airfield and also at a warehouse in the capital city of Kabul.

Though the troops within the capital were close enough, in theory, to provide support, they might as well have been two hundred miles away given how many Taliban fighters they would have had to fight through. Plus, there weren't enough vehicles to get them safely to the fight.

Nick had learned some hard lessons in Afghanistan and he didn't plan on repeating the same mistakes.

One unexpected surprise to bringing along the logistics and security men was that their moral had shot through the roof when they learned they'd be going out on raids. These men were fighters, too. Certainly not the caliber of elite forces, such as were in the five squads S3 fielded, but they all had a military background and were warriors who would gladly drive a vehicle or man a machine gun in a firefight.

Nick had the driver stop the lead vehicle while he scanned ahead with a pair of powerful binoculars. He half-expected a line of Boko Haram to be waiting. Or at least some scouts. But he saw nothing.

"Unbelievable," he said. "There's not a single fighter in sight. Forget driving slow," he told the driver, "let's get this caravan moving."

And with that, the reinforced column of armored Humvees picked up speed and roared toward their target. The real work would begin soon.

CHAPTER THIRTEEN

S3's target on this raid was a mid-level commander. Intercepts of radio transmissions had indicated the Boko Haram commander would be touring the frontline to inspect and rally his fighters for an upcoming attack against them by a large coalition.

The terrorist group was riding a long string of successful victories that spanned more than a decade, but they would soon be facing their greatest threat yet. And it wasn't just S3.

Rather, a coordinated assault had been planned from a coalition of neighboring countries. Forces from the countries of Nigeria, Cameroon, Chad, and Niger had agreed to work in concert to deal with the threat from Boko Haram.

Clearly, Nigeria couldn't handle the foe on its

own, and Boko Haram had committed the strategic mistake of attacking neighboring countries without fully considering the ramifications. Most analysts were already predicting the fall of the ragtag terror group. Even frontline fighters of Boko Haram seemed to sense a sort of doom on the horizon.

Boko Haram's days as a conventional army that held ground and operated as a caliphate, such as the Islamic State, were numbered, unless they somehow managed to score a series of brilliant victories against the coalition. Most likely, the terrorists would be changing to hit-and-run tactics from here on out, instead of trying to protect captured territory against better trained and more heavily armed opponents.

But the coalition was newly formed, and their coordination was still shaky. As a result, they hadn't begun operating yet and would probably have to crawl before they could walk.

S3 was part one of a two-part assistance package the U.S. had promised to the countries to get them on board.

Each country had suffered from Boko Haram and knew the terrorist group needed to be taken down at some point. But none of them wanted to deal with the volatile force or face the possible repercussions that would follow in the form of retaliatory suicide bombings against their civilian population centers.

The United States remained stretched to the max with operational commitments in Afghanistan, Iraq, Syria, and military counter-moves to match Putin's latest threats against NATO and Europe. America lacked the time or resources to pull together a force to take on Boko Haram. Not to mention, Boko Haram didn't get the attention that threats such as ISIS and Russia received.

This mostly resulted to Boko Haram's local reach. They hadn't struck in America or Europe yet. But they still needed to be dealt with.

Thus, the State Department decided to pull together the coalition of African nations and forces to suppress the lesser-known threat before it became another foreign policy shortcoming allowed by the President. Following a marathon session of flights to each country by the State Department, as well as a series of meetings that were incomprehensibly long, the coalition of countries settled on a two-part deal.

Once you removed all the legal language and "whereas's," the deal was pretty simple. For part one, the U.S. would deploy a force of no less than fifty of its elite troops to begin hammering and dismantling Boko Haram through a series of daring raids. The African coalition countries of Nigeria, Cameroon, Chad, and Niger had assumed the U.S. would send the Navy SEALs.

And the U.S. would have if the group had been available, but they were scattered around the globe. Thus, S3 got the call instead.

Besides putting these troops on the ground, the State Department promised that the elite force would have drone support to strategically strike and provide surveillance and intelligence on the terrorist group.

With part two of the agreement, the U.S. would

send each country a strong team of military trainers to help hone their forces, as well as millions in financial aid and military equipment – both of which each country desperately wanted and needed.

None of that affected S3, and Nick didn't care to get into the big-picture stuff. He knew the basics of the deal from a briefing provided by Mr. Smith as well as what he saw in the news, but Nick preferred dealing with what he could see within the next thousand yards. And currently his ability to see a thousand yards was rapidly diminishing.

The column was nearing the Sambisa Forest, which was mostly thick and nearly impenetrable. The forests, along with the Mandara Mountains, were the two major footholds of Boko Haram. Thankfully, the Mandara Mountains were several hours away, so reinforcements from there wouldn't be a concern as long as S3 made the raid fast.

CHAPTER FOURTEEN

Nick could sense the impending action, and a smile crossed his face. He had been seriously looking forward to meeting some of these Boko Haram fellows.

Taking down fanatical bullies was the kind of work he'd gladly do for free.

Boko Haram was one of the most brutal terrorist groups in the world, despite their relatively low-key standing in the American public's eyes. The group did the typical suicide bombings and surprise gunman assaults on civilian populations, but they seemed to have a particular affinity for kidnapping young girls from boarding schools and orphanages. Many of these were ransomed to help fund the group, while others were "married" to the group's fighters.

Nick was of the belief that thirteen-year-old

girls couldn't be "married" against their will, and he couldn't wait to meet up with some of the extremists who believed that was an okay thing to do.

Just months earlier, in fact, the group had abducted nearly three hundred young girls from a school in Nigeria. Three hundred girls, Nick thought, squeezing the stock of his M4. A deep anger stirred in the pit of his stomach. Yeah, he had a particular hatred burning inside of him for this mission.

As Nick saw it, Boko Haram was more despicable than even the Taliban. At least in the Taliban's case, they had some level of religious code that they mostly respected and followed, despite how perverted and backward it seemed.

The convoy of twenty-five armored Humvees entered the first stretch of some moderate forest on the outskirts of the Sambisa Forest. Visibility was as shallow as fifty yards.

"Everyone stay alert," Nick said over the radio.

He didn't need to say it, most likely. The forest was eerie and honestly gave Nick the heebie-jeebies.

Nick's eyes scanned left to right in the lead Humvee, searching for danger. They weren't expecting to make contact in the woods, but he didn't like the way he felt. The hair on the back of his neck was standing up. Nick tried to dismiss it as nerves, since it was his first time back in the saddle since Afghanistan.

Still, one thing was for sure. He trusted his three Scout Sniper teams, and they had reconned the area the day prior and not seen any enemy. The fact no guards were posted along the road broke every military rule in the book, but it made sense. The Nigerian Army hadn't seriously attacked or probed Boko Haram in months, if not years, according to Mr. Smith.

Consequently, S3 had the advantage on this first mission of hitting the amateurs while they had their guard down.

The Humvees pushed deeper into the Sambisa Forest and arrived at their final rally point without incident, just as the Scout Snipers had predicted. Nick cursed the fact that his nerves were rusty, but felt grateful S3 still had the element of surprise.

"Here we go," Nick said into his radio as they hit their final rally point. "Stay alert, ladies and gents."

Up ahead, Nick knew what they would find since he had studied plenty of maps and aerial photos of the small town. The town, or village really, featured a large open area that had been cleared of trees and brush. Villagers had cut and slashed out a home for themselves inside the outer edge of the Sambisa Forest several decades ago.

Somehow, they had scraped out a living, though Nick doubted it was much of one. But perhaps by impoverished African standards, it wasn't that bad.

It must have been an exhaustive effort for the villagers to clear out the massive open area that now stood more than two miles wide. There were about eleven buildings occupying the village center. The structures ranged in size from small homes to two larger ones that had once served as a marketplace and a school.

Unfortunately, all the work the villagers had put

into the town had been for nothing after they were forced to flee it. Boko Haram fighters had threatened and attacked the place several times before the people finally took flight. Now the town was a shot-up, ghetto-like dump occupied by thirty Boko Haram fighters, according to intel and reports from S3's Scout Snipers.

The three Scout Sniper teams currently waited on the north side of the village clearing, while the Humvees approached from the south. The Scout Snipers were there as a simple blocking position in case the targeted commander attempted to escape.

Nick had no idea whether the Boko Haram fighters would stay and fight or turn and flee. The terrorist group had a nasty habit of doing both, sometimes slugging it out and sometimes withdrawing to fight another day. It was just another thing that made Boko Haram dangerous: they fought with complete unpredictability.

There was also the chance that anywhere from ten to a hundred backup fighters would flock to the sounds of the unexpected firefight in the forest to reinforce the group. Sometimes, Boko Haram rushed fighters forward in trucks and on motorcycles, moving troops to the fight at an astonishing speed. They looked and sounded like a pack of rabid dogs when they did this, but their ferocious sprints into battle could be terrifying and cause opposing troops to panic.

Nick certainly didn't expect his men to panic, but he wondered how the fighters in the village would react to the surprise attack.

The good news was he wouldn't have to wait long to find out. Up ahead, sunlight poured through a clearing, and Nick reported over the radio, "It's go time. Get ready."

The column's lead Humvee never slowed down. The driver hammered the gas and the Humvee roared through the edge of the thick forest, emerging in open ground.

"Contact front!" yelled the machine gunner above Nick's head as a fighter dashed toward a home; an AK clearly visible in his hand.

The machine gun roared as a stream of bullets tore up the ground and air around the man, as their vehicle moved closer and closer toward him. The bullets found their target, stitching him up the back of his legs and into his lower back before he hit the ground.

Nick had a huge grin on his face. The grim reaper had arrived in north-east Nigeria and finally some of these Boko Haram bastards would get a taste of the death and destruction they had so venomously spread for more than decade.

CHAPTER FIFTEEN

Boko Haram fighters reacted furiously to the sound of gun fire. Armed men poured out of homes and buildings, grabbing weapons and running toward the threat.

But they were about to get their first taste of action against an organized, well-trained force. In the moments after the lead Humvee's machine gun shattered the early morning's silence, the rest of the column of vehicles burst out of the wooded treeline and plowed forward across open fields that had once been crops.

The fields, merely knee-high weeds now, had been left bare for several years, since the Boko Haram had no interest in raising crops. The Humvees ripped up the dirt with their huge mud lugs, slinging mud and weeds into the air.

A recent rain had drenched the area, but the muddy conditions didn't come close to affecting the performance of the Humvees. The vehicles tore across the open ground hitting nearly thirty miles per hour as they spread out into a line, their machine gunners opening up and engaging targets as Boko Haram fighters burst from homes.

Twenty yards from the line of first houses, the vehicles slid to a stop, and the twenty-four S3 shooters jumped from their vehicles, deploying on foot into a long line facing the village. The driver and gunner for each Humvee maintained their position in the vehicle, ready to provide backup for the individual squads.

Nick took a knee, aiming his M4's red dot sight toward a home straight ahead. He heard movement to his left and right as the Primary Strike Team members adjusted their positions in the line. Nick, like all professional gunfighters, ignored the sounds of the troops around him and kept his eyes and focus on covering the sector directly to his front.

It was a good thing he did so because a man appeared in the shadow of a doorway, the silhouette quickly raising a weapon. Nick snapped his M4 off safe, moved the red dot to center mass, and fired twice. The silhouette dropped, a weapon clattering on concrete inside the house.

None of these village homes had doors as such things were a luxury not found in most poor villages of this part of the world. A few buildings had blankets drawn over the doorways, but most were open.

"We're all set," Red said to Nick's right.

"Let's move!" Nick replied.

The six members of the Primary Strike Team stood and quickly moved toward the home Nick had dropped the man in. They walked in a tactical, heel-to-toe glide, using their weapons to cover the doorway and single open window that faced them.

The Primary Strike Team closed the distance quickly, and no movement was seen in either the door or window. The squad converged and stacked on the wall, the two lead Humvees rolling up behind them to help cover with their M240 machine guns. The gunners had armored turrets with bulletproof glass to help protect them, so it was an intimidating threat to face if you were the enemy.

Shots and yells could be heard at other points in the perimeter, but Nick didn't worry about his other three support squads. He had to focus on his own squad and their objectives.

But as he heard the firing to his left and right from the other squads, he knew this was a one-sided affair. Orchestrated death, if you will. Each of the four squads knew which building to hit, and each had two armored Humvees sporting devastating machine guns to cover and support them.

Nick and Red had assigned which building each squad would hit back at their base, and each squad had rehearsed the assault dozens of times. This wasn't the invasion of Normandy, with its shoddy intel and horrific casualties. This was the new form of warfare mastered by the U.S. military: practically perfect intel, flawless tactics, and experienced vets who'd all been there and done that.

Nick was glad he was on S3's side today – that was for sure. Boko Haram had grown used to massacring innocent victims. This time, the bullies were going to find out what it was like to be on the losing end, bloodied and mauled.

CHAPTER SIXTEEN

The six members of the Primary Strike Team stacked on their target building – the very one Nick had shot a man inside of through the door. Truck was the first man in the stack, followed by Nick and the rest of the team members.

While Truck covered the door, Nick grabbed a flashbang off his gear, stepped around Truck, and heaved the device into the room. The explosion shook the room, and Truck and Nick charged into it, relying on its bright blast and concussive roar to give them an edge.

Inside the door, Truck turned left and Nick went right. Nick focused on his sector, but saw nothing in his corner. Not even a chair or piece of furniture. Just a dirt-floored room, which had likely been impoverished and dilapidated even before Boko Haram spent years neglecting it.

As Nick turned to cover the rest of the room along with Truck, the remainder of the Primary Strike Team rushed through the entrance room toward the two openings of the next rooms. Preacher and Red took the next room on the left, while Lana and Bennet took the room on the right.

Preacher had been with S3 since before they deployed to Mexico. Having been raised by missionary parents, Preacher had grown into a man with a strong moral compass and faith. The prior Marine, who felt "called" to join the Corps, turned out to be a quiet yet crucial cog in S3's machine. Even with several combat tours under his belt, Preacher had managed to maintain his internal fortitude and served as a calming presence in the harshest of storms. He was the consummate voice of reason and a patient peacemaker in high-tension situations, especially between team members. And thankfully, he was also massive enough to motivate a status of tranquility into even the most bullish of their crew.

Lana was a brunette badass that S3 had picked up prior to deploying to Afghanistan. She was a Harvard graduate, who'd been born in Saudi Arabia, and was an expert of Muslim culture and languages. But she was more than a bookworm and genius. She'd also spent years and years working as an undercover CIA operative. Originally, Nick wasn't even sure how much real-world trigger time the woman actually had, since it was all classified. Mr. Smith had inquired discreetly and learned it was enormous. And that her courage was out of this world. Perhaps only exceeded by her hatred of men who she felt had perverted her Islamic religion.

Bennet was one of S3's newest acquisitions, selected in the tryouts just weeks ago. He was a six-foot tall, skinny guy who could run all day, and who had done nearly five years in the Army's Delta Force after serving several years as a Ranger. So far, the man had mostly kept to himself, and Nick secretly hoped the low-key manner was simply Bennet's nature, as S3 had already met its quota on big personalities.

Both rooms were cleared without problem, and the Primary Strike Team quickly confirmed the remainder of the house was empty. The enemy had apparently fled the home after Nick dropped the one fighter who'd appeared in the door. It was time to hit the next one.

CHAPTER SEVENTEEN

While the four assault squads cleared homes in the village with the support of their armored Humvees, the six Scout Snipers watched the action from the opposite side, scanning through their binoculars and scopes for the commander they were trying to nab alive. Capturing the mid-level commander was crucial. Without him, this op would prove a waste of time.

S3 had very little intelligence on Boko Haram, which meant the CIA had very little. Sadly, the Nigerian Army had even less.

You can't win a war without intelligence on the enemy. Where they are. What they're doing. What their goals are.

Nick, Red, Mr. Smith, and Allen had decided that they needed to nab someone in the command element of Boko Haram to peer into the details of the terrorist organization for, frankly, the first time. If S3 failed to capture the commander on this village raid – or mistakenly killed him instead of taking him alive – they were back to square one.

The snipers were spread out in a U-shaped formation, each team divided into the classical two-man team of sniper and spotter. The village had the same barren fields with knee-high weeds at its rear as it had on the other side.

Each sniper team had selected positions that allowed them to see beyond the several hundred yards of weeds and brush to where the homes were. Donned in ghillie suits, none of them had been discovered yet, and they waited at roughly nine o'clock, twelve o'clock, and three o'clock around the backside of the village.

The sniper teams listened to the progress of the battle through their radios, but so far the enemy was attempting to fight and hold its ground. Shouts, shots, and explosions reached the snipers in the treeline, but they couldn't see the battle yet. Nonetheless, it was creeping closer and closer.

Moments later, after eight of the eleven structures had been cleared and secured, the enemy made their move. The Boko Haram fighters broke, deciding to fight another day.

Instantly, targets appeared for the sniper teams. A Boko Haram fighter ran from cover, glancing behind him in fear and firing a final burst over his shoulder toward the S3 assault squads. A shot cracked from a sniper in the treeline. The fighter fell hard, crumpling and twisting into a pained position.

This was the case with each running soldier, and the sniper teams dropped them as easily as a toddler swiping down a stack of blocks. None of the shots exceeded three hundred yards and each sniper was accustomed to shooting eight hundred to a thousand.

It was a shooting gallery, and the snipers were firing at men who had already snapped. The surprise and shock that a force waited behind them sent sheer terror through them. None had encountered troops this well trained. None had lost a battle so decisively.

The remaining Boko Haram fighters dropped to the ground in horror. Some threw their hands up in desperate surrender.

But there was one who didn't. Suddenly, a man wearing a red beret bolted from behind a building and sprinted toward a parked truck. The snipers recognized that this was the commander they had been watching and studying, but they also knew they couldn't kill him.

As he raced toward a white Toyota truck, a sniper fired toward the driver's side window. The commander reached for the door when the glass exploded into thousands of shards.

He flinched, but yanked the door open anyway.

"Stop that truck," a spotter said with urgency across the radio. The man wanted to ensure all the sniper teams had noticed their primary target. With such small fields of vision in sniper scopes, it *was* possible that not every team had noticed him.

The other sniper teams rotated onto the target and fired into its engine block as a first course of action. The truck's engine screamed and groaned as the Boko Haram leader attempted to start it, but three more rounds slammed into it, rendering it dead for good. It wouldn't even turn over now, as fluids and oil drained to the ground. Smoke rose from the shattered heap, and the snipers laughed as the commander slapped the steering wheel in frustration.

They couldn't hear his torrent of curse words, but they could easily guess what he was thinking. He sat there defeated, knowing that if he ran he might be gunned down like the dead fighters around him.

It took another ten minutes for the four squads of S3 to finish clearing the village and approach the cornered commander, but they had their target. Nick and the gang had struck their first blow against Boko Haram, capturing the mid-level commander and eight other fighters in the process.

S3 could now begin dissecting and breaking apart Boko Haram, one piece at a time.

CHAPTER EIGHTEEN

While S3 was striking its first blow against their enemy, one of Boko Haram's own legendary fighters was leading an operation more than two hundred miles away. An insanely ferocious militant, who had earned the title of Colonel Owan, inched forward along the ground, slithering forward to the edge of some brush.

A Nigerian Army outpost lay five hundred yards ahead, and Colonel Owan studied it through a pair of binoculars. Two men were visible at the small, one-room guardhouse. They sat on metal chairs, smoking and talking.

They looked bored, and why shouldn't they be? Boko Haram had never been within a hundred miles of this village. The guards were so at ease that they had their weapons leaning against the white guard shack behind them. In front of them, two cheap sawhorses and a single strand of circular concertina wire blocked the dirt road into the village.

This was all that stood in the way.

Owan snickered and lowered the glasses. He had come to expect this kind of behavior from the Nigerian Army. The great defenders of Nigeria's territory were drastically underpaid, woefully unprepared, and usually ordered to defend substandard defensive positions that were poorly equipped.

These two soldiers would probably run at the first shots fired, but Owan couldn't allow them to get away. His goal was to do more than merely make these men flee.

Behind these first two soldiers were thirty more, who were assigned with defending the small, hapless village that Owan intended to raid. If Owan's men didn't hit the checkpoint perfectly, then the raid into the village could easily turn into a failure. Thirty well-armed men could hold off Owan's 150 fighters if they took up defensive positions inside the village's homes and fought hard.

Fighting in urban environments was some of the hardest fighting to do anywhere, even if you were a well-trained army. On the other hand, if these soldiers inside the town were caught by complete surprise and shocked into paralysis, then they'd stand no chance.

Bottom line: it was crucial that Owan's men hit both the checkpoint and village with fast and overwhelming force.

Owan raised the binoculars and inspected the men at the checkpoint one more time. His confidence reassured that the plan would work, and he slowly lifted a hand-held radio toward his mouth. The guards weren't paying attention, but sudden movements could be picked up in anyone's peripheral vision, so he kept his movement to a minimum.

"Sappers, move forward," he whispered in a low voice.

The Nigerian Army had cleared out the brush and trees around the guard shack a couple of years ago, removing any cover the enemy could use to advance surreptitiously behind. That's what any competent army in the world would do. But after an initial burst of diligence and enthusiasm, the soldiers assigned to the post had now allowed grass and weeds to grow higher and higher.

Complacency – that terrible affliction that strikes so many armies who are placed in the defense for months on end with no action – was about to cost these men their lives. Boko Haram fighters hadn't been anywhere near this area for longer than anyone could remember, and with each passing day and week, they had lowered their guard completely.

Colonel Owan noticed one of his men across the road, creeping forward slowly through the grass and weeds. The man stopped crawling and eased an RPG up to his shoulder.

Owan glanced back at the guards, but they were still oblivious. Still sitting. Still laughing and talking in the metal folding chairs. One of them had leaned his chair back against the guard shack. Except for sleeping or abandoning their post, they literally couldn't have been less alert.

"Everyone, be ready," Owan said into the radio.

A convoy of trucks and motorcycles waited around a bend a half-mile back. Owan had led the convoy last night from Boko Haram territory to their current location, using nothing but back trails that cut through woods and unpopulated areas. Several times they had come across people or small, thatch homesites that had cropped up, but an advance scout had always seen the danger first. And though the entire column would have to turn around and backtrack to find an alternate route. Secrecy mattered more than anything, and it was crucial no one in the area know Boko Haram had arrived.

Commanders from rear vehicles checked in with Owan, confirming that they were indeed ready for the assault.

Owan whispered into his radio, "Remember, my friends, we must achieve absolute shock or the Nigerian Army troops inside the village won't flee and they might fight us hard. Let's do this right so that all of us survive and are celebrating tonight. Duru, take your shot when you're ready."

Owan pocketed the radio, confirmed it was securely snapped in, and clinched his AK tightly. This feeling he had right now, his heart pounding so hard he could feel it, was what made all the deprivations worth it. What was hunger, lack of sleep, or fatigue compared to this? Feeling so alive and in command easily surpassed any drug Owan had ever used.

He glanced over to his sapper team, most of whom he couldn't see since they were camouflaged so well. However, he could see the RPG gunner, watching as the man made a slight correction in his aim. Duru pulled the trigger and fired the rocket.

CHAPTER NINETEEN

The RPG hurtled toward the shack, exploding and shattering the peace of the town. The aim had been true and the guard shack exploded, throwing up chunks of wood and metal into a ball of fire and smoke.

Colonel Owan dropped the binoculars and shouted, "Go! Go! Go!" into his radio. Additional sappers, lying hidden alongside the RPG gunner, jumped to their feet and sprinted toward the remains of the guard shack. One of the Nigerian soldiers had survived and lay rolling on the ground holding his arm. Had his weapon not been stacked against the wall, and in his hands instead, he might have resisted. But the weapon had disappeared with the explosion, and he was defenseless.

A Boko Haram fighter stepped over him and fired

an automatic burst into the guard from his AK.

Two others from the sapper team ran over to the circular strand of concertina wire blocking the road. Using thick gloves, they pulled it taut and cut it in the middle with a pair of heavy bolt cutters. Colonel Owan had carefully planned this attack, and they had arrived fully prepared for what faced them.

Each of the sappers grabbed one side of the sawhorse and hauled the obstacle out of the road. Even though the two men had rushed, they cleared the road with only seconds to spare. Trucks and motorcycles roared forward from around the bend, already achieving more than fifty miles per hour. The two sappers barely had time to drop the concertina wire and sling both sawhorses out of the way before the 150 fighters raced by in a cloud of dust and noise.

The rear vehicle, an empty truck, slowed to allow Colonel Owan and the sappers to jump in its bed. The village, named Laha Tesi, was too far down the road for them to run to it.

By the time the last truck with Colonel Owan arrived in the village, it was mostly over.

Boko Haram fighters had flooded into the village like a violent tidal wave, and what few Nigerian Army soldiers who had weapons near them were gunned down in a fusillade from a half-dozen or dozen fighters. They were badly outnumbered and completely surprised.

None of the Nigerian soldiers made it into homes or decent fighting positions.

Most of them shucked their uniform tops and ran

for their lives, trying to blend in with the villagers. They hadn't even bothered looking for their weapons. They knew from all the stories they had heard that being caught with an AK or a camouflage uniform was a dead giveaway that you were a soldier, and the Boko Haram didn't take prisoners. Better to flee unarmed and pretend you were a mere villager who just happened to wear camo pants on the wrong day.

The soldiers weren't the only ones fleeing. So, too, were the villagers. A very small number stayed, but that course of action was even riskier than running.

Boko Haram fighters pursued those who fled on foot from their trucks, easily catching up to the majority of them. The smart villagers ran into the woods, avoiding roads that the trucks could use. A few actually escaped. Sadly, even most of those who ran for the woods were rounded up by fleet-footed, angry fighters.

While the final villagers were gathered up and brought together in the village square, Colonel Owan supervised the scene, standing in the bed of the truck. The elevated position gave him a great vantage point, while also making him an easy target.

This was no accident. He knew great leaders had to show more courage than their soldiers under them, and his men would notice his lack of fear and double down on their own courage.

Once the final shots had ended and the yelling mostly ceased, Owan jumped down from the truck bed, joining his sappers, who were now surrounding him and acting as his bodyguards in case any Nigerian Army fighters had been missed in the hasty search.

Around Owan, Boko Haram fighters tore through the homes of the village. Some of the huts were wood thatch, while others had a few concrete walls for additional stability. Most of the abodes weren't big enough to offer adequate hiding places, and Owan's men continued to yank men and women out of their homes who had attempted to conceal themselves.

A few kids got kicked, and a few men were shot or stabbed if they showed even the hint of resistance. Owan oversaw all of this and said nothing, for it needed to be done. The villagers needed to be subdued, and the children needed to learn to not interfere with adults. Besides, they'd heal. And those who survived this ordeal needed to talk. To describe the terror of the Boko Haram fighters.

The talk of their legendary fighting ability was what weakened the will of the Nigerian people and the bravery of the Nigerian soldiers. Both needed to be sapped.

Owan walked away from the huts, his attention focused on a long concrete hall up ahead. Only Christian-funded ministries, mostly funded from America, could afford such an extravagant expense as this much concrete in such a poor village. His sources had told him it was one of the few Christian schools still operating in the area.

An American man stepped out of the empty hole that served as a door for the Christian school. He was gray-headed and bearded, probably in his sixties, with a pair of round glasses on his face. He put both hands on either side of the door to block the entrance from Owan and his sappers, though he was clearly unarmed and no threat to anyone.

"Please do not take the children," the man said, pleading.

A wooden cross hung from a yarn necklace and reached far down the man's chest. Almost to his stomach. The cross was the symbol so many of the unbelievers known as Christians wore, Owan knew.

The massive, muscled leader never hesitated. He lifted his AK and fired three rounds through the man's chest, attempting to hit the ridiculous wooden cross. A nun, he assumed, screamed from inside and ran toward him. To do what, he had no idea.

She had no weapons and was harmless, but wore the same ridiculous cross around her neck, as well. He nearly couldn't help but shoot her, but somehow managed to control himself and sidestep her charge. With little effort, he knocked her to the ground with the buttstock of his weapon. She was maybe forty, and though an infidel, his men could derive some pleasure from her. He felt confident of that.

Owan managed to not kick or shoot her where she lay, though he wanted to more than anything else in the world. He swallowed down the disgust and stepped past her as his fighters yanked her up and dragged her out of the school by the hair, her screams bringing a smile to Owan's face.

Inside the long hall, more than fifty young boys and girls sat. Many cried. Some looked shocked.

All knew their fate.

The boys would be re-educated into the truth faith: the way of Islam. The girls would be re-educated, as well, and quickly married to loyal Boko Haram fighters who had been patiently waiting for the comfort of a "woman." Well, some of them were a bit young to be called women, but in due time. In due time.

The only shortcoming about this village as a target for his forces was that it lacked a small bank that could be robbed as part of the raid.

Colonel Owan motioned for the young students to come toward him. He and his fighters would need to leave the area soon. Sticking around in a village this far away from Boko Haram lines was a good way to get killed, as the Nigerian Army would be responding soon.

Owan wanted to avoid dying in an unnecessary fight, because unlike most of his men and even his leaders, he was not a believer. Not even a Muslim. Owan was just a man who enjoyed wielding aggression and a gun.

And thankfully, he happened to be skilled with both.

CHAPTER TWENTY

S3 had barely returned to base and begun cleaning weapons when news arrived of Boko Haram's raid on the village of Laha Tesi. Truck, Lana, Preacher, and Bennet, all members of the Primary Strike Team, had just turned over the mid-level commander to the Nigerian Army for interrogation.

The Primary Strike Team now cleaned their weapons outside the barracks with the rest of the squads. The day was sunny, but not too hot. Just one of those days you'd rather be outside than inside, so the squads scrubbed and wiped down their weapons in the warm, radiant light.

Nick was walking among the troops when his encrypted phone buzzed. He stepped away from the group and listened to Mr. Smith's information about the attack. Mr. Smith's source for information was a highly connected brigadier general in the Nigerian Army, and Nick briefly wondered if the intelligence was legally shared and part of the general's job. Or if Mr. Smith had deposited about thirty thousand dollars from the CIA's slush fund into the man's account for some info on the side.

"Let's go after them," Nick pressed. "It makes me sick they've nabbed more kids."

"They're a couple hundred miles away," Mr. Smith argued. "And we don't even know where they are now. The fighters hit Laha Tesi from out of nowhere and fled the area."

Nick spit on the ground, his stomach in knots. He stood outside his office, watching his men and women break down their weapons for cleaning. His troops, oblivious to the seriousness of his phone call from Mr. Smith, were joking and horseplaying in that post-mission glee that hits a vet when they realize they've survived yet another rendezvous with death.

"If we were to spot the retreating force by drone," Mr. Smith said, "then maybe S3 can get approval to pursue. And assuming we even receive approval, we'd still need to figure out how to get you down there quickly and, more importantly, locate the enemy column."

Nick didn't need any more approval than that. He lowered the phone.

"Red!" he yelled back toward his office. "Bring me a map!"

Lifting the phone again, Nick said, "Let me look the situation over and get back to you. I want to at least try to make this happen. No way am I letting them get away with more kids, especially those girls, if I can help it."

With that, Nick hung up the phone before Mr. Smith could form a reply. It was a habit Nick felt pretty sure the man was used to by now.

In truth though, the abducted boys wouldn't be a whole lot better off. They'd be fed hatred and used as soldiers, best case. Or possibly suicide bombers.

Nick desperately wanted to make this mission happen. Regardless of the cost. The thought of losing more kids to Boko Haram sickened him to the point that he just couldn't let it go. These assholes needed to be taught that violating such innocence would be met with swift and painful retribution.

The next hour and a half was a maddening streak of hectic running around and planning for Nick and S3's leadership, the kind that seems to only happen when lives are at stake.

First, Nick called a squad-leaders' meeting immediately after pinpointing the village of Laha Tesi on the map. He informed the squad leaders of the raid by Boko Haram and instructed them to have all their men and women re-issued full allocations of ammo.

Nick assigned Dean, who handled logistics, to coordinate with the Nigerian Army to see what kind of transportation S3 could get. Dean returned twenty minutes later with an interpreter who explained the Nigerian Army only had two Huey helicopters they could spare. Worse, the Nigerian Army planned *not* to respond to the attack.

"We think it could be a trap," the skinny man relayed, looking down as he spoke the words.

Nick wanted to punch a wall in frustration. What was it with third-world armies, anyway? But there was no point in arguing with him. They were worried and scared, and Nick supposed America's armed forces would be, too, if they had been losing to a group for ten-plus years, ceding territory the entire time; mile-by-mile, village-by-village.

Nick swallowed down his protestations and desires to try to sway the man and instead thanked him for their support on the Hueys. Allen went further than Nick, informing the man diplomatically that caution was probably the most prudent course of action.

Nick didn't have time for diplomacy. He turned and studied the map some more with Dean and Red. Hueys could fly 140 miles per hour at top speed, but each one would only be able to ferry six to eight men at a time, depending on how much gear each member carried.

Hueys could only lift so much weight, and these Nigerian Army Hueys probably hadn't been updated with twin engines and more powerful blades, making it harder to estimate speed and flight time. All the team members in S3 had experience with updated Hueys, or newer model helicopters such as Black Hawks, Super Stallions, or Chinooks, so they had to scramble to dig up research on the older models.

Nick used the map and a protractor to calculate the distance of Laha Tesi from their base.

"Looks like it'll take an hour to get there," Nick said.

"Damn," Red muttered. "That means if it's an hour there, it'll take the two helicopters an hour to fly back here and *another* hour to return."

"Two hours on the ground, with only twelve or sixteen guys to duke it out with a hundred and fifty Boko Haram fighters," Allen said, having walked into the office to help with the planning.

"Might even be worse," Nick added. "That raiding party will probably have reached Boko Haram territory before we even get there. And there's no telling how many fighters, plus the 150 who attacked the village, there might be nearby and ready to respond."

Nick wanted to go after these guys worse than anything in the world, but even Red, who was deeply conflicted by the decision and never scared of anything, vetoed trying to pursue them.

In fact, for the entire time they had been discussing possible actions, the typically feisty and loud man was surprisingly silent. His face was set in a harrowed frown and appeared devoid of color. This behavior made sense to Nick considering Red's cherished role as the father of two young girls.

"We can't do this, Nick," he said, shaking his head in disgust. "It's just a great way to get a lot of good people killed."

Allen spoke up again, his tone soft and steady in a clear attempt to help re-center his despondent companions. "We nabbed one of their leaders today. We need to concentrate on our game plan here, continuing to systematically destroy them. One piece at a time."

Nick knew Allen was right. And he seriously respected Red's acceptance of his new leadership role and the realities of such a position, especially in the face of a personally impactful situation. The reckless point man who barely valued his life had grown up right before his eyes. Nick appreciated that kind of tactical realism, as it helped balance his own natural aggression.

But he thought of the boys and girls in that column, and he raged inside. He turned and kicked the side of a metal file cabinet, denting it to the point that no one would be opening the bottom two drawers any time soon. He shoved the cabinet against the wall for good measure before storming off.

"Damn it!" he yelled as he slammed the door behind him and stomped off down the hall.

The boys and girls were in unimaginable danger, and there was nothing he or S3 could do about it in the short term.

Several minutes later, after Nick had tramped off his anger outside the office, he called in the squad leaders for a quick meeting. He informed them about the impossible logistical situation of flying two squads per trip and the need to cancel plans of going after the Boko Haram force.

None of the squad leaders took it well.

"Go brief your squads and tell them we'll get our payback soon enough," Nick said.

Nick asked Red to pull the Primary Strike Team together, and again, Nick relayed that the mission was called off because of the logistical impossibilities. The reaction was immediate.

Lana was bristling with rage. She had stood up and begun pacing furiously, clenching her fists and muttering what Nick assumed were curse words in one of the many languages she was fluent in. As a young girl in Saudi Arabia, Lana had witnessed a slew of abuse associated with Islamic extremism, especially against women and children. Her mother had whisked her away to the United States when her underground suffragette movement was uncovered by Lana's father.

Truck hadn't taken the news much better. He had sat hunched over as he listened, staring at his knuckles which were stark white from being balled up so tightly. Eventually, the big man had stood up and walked stoically from the room without a word. Once out of the room, a barely muffled roar pierced through the door, startling several of those in the room. Nick included.

Bennet and Preacher were both still and silent as usual. Only Preacher had bowed his head, presumably praying for the captured children. Bennet stared ahead at Nick, a look of something cold and dangerous in his eyes.

"I'm sorry, guys," Nick said. "It pisses me off, too. But we need to return our focus on what we can control. We nabbed a man today who will be a crucial linchpin in our effort to tear Boko Haram apart."

A few men nodded, but Nick could still feel the anger radiating in the room. Lana, her strong lean-muscled arms showing below a T-shirt, looked ready to rebel and go after the group on her own.

"Let's get back to cleaning weapons, then get showered up," he said. "We'll have to wait for another opportunity to nail those bastards."

CHAPTER TWENTY-ONE

The next three days were maddening for Nick. Each day felt like a lifetime as he and his men waited while the mid-level, Boko Haram commander was debriefed and interrogated.

Nick fumed, stomped, and cussed, knowing he was being even more ornery than usual. But in the end, there was little S3 could do. Nick had no idea if the commander was being tortured or treated like a king by the Nigerian Army while he was being interrogated, and frankly, he didn't care. All he knew was a bunch of young boys and girls were in the hands of sadistic madmen, and he and his men were sitting around on their duffs waiting for information on when and where they could strike.

Actually, it wasn't accurate to say they were sitting on their duffs. Nick and Red had pushed the squads through brutal training drills. They exercised hard to maintain their insane fitness levels. They shot until the barrels of their weapons were hot and brass covered the ground.

But none of that weakened Boko Haram, and Nick continued taking his frustrations out on the troops. Red and Allen helped keep him in check, as well as Preacher and Truck on one occasion, but only barely. It was so bad that a couple of members in the three supporting squads nearly quit after Nick lit into them, which led to him ordering them to take their asses home. He didn't want them anyway.

Red and Allen helped mediate the situation, cooling both sides down. Privately, the two men agreed that the loss of Marcus had Nick pushing the troops harder than ever.

"He thinks if he pushes them hard enough, we won't lose any more," Red said. "But he knows deep down that's not true."

"And it's all this waiting, feeling helpless and out of control," Allen said.

Not all was for naught though. During the three dark days of frustration, the massive coalition of countries had managed to kick off their military offensives against Boko Haram. Advised by U.S. commanders and with the help of excellent aerial reconnaissance by numerous drones and satellite imagery, the countries of Nigeria, Cameroon, Chad, and Niger immediately started making a serious dent in Boko Haram.

On the one hand, this made Nick's day. He read

the after-action reports on how many Boko Haram were being killed with relish. But on the other hand, he was pissed S3 was sitting behind a fence on base doing nothing. Or out on yet another firing range, shooting the rifling out of their barrels.

"Why the hell did they even send us down here if the coalition was about to kick off its massive offensive?" Nick asked Red and Allen, while all three sat in their office, formulating yet another original training scenario.

"Hell if I know," Red replied, running a huge Ka-Bar knife down a partial 2x4 he had found discarded by Dean or some of his men on the base. A good-sized pile of shavings lay on the ground beneath him.

Allen lowered a week-old copy of *The Economist* and said, "As embarrassing as this sounds, I'll bet the CIA hadn't coordinated with the State Department on the timing of this offensive."

"Typical," Nick scoffed, easing his chair down and taking his feet off the desk. He stood and rubbed his eyes. If they didn't conduct a real mission soon, he was going to go howling mad. "One hand not talking to the other."

"In fairness to our bosses at the CIA," Red said, "who would have ever anticipated the State Department doing such a great job pulling together a coalition like this?"

Nick grunted, knowing Allen was about to lecture Red for the next ten minutes on topics such as the state of the country's current foreign policy, how upcoming elections were playing a role on current decisions, and who the hell knew what else. Nick hated politics and everything about it, so he grabbed his M-14 and said, “I’m going to go walk the lines” before Allen could get started.

Maybe, just maybe, he thought, he’d see something out there worth shooting.

CHAPTER TWENTY-TWO

Things turned for the better for S3 on the fourth day. Apparently, the Boko Haram commander had finally started talking. And he had dropped some incredible pieces of intel on his captors.

"We got a break," Mr. Smith said, through their encrypted phone. "A big one."

Red and Allen were sitting by Nick, listening in to the call through a speaker system that Allen had set up.

"We need a break," Nick replied. "This sitting around is for the birds."

"We've got a big one," Mr. Smith said again, too excited to realize he was repeating himself. "Actually, you could say we have three big ones."

Nick could almost hear the man smiling, and while Mr. Smith drove him crazy for a number of reasons, Nick had always at least appreciated that while the man sat at a desk in a town full of nothing but backstabbing cowards, he was still a hunter at heart in his own way. Just the kind that probably took wet wipes on camping trips.

"We're listening," Red encouraged, an eager smile on his face.

"First, we've learned that one of the reasons the Nigerian Army has made almost no headway against Boko Haram is because Boko Haram has nearly perfect intelligence. The Nigerian Army can't make a single move without Boko Haram knowing."

"Tell me you know the source of the leak," Allen interrupted, recognizing the importance of leaks and the motivations that created them better than anyone. He'd spent thirty years exploiting and printing such things.

"We do," Mr. Smith replied. "He's a powerful general who recently retired, but retains incredible connections within the Nigerian Army. These current officers are men he trained and mentored, who look up to him and regularly seek his advice. They simply have no idea he's passing along this information to their sworn enemy."

"What kind of piece of shit passes on information that literally gets his men killed?" Red growled.

"A man who has an expensive taste in women, travel, and costly toys like cars, mansions, and beach homes," Mr. Smith said. "The worst thing is that this general is a legend in the Nigerian Army and is still retained as a consultant and advisor by the government. You can't underestimate this man's power and influence. He could literally lead a coup against the president here with very few problems."

"Where's he at?" Nick asked impatiently. "We'll start planning immediately."

"He's not our problem," Mr. Smith said. "He's being picked up as we speak. The Nigerian Army is raiding his downtown condo and likely already have him in custody."

"Good," Nick replied. "What's the next piece of news?"

"We finally know the leadership structure of Boko Haram."

All four of them knew the former leadership structure by memory, having reviewed the files about the group at least twenty or thirty times. The initial leader and founder, Mohammed Yusuf, had been taken out in 2009 by the Nigerian Army. His second-in-command, a man by the name of Abubakar Shekau, assumed command but was allegedly killed that same year. However, it was more complicated than that.

Shekau regularly used body doubles as a security measure, and soon, the new leader popped up "alive" again on a video. Since that time, he had been killed a couple of other times by Nigerian forces, yet more videos featuring Shekau were released.

But it was all for show. Further investigations revealed differences in appearances, skin tone, and mannerisms of "Shekau," and the second-in-command had long been considered dead by analysts. But to Boko Haram, he was an important figure used in propaganda and fundraising videos published throughout the world, and the Nigerian Army threatened to kill any man who impersonated Abubakar Shekau.

Bottom line, if S3 and the Nigerian Army now had the true leadership structure of Boko Haram – something no one had known since Shekau's initial assassination in 2009 – then it would indeed be a huge advantage.

"We've learned," Mr. Smith said, continuing, "that Abubakar Shekau is dead, as we all suspected. The body doubles of Shekau are nothing but a recruiting tool for Boko Haram. Especially for fundraising purposes on the net."

"Yeah, he remains a popular figure worldwide," Allen added in confirmation.

Nick knew Allen had read reams and boxes worth of information about Boko Haram before they departed the States. Nick figured Allen comprehended more about the group than most of the CIA's analysts at this point. The long-time reporter and foreign policy junkie was simply a research machine, always reading, marking up books and intelligence reports, and calling experts in the field for more information.

"Shekau may be popular worldwide, but the true leader now is a man by the name of Colonel Owan."

"Damn it," Red blurted, laughing in disbelief. "How many colonels and generals are working for Boko Haram? Does the Army not have enough spots for all the officers they promote?"

S3 had already noted that, like America's military,

there sure seemed to be a lot of high-ranking officers in the Nigerian Army, and damn few true trigger pullers.

"This one isn't necessarily official," Mr. Smith explained. "He's basically just a criminal, however he's a damn dangerous one. One with incredible street smarts."

Nick yanked a pad of paper out of his back pocket and lifted his pen to take some notes on the guy. Nick realized, with slight irritation, that both Allen and Red already had their paper and pen out and ready.

Nick listened to papers shuffling over the phone's speaker, as Mr. Smith pulled up a report on the true leader of Boko Haram.

"Colonel Owan killed his first man as a young boy," Mr. Smith said. "Murdered his own father, who was known to be an abuser, a drunk, and a Grade-A dirtbag. His father apparently put his hands on Owan's mother one time too many. Little boy Owan, merely eleven at the time, snuck up behind him and swung a machete deep into his father's quad."

"He hit him in the leg?" Red asked, confused.

"The mother and father were scuffling and he was afraid he'd hit his mother's hands or arms, which were wrapped around the father," Mr. Smith elaborated. "So he swung hard for the upper leg – used both hands, too – and hit the man with everything he had. The blade cut deep, all the way to the bone. The father somehow avoided falling, turned, and attempted to defend himself while trying to staunch the bleeding, according to an interview with the mom from a detective investigating the case."

"Damn," Allen said. "And he didn't stop?"

"Nope," Mr. Smith said. "Little Owan kept going. The defensive wounds on his father were brutal. Owan hacked off some fingers, cut his forearms down to the bone, and diced him up nicely until the father, in full retreat, tripped over some furniture and fell."

Mr. Smith paused to allow Nick, Red, or Allen the opportunity to speak, but none said a word.

"Owan's mother tried to stop him at that point, reaching for the machete on one of Owan's back swings. But Owan turned and screamed at her to get back. She confessed in her court testimony after the event that he was so enraged that it was almost as though he didn't recognize it was his mother behind him, and she worried he might hack her up, too."

"That boy," Nick said, looking up from his notepad, "had some pent-up rage."

"Well, you can guess the rest," Mr. Smith said. "Owan hacks his dad up while the man is lying defenseless on the ground. His body was almost unrecognizable."

"Yeah, that's definitely some pent-up rage," Red said, his eyes wide.

"So much for a warning or second chance," Allen added.

"Easy," Nick said to Allen. "Let's not go crazy with the liberal, New York values. Who knows what all the dad had been doing to the mother and son."

"I'm guessing there *were* no winners here," Red said.

"They tried him as an adult," Mr. Smith said, getting everyone back on topic, "and punished him with thirty years in prison."

"Thirty years in prison for an abused eleven-year-old?" Nick blurted out.

"That's right. And that's thirty years in a Nigerian prison. Remember, they make American prisons look like summer camp."

"He finally get parole?"

"No way," Mr. Smith said. "Owan killed more than two dozen men while behind bars in the past thirty years. Most of them up close and personal, with either a rudimentary shank or his bare hands. He's a hulk. Six foot, four inches. Two hundred pounds of muscle and mental instability. They barely feed them in prison and don't provide inmates with weights. I assume he's figured out every form of push up and pull up that you can imagine."

"So how'd he get out?" Allen asked.

"This is where it gets good," Mr. Smith replied. "He was so dangerous that they moved him to the northern part of Nigeria."

"To the Muslim part of the country?" Nick said.

"Yes," Mr. Smith confirmed.

In all of their research, it had come to be understood that Nigeria was divided between the southern part, mostly Christian and rich, and the northern part, which was mostly Muslim and poor. Complicating matters, the southern part was fertile and wet, while the northern part was arid and partly desert. Both religion and income disparity had led to the rise of radical Islam and eventually to formation of the misguided and brutal Boko Haram.

"So he converted to Islam then?" Red asked.

"Well, he at least went through the motions," Mr. Smith said. "But there's always been serious questions about his convictions. And we know this because of intercepts in which he laughs at the religion privately with former crime-pals. The times he's been called out on his fake beliefs, his inquisitors have either wound up dead or were never seen again. But I'm getting ahead of myself."

"So why go through all the effort of pretending to believe?" Allen inquired. "And how'd he get out of prison and somehow end up commanding Boko Haram?"

Allen's reporter tendencies to ask lots of questions were popping back up, Nick thought.

"Owan was all about running whichever prison he was in," Mr. Smith said. "Had pretty much run every single one he was ever placed in, except for when he was younger. And even then, he learned from the best enforcers on how it should be done."

"Sounds like this guy has a PhD in thuggery," Red said. "Thirty years of it."

"Absolutely," Mr. Smith said. "He's mastered leading, fear, and intimidation. But up in the northern part of Nigeria, Islam dominates the prisons, and people lean on the religion for some kind of hope or sense of purpose. Colonel Owan had to convert to Islam if he ever wanted to climb up the criminal hierarchy in the prisons up north where you all are."

"So how did he get out again?" Allen asked, repeating his unanswered question.

"Easy. Boko Haram broke him out in that infamous mass prison break of theirs in 2010. Matter of fact, he's the one who convinced them to do it, through some of their former members who were true believers but facing life in prison. Bottom line, the man's persuasive, smart, and violent as hell."

"And," Nick said, "he's running the world's second largest terrorist organization and completely behind the scenes."

"Impressive, honestly," Allen noted.

Nick couldn't argue with that.

CHAPTER TWENTY-THREE

"You still didn't say how Owan got his title," Nick said. "How's a low-life criminal, who's never served a day in the military, and who fakes being a Muslim, ever earn the title of colonel?"

"He got the title just like any other criminal would!" Mr. Smith said, laughing. "He lied about it."

"So what's the story with that exactly?" Allen asked. "This has to be good."

"It's a little fuzzy in the beginning. I'm just regurgitating what the Nigerian Army has come up with based on the recent interrogation of the commander you apprehended and a quick personality profile pulled together after talking with the prison wardens in charge during Owan's stay. But we think the 'colonel' title started when he was in his early twenties."

Mr. Smith paused, gulping a few times, and they

heard the crackle of a plastic water bottle.

"Owan was transferred to a new prison after amassing too much power at the one he was at. And remember, this was when he was just twenty-four, which tells you something about his talent of ascending to the highest rings of power in prison. Anyway, Owan had been threatening a riot or discussing privately an attempt to abduct some guards and stage a mass breakout. The prison warden wisely decided to transfer him. The very day before he had planned to act."

"You threaten a riot or hurting officers," Nick said, "and they'll transfer you every time."

Mr. Smith ignored Nick's comments and continued, "Owan knew when he arrived at a brand-new prison, without a single ally or friend, that he'd possibly be seen as a threat by their current prison boss, so he stayed to himself, which is standard practice for new inmates. But Owan took it a step further to help protect himself, claiming he'd been a former sergeant in the Nigerian Army's elite 72nd Special Forces Battalion. This cover story, along with Owan's impressive size and demeanor, helped convince some of the heavy hitters to leave him alone in the beginning."

"Let me guess," Allen interrupted. "He gathered some allies, starting a rival group. Or, he joined the primary group, slowing working his way up the ranks until he could topple its leader."

"Precisely," Mr. Smith said. "He did this act over and over, according to the various wardens, in each and every prison that he was transferred to. But as he got older, his cover story went from him being a 'sergeant' to a 'lieutenant' to a 'captain.' He was obviously smart enough to know that no one in their thirties was only a sergeant in the 72nd Special Forces Battalion."

"Until he was finally telling these dopes he'd been a colonel thrown in prison," Red offered.

"Exactly," Mr. Smith said. "And with that kind of rank, he could drop the bullshit about the 72nd Special Forces Battalion. The prisoners respected him purely on the fact he was a colonel, and they presumed he had money on the outside, as well as incredible connections. The funny thing is that Boko Haram literally thought they were breaking out a colonel with command staff experience, who could assist them with their planning of attacks across the country, as well as with their overall military strategy. Remember, at one point they controlled more than twenty thousand miles of territory, so Boko Haram faced complicated logistical problems of moving men and supplies over incredible distances."

"Well, he must have done a hell of a job acting like a colonel since he's still in charge," Nick said.

"He's done well," Mr. Smith said. "What he doesn't know in military tactics, he makes up for in street smarts. He hits weak targets, catching them by surprise. He avoids clashes where his forces are at a disadvantage. Basic guerilla tactics. Plus, he leads from the front and is clearly half-crazy. His troops worship him, completely convinced of his claims to being a prior colonel."

"Where do we find this guy?" Nick asked. "I'd like to meet him."

Allen interrupted Nick, pointing to the phone. "He hasn't told us what the third big thing they've found out about Boko Haram from the mid-level commander."

"Correct, Allen," Mr. Smith said. "I'm glad to see you're *already* the brains of the operation."

"Make your point," Nick growled. "It's hot here, and this damned office isn't air conditioned."

It was 92 degrees, which was quite a shock from the late winter weather they'd left back in the States. Matter of fact, it had been 40 degrees in Quantico before they departed.

"The third piece of information," Mr. Smith said, "is we found out who Boko Haram's financier is within Nigeria. This is a crucial piece of information for dismantling the group, but it doesn't affect S3. The Nigerian government, either their police or army, will go after him after they nab the general."

"Seems stupid to wait," Nick said. "What if he runs?"

"They claim he's nothing but a banker and won't run, even if he were to get advance notice. He's more the kind of guy who'd fight the charge with a high-priced attorney. They're more than confident he'll be easy to pick up once they've grabbed this general that's been leaking out illegal information."

"For an army that's had their ass handed to them by a terrorist group the past decade, not to mention lost complete control of territory the size of West Virginia, they sure are confident," Nick said.

That elicited some chuckles, but what could they do? They were invited guests in a host country that had apparently gone from needing their help to suddenly not wanting it, now that the coalition of forces had begun their offensives.

As Nick cut off the call with Mr. Smith, he told himself they'd better be getting some real trigger time soon or he was packing up his toys and going back to their farm outside Quantico.

CHAPTER TWENTY-FOUR

A mere three hours later, Nick, Red, and Allen were back on the phone with Mr. Smith. But this wasn't a planned phone call.

Nick knew when the man on phone-watch duty came to get him that this wasn't good news. Once Allen and Red arrived, Nick announced into the speaker. "We're all here now."

"As you guessed, Nick," Mr. Smith said, "this is bad that I'm having to call you back so soon."

"If it means," Red said, "that we're finally going to get off base and see some action, then I'm not entirely sure it can be all that bad."

"Yeah," Mr. Smith said. "I know it's been a slow few days for you guys, but things aren't just heating up. They're blowing up. The Nigerian Army raided the general's condo as planned, but he wasn't there."

"They didn't even confirm he was inside before hitting the place?" Nick asked. "Don't they have any snipers or men working undercover?"

"They thought it'd be easy," Mr. Smith said, weariness in his voice. "Plus, they wanted to move fast and avoid tipping off the general. And apparently there were lights on and a manikin inside that they mistakenly thought was the general. A platoon of elite soldiers hit that house in full combat gear – these were some of Nigeria's best men – and not only was it empty, it had been packed with explosives."

"Son of a bitch," Nick said.

"Yeah," Mr. Smith sighed. "They called in the detail about the manikin just before the place went down in rubble. Thirty good men died almost instantly."

"And the general is now on the run," Red added.

"As well as in the know that he's wanted," Allen said with concern.

"Guess this thing isn't going to be over by the end of the week after all," Nick said. "Where's the general now?"

"Nobody knows, but clearly he still has first-rate intel of the army's moves. And we at the CIA and Department of Defense are pretty doubtful they can root out his moles and capture him anytime soon. But if they determine his location, they've already said they'll use S3. They definitely plan to limit the number of Nigerian officers involved in future ops against the general."

"Did they nab the financier yet?" Nick asked.

"No. That's the other thing I'm calling about. They're afraid to raid his home. Afraid it's rigged with explosives, too."

"You've got to be shitting me," Nick said. "Where'd all that confidence go?"

"They lost a lot of men," Mr. Smith said. "And they're still digging them out of the rubble. This general really was one of their best. Now, he knows he's been found out and is in their head. Remember, he trained and mentored most of the current crop of generals. He was also consulting for them up until today. He's really, really good. I probably should have said earlier, but didn't think it would matter, but this general actually trained at the U.S. Army War College in Pennsylvania. He's the real deal."

"What do they need?" Nick asked, sounding more tired than he wished. But damn it, he was sick and tired of America training and teaching folks who ended up turning their guns against the U.S. and its allies.

"They're wondering," Mr. Smith said, "if S3 will handle the raid on the financier's house."

"They're not too keen on sending their own men into another home possibly filled with explosives?" Red asked.

"That's why they pay us so well," Nick said. "I'm good with it. Red?" he asked, looking over at his second-in-command.

"If we can't take down a banker, then we're in the wrong line of work," the short prior Marine said.

CHAPTER TWENTY-FIVE

Nick checked his watch, noticed it read 0300, and whispered into a mic, "Let's go."

He slipped out of a gray Volvo along with three other members of his Primary Strike Team. Two others emerged from a red Mazda truck across the street. But nobody bothered to shut their vehicle doors for fear of the noise it might make. They gently pushed the doors against the frame, but stopped short of latching them closed.

The six members of the Primary Strike Team had ditched their Nigerian Army uniforms for undercover attire. Jeans, hoodies, and sneakers served as the "uniform" of the day for this mission.

The six members, pistols drawn, lightly snuck up six steps to the front door of the financier's ground-floor condo in the capital city of Abuja. Abuja, located in the middle of Nigeria, was closing in on a population of one million and was far more upscale and high class than Nick would have ever guessed. It put quite a few capital cities in the southern states of America to shame, which helped change his prior perception of Nigeria for good. Whoever said world travel broadened the mind might have been right, Nick begrudgingly admitted.

At the top of the steps, Red covered the front door with a Smith & Wesson M&P40 pistol, while Nick waited just behind him with his own 9mm Glock 19 pointed at the ground. Truck moved up with a battering ram and looked to Nick for the signal.

Nick nodded, and Truck swung the 30-pound battering ram with all his might. The heavy device nailed the door just above the handle and made a thunderous crash. But the door was well constructed and expensive. It didn't give. Truck swung the battering ram again, even harder.

This time, it knocked the door wide open, and Truck pivoted out of the way as Red and Nick burst into the condo, high-beam flashlights held alongside their pistols.

The lights cut through the blackened house as the Primary Strike Team cleared the condo room-by-room, staying in pairs and working together.

The teams zipped in and out of rooms quickly, moving as fast as they could since they did not have approval from the local police for the raid. Matter of fact, they hadn't even alerted the police. There was too great a chance that informing the local police might unearth another mole who might warn the financier, the same way that an army mole had warned the colonel.

And none of the Primary Strike Team were excited to be entering a condo possibly rigged with explosives, so they'd take their chances with pissing off the police.

They'd probably avoid any interactions with the police, Nick figured, unless some officer just happened to be patrolling nearby. Nick had started a stopwatch count on his watch and he glanced down to see that they had spent less than thirty seconds in the house so far. He assumed for a moment that either its occupant or a neighbor had called the police upon hearing their loud entry with the battering ram. That would mean they had less than two minutes to get out of there.

However, none of them had made a sound since the breach, so perhaps a half-alert, half-asleep neighbor might have assumed a dog knocked over a trash can. Then after hearing no further sound, the theoretical neighbor might have decided to just go back to sleep.

Their biggest concern was with the financier himself. As it would be his condo they were invading, he'd probably still be making the call to the police. But he might have been torn on what to do. With the sounds of people moving through his home, he might have been reaching for a gun instead of calling cops who'd be at least three to five minutes away.

Nick and Red cleared a second room together,

and Nick knew they would have the entire condo cleared in probably sixty more seconds. That meant they'd probably be safe from cops, which was a huge relief.

And that was when he and Red heard movement on the other side of a closed door just ahead. The sound caught the two of them by surprise and they split, stacking on both sides of the door.

The door opened just as they doused their flashlights to hide their position. But Nick realized in the temporary darkness that other lights were swinging back and forth in the house from Preacher and Bennet in one team, as well as Truck and Lana in another.

The person in the doorway, most likely the financier, extended a pistol and rushed to his left toward the nearest light behind Nick. The man moved quickly, heading toward Nick.

Nick was behind the wall and hadn't been seen yet. Without a second to waste, Nick knew he didn't have time to pocket the pistol or flashlight. And he certainly couldn't shoot the person since it was probably the financier, who they desperately needed alive.

Nick chucked the flashlight and pistol behind him, where it thankfully landed on carpet and made only the lightest of sounds. Then, Nick lunged for the opponent's weapon, which he could just barely distinguish in the pitch black room. On the bright side, his hands responded perfectly to the target he lunged at and wrapped nicely around the man's wrists, just where Nick wanted to grab. On the down side, he knew the moment his hands closed around the opponent's wrists that this was not the financier.

This was not some soft banker or lawyer. This was a trained man who was ready for a fight.

Nicely done, Nick. Now where's that pistol when you need it.

CHAPTER TWENTY-SIX

When Nick first wrapped his hands around the man's wrists, the man gasped and nearly screamed in shock. But – clearly well-trained – he seemed to rebound quickly, repressing the fear and muffling his surprise. Instantly, Nick felt the man's arms resist and pull powerfully away from him and toward the wall. Nick quickly registered that this man was stronger. Much stronger.

Nick fought the man's strength, realized he couldn't win, and yanked the man's wrists to his own left. This pulled the man forward, unbalancing him. Nick extended his right leg in front of the man's ankles and jerked him harder in the direction the man was already going. It was a basic, but formidable move, which usually swept an opponent to the ground.

But there was a problem. The man sensed what

Nick was doing and countered it by stepping around Nick's outstretched leg. Worse, the man accelerated the move forward, now sending Nick off his balance. Then the man stepped his left leg forward and swung it in front of Nick's legs, mirroring the move Nick had just attempted. Nick failed to anticipate the reversal – and was off balance anyway – and like an absolute newbie in his first fight against a trained opponent, Nick tripped and fell right over the man's legs, falling forward and fast toward the wall.

The only thing that prevented Nick from going face first into the ground was his hands around the man's forearms and the wall of the hallway opposite the door. Nick barely slowed before his face and shoulder found the wall in the darkness. Actually, found the wall was an understatement. His face and shoulder tested the wall, and it was solid.

Nick grunted in pain, but held onto the man's wrists for dear life.

Where the fuck was Red? he thought.

This man was some kind of giant bodyguard, easily 6'4" and 220 pounds, and he clearly knew hand-to-hand as well or better than Nick. Or maybe it was simply the fact he was twenty years younger. Regardless, Nick felt a jolt of fear and grasped the idea that this man might best him and put a few bullets in his body.

No sooner had Nick slammed into the wall than the man yanked back with his two-handed pistol grip, pulling Nick's face and shoulder off the wall and back toward the bedroom's door. Just as Nick caught up with the momentum, got his feet under him, and had nearly regained his balance, the big hulk reversed course and slung him backward. twice as hard as before.

As Nick's face and shoulder slammed into the wall for a second time, he realized this bastard must have been some kind of judo expert.

Damn it to hell, he thought. He really should have stuck to sniping.

Gratefully, his eyes were adjusting to the darkness that permeated the hallway, given that his flashlight lay useless behind him, so maybe he'd be able to see as well as his opponent soon. The man had retained his night sight since he hadn't been waving around a bright tactical flashlight like Nick. But two other realizations arrived at the same time.

He heard Red sprinting into the bedroom after someone, and he neither heard nor saw the lights of his two other teams. They must have moved away toward other rooms, having not heard the scuffle in the hallway.

The cavalry wouldn't be coming to rescue Nick this time.

The man spun back again and pivoted his arms to jerk Nick toward the door he had exited, but this time the man used his right arm to deliver an elbow to the side of Nick's head. Despite the dulling pain, Nick had figured out the game and kept his footing better this time.

Nick also managed to maintain his grasp on the man's wrists, but his fingers were slipping. Neither of them could risk losing the pistol.

The pistol was pointed up between their heads for the moment, but it had been yanked left and right several times with all the off-balancing. Both men were very aware of where it was pointing at all times, and not once had the barrel of the weapon covered either man's body.

Nick confirmed the position of the barrel one more time and then stomped down on the man's in-step, which was barefoot. The man must have been sleeping because he was only wearing shorts and a T-shirt. The man grunted from Nick's stomp, and Nick seriously wished he'd been wearing his boots, so that he might have broken a bone in his foot or toe.

Quickly, before the man could react, Nick reared his right leg back and kicked him in the shin. The man yanked back his leg, weakening his center of balance. And in the millisecond of weakness, when the man's brain was computing the pain of the kick and the fact he was off balance, Nick drove his right knee up into the man's groin.

The man gasped and bent double, but Nick was a step ahead of him. Guessing his reaction would cause him to jerk forward, Nick stepped closer and drove his forehead right into the man's face.

One of Nick's favorite weapons was his head, a weapon most people forgot about. But not Nick. He'd once had a hand-to-hand instructor from the Marine Corps tell him that a person's head was no different than a bowling ball, and Nick had been using his head in such a manner ever since.

Nick had used his own head to break many a man's knuckles and wrists from an errant punch that was too loose and high, which Nick had avoided ducking and instead driven his forehead into. In this case with the bodyguard, Nick smiled with delight as he heard the man's nose crunch as it violently slammed into his head.

The man screamed and yanked back out of danger, but Nick anticipated that, as well. Nick drove his knee even harder right back into the man's groin, which had been pushed forward by the man's reaction to the head butt.

Finally, things were going in Nick's direction.

CHAPTER TWENTY-SEVEN

As the bodyguard bent double again, Nick felt the man's strength dissipate. Nick twisted his body around so that he faced the same direction as the staggering bodyguard, and with expert ease, Nick hip tossed the man over his leg. Nick had perfected the maneuver many, many years ago.

Nick made sure to drive the bodyguard into the hardwood floor as hard as he could, and the man yelped in pain as something cracked. Nick wasn't sure if it was the man's back or collarbone, or maybe even an arm. And he certainly didn't care.

Still holding the man's wrists and controlling the weapon, while the man lay defenseless on his back, Nick kicked the man in the lower ribs with the ball of his foot, no different than how you'd kick a football or heavy kickball.

The man gasped in pain, and his arms naturally pulled back and in. Nick used that moment to slide his hands up from the man's wrists to the gun, yanking the pistol free, once and for all. And as the man's arms dropped to protect his ribs from a second kick, Nick lifted his right knee high and stomped the man's face with the heel of his shoe.

Nick stomped him so hard that it hurt his own foot, even with the cushioning of the tennis shoe to dampen the blow. No doubt it had loosened a few teeth and further rearranged the cartilage in the man's nose. The guy clearly hadn't seen the stomp coming in the darkness, or he'd have turned his head, which Nick had half-expected. Had he done so, Nick would have followed up with a second kick to the side of the head, to finish this little shindig.

But the darkness had cut this dance a tad shorter than Nick expected, which was probably for the best. Nick stepped back, breathless.

Bennet and Preacher darted around the corner into the hallway, nailing him with their 600-lumination flashlights. They clearly had thought Nick was a bad guy, since he was alone and out of position, or they would have never blinded him.

"Jesus, guys," Nick said, as he raised his arm to protect his eyes.

But he had been too late, and blots of darkness and painful bright spots blinked on and off behind his eyelids. He cursed not only because it hurt, but also since he knew it'd take two or three minutes before he could fully see again.

"Sorry, boss," Preacher said.

"Cuff this man and search him," Nick commanded. "I can't see a damn thing. And Bennet, go check on Red. He's in the next room. He went in after somebody."

Nick could barely see as Preacher flipped the man over and yanked his arm behind his back, applying pressure until he had both wrists ziptied. Then Preacher searched the man, but found nothing on him in the pockets of his shorts.

Nick tried opening and closing his eyes quickly, but it didn't seem to help. He stood there, still bent over at the knees, feeling helpless as Preacher finished the search. Nick could feel blood coming down his face from some kind of wound on his head, but it wasn't serious. Hell, maybe it was more than just his eyes that had him groggy. Perhaps the guy had given him a mild concussion when he had slammed Nick's head into the wall twice.

Hearing Nick and Preacher's voices, Truck and Lana came around a corner with their lights, keeping their lights low to the ground.

"Damn, Nick," Truck said. "You look like you got your ass kicked."

Nick cursed and tested his left shoulder. It hurt like hell from the impacts in the wall, but the collar bone wasn't broken and it didn't feel like the shoulder had been dislocated. It would be terribly sore in the next few days, but unless he was wrong, no tendons or ligaments had been torn.

Lana stepped forward, pocketed her pistol and

flashlight, and ripped the sleeve off her T-shirt, applying pressure against Nick's head.

"Hold this against it," she instructed.

She stepped back as Red and Truck emerged from the bedroom, pulling a fat, soft man behind them.

"This is our financier," Red said. "Looks exactly like the man we have a picture of."

"Everybody else okay?" Nick asked.

Truck looked around and said, "Yep, we all look fine. You're the only one who got whooped."

Nick ignored the additional comment and said, "Let's get the hell out of here. Lana, I need you to guide me. I can't see shit after getting hit in the eyes by a couple of flashlights."

As Lana grabbed his arm, he asked her to pick up his flashlight and pistol. He still couldn't see more than a foot or two in front of him, and his eyes hurt less if he kept them closed.

"Preacher," Nick said, "grab the man on the floor and bring him with us. I think he's just a bodyguard, but I want to make sure. Would hate to leave him if he's a terrorist or member of Boko Haram."

Red pulled a radio out of his back pocket, reporting, "Second Squad, we're exiting the building. We need pick-up on two targets."

CHAPTER TWENTY-EIGHT

The six members of the Primary Strike Team exited the financier's condo, holstering pistols and trying to look as nonchalant as possible. This was a nice part of Abuja, well-lit by streetlights. Being seen was a real possibility on the crowded downtown block, but they had been quiet, so with luck, no one had been awakened or alarmed enough to look out on the street.

A white cargo van pulled to a stop in front of the condo, and Preacher and Bennet half-tossed the financier and bodyguard inside it. Four members of 2nd Squad were waiting in the back of the van, and they grabbed the two men and closed the doors.

As the van drove away, the six Primary Strike Team members split up and moved to their two vehicles, keeping their heads down and walking calmly.

Lana had her forearm hooked around Nick's upper arm, guiding him toward their Volvo. Despite the brighter environment, Nick still couldn't see well.

Had anyone looked out their window, they would have seen what appeared to be a group of six friends walking down the street after a late-night party.

Lana opened the rear door of the Volvo for Nick, and he climbed in. She circled to the other side and sat next to him. Truck hopped in the driver's seat, while Red took the passenger seat. Meanwhile, Preacher and Bennet loaded up in the Mazda truck parked four spots down.

Both vehicles pulled out onto the road, making sure to control their speed. As S3 cleared the area, Allen radioed them to say, "So far, nothing on the police scanners. I think you all made it out without a single call to the police department."

Nick squeezed his eyelids with his fingers, and then tried opening and closing them. Slowly, but surely, they were starting to work better. Still, he was glad he had taken the backseat and told Red to sit up front, as he was still in no position to command.

"Red," Nick said, still rubbing his eyes, "tell 3rd Squad to pack up."

Red nodded and made the call on their encrypted Motorola radios. Third Squad had been set up a couple blocks away, waiting in two vehicles as a back-up force in case Boko Haram had some troops on the scene protecting the financier.

Or, as Truck had said in their briefing with his typical dark humor, in case the Primary Strike Team needed to be dug out.

Nick started to relax as they moved further and further from the target's house. The 0300 raid time had paid off. The team members had bitched about such an early time, but the fact was that most people were dead asleep at three in the morning. It was the perfect time to pay someone a visit.

The six undercover vehicles of S3 departed the capital city without any incident, staying nice and spaced out on the highway out of town. They had a very long drive north ahead of them, back to their base, but they had nabbed the financier and one other unknown captive, who was likely nothing more than a bodyguard. That made each of the members feel good as many leaned back to grab some shut eye on the return trip.

Soon, both men would be debriefed by the Nigerian Army. Even better, with luck, S3 would be working with the CIA and the Nigerian government to drain the accounts of Boko Haram in just a few hours.

Like a game of chess, Nick was already contemplating the next moves ahead. As he saw it, S3 would need to go after the recently retired Nigerian Army general next. And after that, there would just be Colonel Owan for S3 to deal with. Though having said that, Nick seriously wanted to rescue the boys and girls who had been abducted by Boko Haram. He wasn't sure how they'd locate them, but he planned to make every effort he could.

Back at the base, the team exited their vehicles and gathered in a room to be debriefed. Dean collected the keys for all six of the undercover vehicles and assigned his men to get them returned to the rental agency.

The debriefing was boring and monotonous, minus a few jokes at Nick's expense. It didn't matter that the bodyguard had forty pounds on him and was twenty years younger, nor that most of the folks in S3 would have had a hell of a time taking down the bodyguard. No, all that mattered was that the old man had gotten his ass kicked before finally getting the situation under control.

The story had grown and grown, and some were saying Red – the smallest man in S3 by far – actually had to save Nick's ass, before disappearing in the room to nab the financier.

"I can see it now," Truck blurted out over the laughter. "Nick is getting his head slammed in the wall, just BAM, BAM, BAM, when Red decides he has to leave the financier and come rescue him!"

The story irked Nick to no end, which they could see, and this only added fuel to the fire. Nick figured he'd be catching twice as much hell if Marcus were here, so he allowed himself to smile and shake his head a bit.

The debriefing continued, long and repetitive. Several CIA intelligence guys, none of them trigger pullers, kept trying to keep the S3 members focused, but it was a losing battle. There was nothing to see or share. Merely a simple condo and a rich banker who'd been rousted from his sleep.

It wasn't like the various squad members had seen the enemy or been in some complex firefight that needed to be unwound, sorted, and reconstructed. Nick was about to say "enough" – no matter how much it pissed off the intelligence guys, and no matter how much they bitched to Mr. Smith about Nick pulling the rug out from under them – when Julia stuck her head in.

"I'm sorry to interrupt," Julia said, "but I heard there was an injury?"

Equipped with her medical bag, her eyes searched the room, as catcalls and hollering ripped through the air. Nick begrudgingly stood up, and Truck roared above the noise, "Put him on a stretcher and secure his neck. He's incurred some serious trauma!"

That elicited more laughs, and Nick could only stare at his men, snarling. On one hand, Nick knew that harassment was a sign of endearment. He'd seen too many units where a cold distance between its leader and the troops usually led to hot heads and insubordination.

But on the flip side, Nick was still an introverted sniper at heart who preferred to be in the background. Certainly not a man used to being ragged and laughed at. And it certainly didn't sit well with his ego that the doctor was present for the ribbing.

Red finally stood and lifted his arms to quiet the crowd. "All right, that's enough. Everyone grab your gear and get out of here. Get whatever rest or food you need now and be ready in case we get called out again."

As the room emptied with more laughs and jokes at the old sniper's expense, Nick found himself standing alone with Dr. Julia Clayton. He hadn't seen her in a couple of days.

She seemed to keep herself busy, meeting and mingling with most of the S3 membership. At first Nick thought it was just socializing, but after overhearing a conversation here and there, even participating in a couple himself, he realized that the doctor was pulling double duty. Not only was she connecting with people, but she was also subtly checking on the overall health of each individual.

To add to her busy schedule, Julia was spending a great deal of time at the firing range with Lana. The determined doctor, Nick had learned, was insistent on being as prepared as possible. And according to Lana's casual remarks, Julia was either already familiar with guns or just a natural. Nick supposed it made sense that the steady hands of a surgeon might easily function just as well in other high-stress situations, such as shooting.

She was certainly steady. As a distinguished surgeon who seemed to have a special talent for trauma, her career had started in Baltimore where she sewed up and kept hearts beating from the gruesome realities of an environment prevalent with gang-related activity and violent retaliation.

Years of witnessing such brutality and pained

death hadn't broken the doctor's spirit, as she soon found herself deploying to Afghanistan to patch up wounded soldiers. Her life very clearly painted Julia as a woman who was both passionate about her profession and physically and mentally fearless.

Despite his initial objections to bringing the doctor on board, Nick had to admit that adding a second woman to the S3 team had been a welcome experience. With both Julia and Lana individually able to hold their own, even against a tide of testosterone, there hadn't been nearly the amount of drama that Nick might once have worried about. In fact, as best he could tell, his men seemed to behave and get along better, rousing fewer fights and limiting the number of childish shenanigans with the women around.

Somehow S3 had found a perfect balance. With the personal boundary lines being clearly drawn and held by their female co-workers, it seemed that his men had a safe outlet for their harmless flirtations without serious distractions. The arrangement appeared to help ease both parties, male and female.

The only real problem the integration had caused was with Nick himself. While Lana had always felt more like a daughter or niece to the old Marine, Nick's immediate and intense attraction to the beautiful doctor was driving him mad. And that attraction made Nick feel riddled with guilt, given his recent breakup, or separation as he liked to think of it, with Isabella.

He knew it wasn't technically cheating, since he and Isabella had never been anything close to official, but that didn't help Nick feel any better about it.

Nick also felt awkward and insecure around the smart, clever, gorgeous, and yet perfectly normal woman. He'd never met anyone like Julia Clayton before, and unable to quell his growing interest in her only reminded him of how lonely he was. Not to mention how lonely he expected the rest of his life to be. It was like hoping for heaven and knowing you were doomed for hell.

As she walked toward him, he closed up a small binder, taking her in with his peripheral vision. Curvaceous, and still as down to earth as a woman could get, Dr. Clayton was like crack cocaine to Nick's miserable and mutilated soul. Nick tried furiously not to look at her chest again, but failed. Same as he always did.

At least she was out of his league, though that's probably why he wanted her so bad. She was far better educated and ran circles around Nick with her ideas and thoughts, whenever the two talked. In addition, she'd been hired by Mr. Smith and reported directly to him, so there wasn't the inappropriate "commander and soldier" feeling.

Unlike most men, Nick also found Julia's age, which was closer to his own, to be sexy as hell. Although he purposefully limited his interactions with her, their conversations at least felt familiar. When Julia was around, it was, well, electric. It was like –

"Nick, are you listening?" Julia's voice suddenly burst through his tangled mind.

"Yes," he said, embarrassed and frustrated at himself. "I was thinking about something else... The mission."

"Hmm. Maybe you do have a mild concussion?" she suggested. "Your responses are slow, and you appear inattentive and absentminded."

She placed her hands on his face to look at his eyes, and her fingers felt heavenly. Nick wanted to tell her that the only thing distracting him was her, but he knew that really wasn't on her. She was surely just doing her job. He was the one daydreaming.

She turned from looking in his eyes and removed the field-expedient bandage that Lana had created.

"Pretty smart of someone to use this," she said.

"It was Lana," he replied quickly. "We didn't have our medkits and well, women have all the brains."

"Yes, we do," she said, still examining the wound.

"We raided the house without assault gear in order to appear as inconspicuous as possible," Nick said, "but that meant we had no first-aid gear inside the house."

"You also didn't have a doctor nearby," Julia added, reprimanding him slightly. "Wasn't that financier's condo several hundred miles away in the capital city?"

Nick didn't say anything at first. She was right, of course, but he was slow to admit it.

Julia cocked an eyebrow and said, "I'll let your silence speak for itself."

"I guess in my mind," Nick replied, "I was thinking we would have taken any casualties to one of the hospitals in Abuja since this wasn't some top-secret mission that the host nation was unaware of."

"It still would have been nice to have gone," Julia said. "I know they have first-rate hospitals there, but I could have helped stabilize anyone wounded until better medical care arrived."

Nick wanted to kick himself for not even considering it. Even though he wasn't exactly used to the option of having a doctor on hand, it was still his responsibility to use every means available to him to keep his team safe. Nick didn't even want to think about why his mind had blanked on the opportunity to have expert medical care ready and available.

"Let's get this wound cleaned up," she said, changing the subject. "We'll probably need a couple of butterfly stitches on it."

"It'll be fine," Nick said, pulling away.

"Mr. Woods," she snapped, "if you don't come with me to the aid station, I *will* call Mr. Smith and tell him you're incapable of command due to a significant head injury."

Nick looked at her, surprised to see a very clear warning flash in her eyes. This lady was serious. But almost before he could blink, those brown sparkling eyes were soft again, swaying him to comply. Though feeling a bit sideswiped by what he'd just witnessed, Nick didn't resist as Julia lightly grabbed his arm and pulled him toward the door.

"Mr. Woods," she said with a small chuckle, "I'm starting to get the impression you're scared of me."

Nick couldn't think of a response better than mutely staring at the floor as they walked. Like so much Julia said and did, he couldn't tell if she was flirting, teasing him, or if he was just making stuff up in his mind. And considering what he'd just seen, it was probably best not to assume anything.

Wow. Maybe he was a little scared of her.

And with that, he'd settled it in his mind to let the doctor do her job and not bother thinking on any of it. Besides, he could take off the butterfly stitches later that day without her knowing.

Although it might be better to avoid risking another medical visit and just deal with the things he could control. So he'd keep the stitches, but he'd be damned if he'd take one more lick of shit from Truck or the rest of the team.

Nick smiled as he silently resigned his mind to the task of devising all the different horrors he could employ to keep his men too busy to even think of busting his balls.

CHAPTER TWENTY-NINE

Julia cleaned up Nick's head wound and applied the two butterfly stitches. Nick managed not to stumble over his words too badly as she made small talk with him. Nor did he get overtly caught checking out her incredible curves.

But still he'd need to watch himself, because damn, that woman was dangerous.

So dangerous, in fact, that Nick decided to repeat that thought over and over to himself as he made his way back to the office. Maybe, just maybe, the message would somehow latch itself permanently to his brain.

Neither Allen nor Red were in the office, so he nabbed a bowl of Cheerios and milk from their kitchen. While he gulped down a couple bowls of cereal, he studied the day's intel report from Mr. Smith. But it seemed the Nigerian Army hadn't learned much additional information of relevance from the incarcerated commander.

There was no info about the financier or the bodyguard yet, since they had just gotten started on them. Satisfied with both the meal and latest news update, Nick left a note with the duty officer that he wanted a noon wake-up call for all hands. They were then to be informed of a 2 p.m. formation, from which they'd do an hour's worth of exercise and then a couple more hours of shooting and rehearsing of squad maneuvers.

Just another day living in a war zone, Nick thought. He was tired and wanted to go sleep, but decided to ignore his pain a little longer. He grabbed his M14 to walk the lines instead. He needed to make sure Cormac's security men were standing post fully alert.

With the seizure of the financier and the near miss capture of the retired general by the Nigerian Army, Boko Haram had to know that they'd been hit in the mouth by a new unit. The last thing Nick needed was for some attack on their base to go down and catch S3 unprepared.

Given Boko Haram's strong source of intelligence through the retired general, Nick felt confident Boko Haram probably knew of S3's existence in the country by now.

The PT session and training afterward went fine, and Nick drifted back to his office after showering and throwing down some dinner. Dean, taking care of logistics like he always did, had brought in a local caterer, who had cooked up steaks and baked potatoes for the entire unit.

Nick instructed the squad leaders to coordinate with Cormac so that the security men on the line could be relieved from their posts and provided the chance to throw down the special meal of steaks, as well. After the food was devoured and morale had skyrocketed to impossibly high levels, Nick sauntered into his headquarters office feeling nice and full. And he also had that amazing feeling all commanders experience when things are going their way. S3 had just been fed better than probably any unit currently in a war zone, and his boys were already kicking the shit out of Boko Haram – and they'd only been in country a couple of weeks.

Sometimes, he thought, being in charge wasn't so bad.

Red and Allen were in the office when he stepped in it. They were sitting around his desk in the two chairs that had probably served as great guest chairs forty years ago. Now, they barely supported their occupants, sporting ripped vinyl and rusted legs. As was par for the course, S3 had been placed in an unused part of the base, though Nick was okay with that. It helped keep them out of sight and out of mind, which boosted their already over-the-top security measures.

Inside the office, both Red and Allen looked up

and smiled. Nick nodded in return, and both men resumed to what they'd been doing. Red, whittling again on his board. Allen, studying some highlighted and marked-up reports.

"I should've brought me a fine piece of cedar," Red said, trying to make some conversation. "This pine 2x4 isn't worth a shit for whittling."

Nick smiled and took a seat behind his desk, kicking his boots up on it. Nick wore a camouflage Nigerian Army uniform again, same as the rest of S3. He felt confident the uniforms helped S3 blend in with the rest of the Nigerian Army, should Boko Haram have only half-assed intelligence and be scouting for S3 along the base. If they didn't look closely, they might disregard the new unit on the outskirts of the abandoned base.

"Whatcha reading, Allen?" Nick asked.

He had been updated on the fact that the financial accounts of Boko Haram had been identified and raided. Apparently, the financier had decided to avoid retaining a lawyer, choosing instead to cooperate with local authorities. The Nigerian government had offered to give him a new identity and allow him to avoid jail time if he fully cooperated. Nick figured the banker had made the right move.

Allen set the papers down and rubbed his temples.

"I'm missing something," he muttered.

"He's been sitting there looking at those papers for so long that even I have a headache," Red said.

"It's beats whittling," Nick said, laughing.

"Not really," Red replied, "but you're not the type to relax and sit awhile."

That was true. Nick used to be decent at biding time, but these days he always wanted to be doing something. Perhaps "Nick the Sniper was dead," and "Nick the Leader" was all that remained? This thought was interrupted as Nick remembered dropping Senator Gooden before they left the States and he smiled. Well, he could still man a rifle when it came down to it.

Maybe he had changed. He'd need to chew on that some more some time.

Nick leaned back and scratched the scalp below his short, blonde hair. He kept it short on top – basically just a tuft – and even shorter on the sides. But he was already wanting a haircut, as he typically cut his hair every two weeks when he was back in the States. Once a Marine, always a Marine, he thought.

He could worry about the haircut later. He glanced back at Allen, who looked mentally zapped.

"You never answered my question," Nick said. "What are you chewing on?"

"I've been working on how we nab this retired general," Allen said. "It has to be S3 because he knows how the Nigerian Army thinks, and they will think exactly as he expects since he trained most of them."

"True," Nick said. "So, what have you got?"

"I've been working over the idea of somehow using the financier to reach the general."

"I thought the reports stated the financier has no idea on his location," Nick said.

"That's correct, but what if we somehow contacted the general as if we're still the financier?"

"You don't think he already knows the financier has been captured?" Red asked, shaving another small strip of wood into a curled circle that fell from the board and slowly drifted to the pile below.

"Good point," Allen said, sighing and squeezing the bridge of his nose. "See, I'm not even thinking straight anymore."

"We've already emptied Boko Haram's accounts, so he has to know," Nick said.

No one said anything for a moment, the office quiet except for the gentle whittling noise made by Red.

Then an idea struck Nick.

"Allen, why don't you get with the hacking gurus and track his cell phone history, or maybe his email history, to see if that leads to any clues on the general's location? Even if we could get it narrowed down to a couple of cellphone towers, we'd be closer than we are now."

Allen nodded his head in agreement.

"Yeah, I like that idea," he said.

CHAPTER THIRTY

While Allen contacted the CIA computer hackers back in the States to try and crack the location of the general, Nick called for an update from Mr. Smith.

Mr. Smith said the coalition operating against Boko Haram continued to score big wins. As Mr. Smith outlined the recent successes of the various country's military units, Nick realized the combined armies were truly destroying the terrorist group one piece at a time by using first-rate intelligence, renewed confidence, and excellent coordination and logistics. The modern-day armies had incredible communications, which was usually half the battle. In addition, they were well-supplied, which was usually about the other half.

The ragtag structure of Boko Haram, with its limited communications equipment and various cells that worked in solo operations, was suddenly no longer an advantage for the group. Their fast-moving light trucks and troops, all of which lacked armor, were no longer assets either.

The unprotected equipment and fighters were getting pummeled while operating in the defense, especially against the precise and deadly air, mortar, and artillery attacks. Nick listened to Mr. Smith recount the numerous air strikes and battles the coalition armies were winning (both providing incredibly high body counts) and he smiled.

But he also knew that eventually Boko Haram would break. They'd be forced to give up territory and their attempts to become their own country or caliphate. Then, as the group was forced to break up into small units, they'd certainly revert back to guerilla tactics, and the traditional armies working against them would again become ineffective. Like using a heavy sledgehammer to swat at gnats.

That's when S3 would once again be called into the fray. Of that, Nick felt certain.

Nick signed off with Mr. Smith and checked in with Allen. He said the CIA hackers had some ideas on how to track down the general's location electronically. And that he planned to stay up most of the night to get his arms around the former general's location.

"Time is of the essence," Allen said. "He might flee the refuge, or even the country, at any time. Doesn't matter if I don't get any sleep at all. We have to find him immediately."

"You're a good man," Nick said. "Wake me if you need anything, but I'm calling it a night. With luck, you'll find something we can jump on in the morning."

"Agreed," Allen said.

Nick headed off toward his rack for the night. All of S3 was housed in an open barracks, so Nick slept just a few feet from his men. Most of them were either lying down, playing cards, or already asleep. Nick lay down on the concrete floor by his rack and knocked out a couple hundred sit ups, doing sets of fifty while he worked his way through a couple dozen emails on his laptop.

Nick's body was sore, and his shoulder still hurt from his fight with the bodyguard. That had indeed been his job, according to the Nigerian Army's interrogators. The man's credentials with a top-rated security firm had been confirmed, and he'd already been released, albeit he'd be needing some serious medical work on his face after the swelling went down.

Nick felt a little bad about the stomp to the man's face. But he'd had no idea the guy was a privately hired bodyguard. And he'd been good. Had damn near taken Nick out.

Nick was doubly glad that neither man had killed the other, despite the high risk of possibility. The bodyguard had told his interrogators that he assumed the noise he'd heard was from a single burglar, and he intended to take action since the financier hadn't wanted to call the police.

After all, the financier had computers in the condo that had verifiable evidence on them that he was transferring money into Boko Haram's accounts. The bodyguard had suggested waiting in the room, but the financier ordered him to leave the room and deal with the burglar.

Nick shook his thoughts away from the fight with the bodyguard. That was in the past, and he needed to move.

Nick scanned the emails, answering the ones that needed his immediate attention or could be handled quickly. His CFO constantly sent him emails with questions and updates about the other side of the company.

Nick regularly told the man to handle whatever came up as best he could. Nick didn't have time to run both the Nigerian operation, as well as the rest of the company. He fired back a few answers and closed the laptop down for the night.

He stretched out on the cot and told himself that if the CFO didn't start stepping it up soon and handling everything on his own, he'd talk to Mr. Smith about replacing him. It was a tangled legal mess anyway. Technically, Nick was the owner and founder of S3. The title had been dumped on him just prior to him taking what he had assumed would be a task force into Mexico.

But after the successful mission to Mexico, it was decided by some of those in the CIA to keep S3 going. And a cover story was suddenly necessary if they were going to keep operating. For that reason, Mr.

Smith had hired the CFO and poured a lot of money into the company for the above-board side to operate in a very public way.

On the one hand, it provided the cover story they needed. On the other, if one of these guards or squads in a country such as Kuwait accidentally shot a local police officer, even while under the CFO's direction, it would still be Nick's head on the chopping block. It didn't matter that Nick had no oversight of that operation, and had argued all along that he didn't want that responsibility. Nick wondered who in their right mind wanted to run a company with several hundred employees.

Mr. Smith had always said the U.S. government would handle any such legal catastrophe, if a massive lawsuit came up against the company. And Nick mostly believed him, but he also knew that if the media began digging and congress scheduled hearings, then his ass was grass.

That's why Nick had taken his two million dollars and hidden it away so that he could flee at a moment's notice to either Canada or Mexico. Isabella had helped set up the southern escape, while an old Marine buddy now living in Canada had helped Nick locate a secluded cabin hideaway that was completely off the grid.

Nick had been sold out twice already. He could really only count on one person to watch is back, and that was him. Not some bureaucrat named Mr. Smith, who he'd never met or even gotten his real name.

CHAPTER THIRTY-ONE

The next morning, Nick awoke to discover that Allen and the hackers had nailed down the general's location to a roughly twenty-mile area. But they couldn't tighten the circle any more than that.

With most people, they would have been able to pinpoint the location down to a single street, but this general wasn't most people. He was bouncing signals off multiple towers, using serious encryption, and going through burner cellphones and tablets like they were candy.

"I'm sorry we couldn't do better," Allen said.

As promised, Allen looked as if he hadn't slept at all.

"Twenty miles beats ten thousand miles," Nick replied. "And maybe we can study this area and see if anything sticks out as an obvious place he might be hiding."

With that thought in mind, Nick called an all-hands meeting and broke up the twenty-mile area into grids, designating each squad an assigned area to study. Using a CIA-created version of map overlay, which made Google maps look like it was created in the '60s, each squad analyzed its sector, trying to determine just where they'd hide if they were the general or on the run.

But all the team members realized what an impossible feat this would be just minutes into the task. It was actually worse than the proverbial "needle in a haystack." But Nick believed in trying, so he encouraged everyone to keep pushing.

The problem stemmed from the fact that none of them had any idea if the guy would be in a tiny apartment, a small home, a large home, or a fortified mountain cabin. As luck would have it, the twenty-mile area fell in about the worst area you could have imagined. It was about half-rural and half-urban. In the rural part, there were large homes with massive yards. Further out, cabins clung to the side of steep hills. On the flip side, in the urban part, dense homes were packed together on expensive real estate, and large apartment complexes, holding hundreds of units, were squeezed in on small plots of land.

Twenty miles sounded small until you started looking closely.

Four hours into the hopeless exercise, Red motioned for Nick, and the two stepped away from the troops. All of the team members looked exhausted and near delirious by the research challenge.

"What the hell do we do now?" Red asked.

"Hell if I know," Nick said.

Nick believed in creating your own luck and making something happen, but even he had to admit that this just wasn't going to work in this instance.

Allen walked over to them.

"Doesn't look good, does it?" he said.

"It sure doesn't," Nick said. "Any ideas? We've got to get this guy. He's our next link."

"You really want to know?" Allen asked.

"Well, *we* certainly don't have the answer," Nick said. "So whatever it is, I guess we really need to know."

"We're going to have to go old-school journalist mode on this one," Allen said. "Obviously, we can't put the man's picture out or alert him that we're so close to his location. If we do that, he'll bolt."

"True," Red said.

"So we need to be discreet," Allen continued. "We need to check property records, utility accounts, you name it. Until we finally figure out where he's hiding."

"If he's smart, then he's used one of his mistress's names to put the property under," Nick said. "Or maybe a son or daughter. Hell, maybe a cousin. Or maybe he's renting from someone. How do we figure out where he is then?"

"Exactly," Allen said. "We're talking about a bitching amount of work here. But we've got what, thirty or forty people here? I never had that many on any reporting team I was on. We were lucky if we had two or three on the same assignment. I could lead this though, break up tasks into manageable chunks, and with this many bodies, we'll catch a break at some point."

Nick looked at Red.

"What do you think?"

"Beats whittling and sitting on our duffs," Red said. "Besides, if we don't do this, we'll get cut out of all the action while the coalition pushes Boko Haram back. And the worst part of that plan is knowing this guy will bolt at some point and easily get away in the chaos."

"Tell us what we need to do," Nick said.

And that's what the superbly trained shooters of S3 did for the next five days. Dean purchased a couple dozen laptops for the team members to use. He also set up higher speed internet to support them by literally paying the Nigerian government to string a direct, temporary line to their corner of the base.

But Allen hit an unexpected problem pretty quickly. He was used to doing his research and public records magic in American. Unfortunately, this was Nigeria, and many of the records weren't online in this part of the world. So they had to do things the old fashioned way. Allen was constantly sending out squad members to check out records in various government offices.

The squad members used cover stories when they stopped in the various offices, claiming they were working for either bill collectors or real estate research firms.

The men also ditched their Nigerian Army uniforms and put back on their undercover clothes, packing only a pistol with them on their trips off base. Dean was pissed he had returned all the undercover rentals from the raid on the financier, but quickly got S3 hooked up with a bunch more.

And for the next five days, Nick's men flipped through pages and searched dusty records while under Allen's direction, until they finally discovered the general's location. The barracks erupted in an explosion of celebratory shouts at the announcement.

The retired general was hiding in a hillside hideout, on the very edge of the twenty-mile circle that they had been searching through.

The home – really, an almost fortress – was owned by a sergeant major that had worked directly for the general for better than seven years. But the cost of the hideaway was several million dollars – a price that no sergeant major in *any* army in the world could afford.

Thus, they knew it was the general's hideout. He had somehow managed to buy the property and place the sergeant major's name on it as a way to give him cover from being discovered.

The general's plan had worked, almost. Actually, Nick told himself that it *would* have worked had they not been able to limit the search down to a mere twenty miles. And even then, it had taken hundreds of man hours and one of the world's greatest researchers leading the effort to crack the puzzle. They had studied and compiled a list of family members, fellow service members, and serious dates he had been photographed with at various military balls and political functions.

Allen reasoned that the general wouldn't just sign his home over to simply any woman, but rather would choose a woman he had spent some time with and trusted. He further reasoned such a woman would be the kind that he was not ashamed to take out in public, and thus she might show up in some photos available on the internet and newspaper websites.

The angle on using a woman hadn't panned out, but Allen's overall thoroughness had carried the day anyway. Allen's idea to search for members the general had served with paid off. S3 discovered the sergeant major's name by studying unit annuals for each division the general had served in. And this was actually easy work, since the general, like most generals, had a publicly available biography and military history posted on his consulting website.

Allen had yet again come through, and as Nick thought about the general and how well he'd covered his tracks, he told himself he'd be especially careful with this particular target. He might be a piece-of shit traitor, but he wasn't an idiot. He was thorough and talented, and had nearly eluded some of America's best talent.

No wonder he'd been giving the Nigerian government fits without them even knowing it. This man was good.

Nick didn't plan on underestimating the general.

Now, Nick only needed his sniper teams to confirm the man was actually at the mountain-like fortress. Then, they'd finally get to pay the man a visit. One he probably wouldn't like.

CHAPTER THIRTY-TWO

The retired general's home was the ideal hideout. It was incredibly remote, sitting more than three miles from the nearest home. In addition, it had been built high up on a hill, with no approach available from the rear. The backside of the hill on which it sat was practically sheer cliffs, which Nick doubted even the most experienced mountain climber could have scaled, even with the most expensive gear on the planet.

Nick certainly wouldn't try it.

An unpaved, gravel road wound up to the mansion, and it was blocked at the bottom by a massive, motorized iron gate. Thankfully, the satellite photos provided by CIA showed that no large iron fence surrounded the property at the top.

Nick hoped the property didn't have ground sensors. Those were a bitch to get around. Even more, he hoped the traitorous general was actually there. The good thing was that Nick would know that soon.

S3's three sniper teams were working themselves into position and would be reporting any moment now on the details of the hideout. They had been dropped off in the middle of the night, riding in the backseat of rental cars to remain inconspicuous. Each car's driver had slowed and allowed the snipers to peel off into the woods. And unless you were closely listening or watching the road, you would have never noticed six men enter the woods.

The snipers had gone in with heavy packs, prepared to stay up to seven days should it prove necessary. Nick didn't expect more than three days, max. But they had wanted to be ready for the worst-case situation.

The teams had been assigned three different sectors. From the home's position, the teams set up at a three o'clock, six o'clock, and nine o'clock position. Obviously, no one could approach from twelve o'clock because of the ferocious cliffside.

The team at six o'clock would study the front entrance and the automatic gate. Nick primarily wanted to know which way it opened and whether an armored Humvee could possibly knock it down. Once the team ascertained that, they'd recon the road from the treeline alongside it. Their mission was to confirm whether or not it had any anti-vehicle barriers that could spring up from the ground.

Motorized, solid steel barriers used to block

roads were becoming more and more common in the new world of terrorism, as truck bombs were one of the greater threats most frequently wielded. And in this case, since the road was flanked with trees on both sides, there'd be no fast way to get around a well-placed, anti-vehicle barrier.

The other two sniper teams were approaching from opposite sides of nine and three o'clock to recon the objective and get eyes on the defenders at the place. Nick needed to know how many there were, how well-armed they were, and how often they changed shifts.

Right now, he didn't know shit. There could be two rent-a-cops or there could be a hundred heavily armed guys, who were prior military. Hell, there could even be a couple dozen Boko Haram terrorists helping guard the place.

Nick needed to know before he, Red, and Allen could plan their strike. And it was all driving Nick nuts. The next few days were guaranteed to be painfully monotonous while they sat and waited for information.

Thankfully, the hillside fortress was only an hour from their remote base that was situated near Boko Haram lines. The retired general clearly felt comfortable being close to his Boko Haram buddies. If anyone in the Nigerian government had known about the property, there would have been red flags all over the place. With its close proximity to the terror group, the place was a dead giveaway of his villainous collaboration.

Nearly everyone who had money and influence in the area had long ago moved away from Boko Haram and its expanding borders over the past four or five years. Choosing to stay anywhere less than a hundred miles from the Boko Haram was simply inviting trouble to your doorstep. So those who could afford to do so had fled and moved closer toward the capital and the safety it provided.

Still, while the hour's drive from the base would make their eventual assault much easier, it was currently creating a logistical nightmare for S3 and their snipers. An hour would turn into a lifetime if any of the three Scout Sniper teams were discovered and attacked by a much larger force. So, S3 had stationed a squad with four armored Humvees just ten minutes away in case the sniper teams needed rescue.

Of course that emergency squad had to be relieved every eight hours by another squad, who had to drive an hour just to get there, so all of this was quickly causing unnecessary exhaustion and tension. Nick was itching to make this hit happen. He wanted to apprehend the general and make him pay, but Nick also really just wanted to end the monotony of waiting and the stress of having his unit so dangerously spread out.

Damn, he hoped his sniper teams gathered their intelligence quickly. Waiting three days might just kill him.

Thoroughly frustrated about the delay, Nick found himself grabbing his M-14 to walk the line. And then he'd knock out some pull-ups, push-ups, and sit ups.

Hurry up and wait. Hurry up and wait. No matter how many times you've done it, it still makes you want to beat your head against a brick wall.

It didn't quite take three days for everything to fall into place, but it still took two and a half before the mission was a "go." In that space of time, the snipers had located the retired general as he peeked out a window one morning. And they had also pulled together decent intelligence on the guards there.

As the information from the three Scout Sniper teams had filtered in, Nick, Red, and Allen developed a plan for taking down the hideout. The plans were then submitted and finally approved by Mr. Smith.

Next, Nick made a request and had a Nigerian Major attached to S3. The Major had no knowledge on what target they were hitting, but Nick wanted him tagging along in case they ran into any problems with police or other Nigerian Army units, either en route or on the return trip.

With all planning and preparation taken care of, all the troops grabbed some shut eye while they could. The next day, at 0300, S3's armored column of Humvees pulled out of the Nigerian Army base, half-waking the barely alert Nigerian soldiers at the front gate.

These men were supposed to be alert and protecting the base, though clearly that wasn't the case. Nick patted himself on the back for once again not trusting the host nation's forces for security. He also reminded himself to thank Cormac for the excellent job he'd done overseeing security on S3's inner perimeter.

The eighteen Humvees drove away from the base and toward the remote fortress. Along the way, they didn't encounter a single vehicle. It was absurdly early, after all. And not a lot of folks this close to Boko Haram territory came out in the dark hours.

It was an excellent way to get robbed or killed.

The Humvees went lights out as they hit the more remote roads and closed within several miles of the retired general's home. As the roads were deserted, a large string of lights in the distance would quickly gain the attention of whatever guards were currently watching the home's perimeter.

The drivers were forced to rely on night-vision goggles, causing them to traverse slower, but it was worth the headache to maintain the element of surprise.

Two miles away from their target, the column stopped. The rural, country road they were on barely got traffic, even during the day, so Nick felt confident no one would drive up the road before daylight hit. They set the Humvees up in a blocking position on the road, at both the front and rear of the column, just in case a car attempted to pass the column heading toward the general's home. The Nigerian Major would then explain to the theoretical traveler that they were being temporarily detained because of a military operation taking place further up the road.

The rest of the Humvees pulled off the road to the left and right. Nick also doubted the Boko Haram had any raiding parties out, but he didn't plan on ignoring the possibility no matter how unlikely.

So Nick, sitting in the passenger seat of the lead vehicle, scanned the road ahead with his night-vision goggles. But neither he nor the Scout Sniper teams, who'd stayed in constant contact, detected any movement within the area.

Nick stepped out of the lead vehicle, adjusted his heavy assault vest, and tugged at his sling to get his M4 perfectly centered across his chest. S3 members were outfitted in Nigerian Army camouflage uniforms, along with heavy assault vests, helmets, and lightweight packs crammed with ammunition.

Waiting for them and guarding the retired general, would be more than thirty security men. And besides having a serious amount of firepower, these men had the home-field advantage. More than likely, they had defensive protocols in place, all rehearsed and perfected.

And these protocols might also include some nasty surprises for any would-be attackers. Nick knew all too well that S3 was pushing its luck, attacking such a large force with only fifty men, but he was counting on their stealth and superior training to carry the day.

CHAPTER THIRTY-THREE

Nick rolled his shoulders and took a couple of deep breaths, mentally preparing himself and feeling the weight of the vest and pack. Nick liked to go in a Zen-like, live-in-the-moment state before combat. He liked to feel very alive and sharp, his senses at the highest state of alert.

He wriggled his toes, flexed his arms, and rotated his neck, allowing the weight of the helmet to really stretch it out. He sniffed the air and said a quick prayer for his men. With that, he was ready.

It was a three-quarters moon, so visibility was twenty feet along the road thanks to the night sky. Nick glanced down at his M4 and confirmed it was on safe. He did a brass check to ensure that a round was in the chamber, despite having already done so back at the base. With that, he closed the ejection port cover, tugged on his magazine to confirm it was fully inserted, and took one final, deep breath.

Nick checked that the machine gunners on his Humvee and the one parked parallel to it were covering the column's front. They were, aiming their big .50's down the road.

Nick turned and watched his men behind him as they dismounted, checked gear, and formed into squads. The scene was deathly quiet as everyone moved in with an orchestrated and silent fluidity. They all knew the danger of being discovered, and Nick had gone as far as issuing orders before moving out that no was to speak.

Two miles was probably far enough away that they could have cut up and joked and not been heard, but sound tends to travel farther at night so they'd take no chances.

Truck approached, carrying a M249 light machine gun. Nick, seeing a couple of men farther down the line check their sights, decided he should do the same. He pointed his weapon away from the others and out into the trees, raising it to his shoulder and checking that his Aimpoint sight was working. Being an old iron sight guy, Nick hated to admit it, but he had fallen in love with the red dot sight in the past year.

He returned his attention to the column of troops just as Lana walked up, followed by Red, Preacher, and Bennet. Each of them carrying M4s.

With all six members of the Primary Strike Team formed up, he looked behind him and saw another group of six figures huddled together. That was 1st Squad. And then behind them, another huddle of six men formed 2nd Squad.

That was three squads of six men, loaded for bear, approaching the target from its flank up in the woods. Both squad leaders behind Nick held up a thumb, signaling they were ready to move. Nick tapped Red and pointed toward the treeline ahead.

It went against typical tactics and common sense to place your second man in charge on point, but Red had been point man for so long that Nick didn't believe anyone could do it better. Nick was counting on Red to successfully lead the column of troops to a link-up point with the Scout Snipers. This needed to be done silently and right the first time, since their schedule lacked any extra time for fuck ups. If they failed to properly link up, not only could it ruin the timing of the attack, but they could inadvertently find themselves walking right into the enemy's sightline.

That would kill the element of surprise and screw up the entire attack.

Red shot an azimuth on his compass and stepped into the woods. Nick followed, despite also knowing a unit's commander should never be the number-two man in the column. But Nick as well had been leading from the front so long that he didn't know how to stay where he should.

The forests around here featured open woodland, with very little undercover or low brush. The trees themselves weren't very dense either, so visibility was much better than Nick had expected. He followed

Red with very little effort, raising a pair of night-vision goggles from time-to-time to search some piece of cover where the enemy might be hiding.

The eighteen shooters of the three squads took several breaks, but progressed through the woods making excellent time and with relative ease. Compared to humping forty miles into Pakistan, this two-mile trek was nothing, Nick thought.

And an hour and a half after starting, they linked up with the Scout Sniper team positioned at three o'clock on the perimeter. Nick checked his watch and saw it was 0602. Sunrise was at 0618, and that was when they would strike.

So far, so good.

CHAPTER THIRTY-FOUR

The three squads fanned out into a single line, facing their target. Each man pushed forward until they had a clear view of fire, staying low by crawling and sliding ahead.

At Nick's position, he could just see a single guard with an AK slung across his chest. It was getting light enough to finally distinguish the hillside home. Nick was a little surprised the home lacked an iron fence around it, but clearly, the retired general was relying on the remoteness as well as the concealment provided by placing the property in the sergeant major's name. And despite the lack of an iron perimeter, the man *still* had thirty-plus guards protecting him.

The kind of money it would cost to pay for that many high-quality guards was something Nick had never considered. But having just thought of it, he made a note to himself to track that down. Surely the man was into more than just feeding Boko Haram information. Was he selling something? Drugs, maybe? Leading hits or working as muscle for some kind of cartel? Nick would need to check this out after the mission. But first things first.

Nick checked his watch and saw they were one minute out from "go time." He radioed the Humvee column to confirm they were loaded and ready to go. Once they acknowledged and affirmed, Nick pressed the button on his radio and said, "Three, Two, One…"

As Nick had said "three," he shifted his weapon off "safe" as quietly as he could. As he said "two," he lined up the sole guard he could see in his sights. And as he said "one," he placed his finger on the trigger.

If the man so much as twitched wrong, he was a dead man. Especially given the short distance separating him from the hidden S3 men. In fact, only fifty yards separated him from Nick and the rest of the line of men lying in the woods.

Nick "tsk-tsk-ed" his radio, and the raid began. Without a single warning, the members of 1st Squad to Nick's right busted out of the woods, screaming, "Freeze, police! Freeze, police!"

They were screaming like insane shock troops – confident and anxious to take down their target. The Nigerian uniforms should have been enough to make most law-abiding men drop their weapons, and the heavy assault gear and weapons in their shoulders should have deterred even the non-law-abiding citizens.

"Freeze!" they continued to scream. "Freeze! We have a search warrant!"

Well, technically, that last part wasn't true, but Nigeria was in the middle of a war, and the lines tended to get blurred in the middle of war.

S3 was lucky in that English was the official language of Nigeria, and nearly all of its military members and educated class spoke it. And even if this guard didn't speak English, seeing six men sprint forward in army uniforms with weapons pointed at you should be enough to keep you from moving the AK you're carrying – no matter what you're being paid.

But this man was either stupid, extremely loyal, or a terrorist who didn't want to be taken alive. As he went from total shock and surprise from the squad breaking out of the woods to a decision, he spun and lifted his AK. Bad move. Nick's red dot sight was already resting on the man's chest, and he pulled the trigger, firing his M4. He watched the guard jerk in surprise as a bullet slammed into his chest.

Nick felt confident that his bullet had exploded the man's heart. And while Nick had been the first man on the line to fire, the man jerked milliseconds later as several other bullets cut into him from other S3 members lying to Nick's left and right.

He wasn't wearing any body armor, only a blue, semi-official-looking SWAT uniform. With the exception of the big arms pushing against the T-shirt, and the combat boots and AK, you might have assumed he was just a step above your typical security guard type.

A big question S3 had prior to stepping off on the mission was how would these thirty-ish guards react to the raid? Would they see the Nigerian Army uniforms and vehicles and immediately lay down their weapons? Or were they former soldiers of the retired general who would remain loyal and fight to the death?

It looked like with the guard's attempt to go for his weapon that S3 finally had its answer. This was going to be a bloodbath.

So be it, Nick thought. If the men were *that* loyal, then it meant they probably knew their boss wasn't your typical, law-abiding citizen. And that meant they were in on it, and probably had been getting paid exorbitant amounts of money. Possibly even actually participating in illegal acts with Boko Haram.

Nick wouldn't lose any sleep over the death of these men.

The 1st Squad members had stopped their rush toward the home, and now waited in the kneeling position. They were hesitating, and Nick couldn't blame them. He wasn't sure what they should do either.

Rush forward the forty yards and stack on the home? Or run back to the safety of the woods, where they couldn't be seen?

The guard wasn't moving and Nick knew he was already dead or only seconds from it. Nick decided the squad should withdraw.

"First Squad, pull back," he yelled, since there was no point in using a radio at such close distance. Besides, with a shot already fired, the morning's silence had already been shattered.

And that's when a shot rang out from the home, and a squad member from 1st Squad was knocked to the ground, screaming in pain.

Oh, shit, Nick thought.

CHAPTER THIRTY-FIVE

"Cover them!" Nick yelled.

He aimed his M4 into the nearest window as the rest of the two squads opened up from the treeline. The two squads could see the front and three o'clock side of the stone mansion, but no windows had been shattered or fired from. Could the home have murder holes? That seemed impossible, but there wasn't time to find out.

Now both squads, and part of the members of 1st Squad out in the open, were lighting up the home, pouring bullets all through it. Nick fired his M4 into the windows on the side facing them, and then angled shots into the windows on the front.

With so much suppressive fire going out, two members of 1st Squad grabbed the fallen man and dragged him back to the woods while the three other members of the squad helped cover them with their fire.

"Where are those trucks at?" Nick yelled on the radio.

"We've made breach and will be there in a moment," came back over the radio.

Nick returned to firing into windows, which lacked any targets that he could see in the early morning light. But better safe than sorry. Six rounds later – fired on single shot – he could hear the Humvees coming up the hill along the curvy, gravelly road.

Thank goodness for that. That would help discourage any serious resistance. And if it didn't discourage it, all those machine gunners letting loose from behind their armored turrets would quickly silence anyone stupid enough to try to take them on.

A guard came tearing around the corner of the left side of the home, an AK in his shoulder aimed toward the treeline. Nick shifted to shoot the idiot, but numerous bullets cut him down before Nick could get his red dot on the man. That had been one of the stupidest acts in war that Nick had ever seen in quite a while, but he pushed the thought from his mind.

With 1st Squad back in cover with their wounded man, and no return fire coming from the home, the two squads on the line slowed their rate of fire to conserve ammo. They were raking the home at the sustained rate, waiting for any additional orders from Nick.

The roar of the large convoy erupted as the Humvees burst from the woods and into the open of the general's yard, tearing up sod and throwing it ten feet into the air. As the Humvees cut left and spread out, their gunners covered the home with .50 cal's and 7.62 machine guns. Nick yelled for his men on the line to cease firing, and the order was passed up and down through the three squads.

Nick hated to ease up the pressure, but this was that gray area between combat and mere police work. Without question, Nick would have preferred the Humvees just blister the building with firepower. But only one shot had been fired, and it had probably been the idiot who came running around the corner.

"Red!" Nick shouted. "Go check on that wounded man with 1st Squad."

"Roger that," Red said, rolling off the line and jogging down to the squad.

Nick depressed the mic button on his gear.

"All vehicles, hold your fire unless we're engaged again."

A series of "roger's" came back over the net, and Nick returned his attention to the building. What the hell were the security guards doing in there? Holding a pow-wow? Deciding whether they should surrender? Or setting up defensive positions, moving couches and furniture in front of windows and doors?

Red came jogging back and slid down next to Nick.

"What's the verdict?" Nick asked.

"It's Cooper," Red said. "He took one through the chest, above the plate and almost over by his shoulder. It missed the lung, narrowly, so he'll survive. But he's hurt bad. I've got two men from 1st Squad carrying him over to Dr. Clayton."

Julia, Nick thought, suddenly hoping she was staying low if she had exited the Humvees to help Cooper. Why the hell hadn't he decided to place Julia further back away from the house when he was drawing up the plans?

No time to second guess himself now. He had to return to the situation at hand, which was clearly a damned mess.

"Looks like the back door is opening," a man on the far right of the line yelled. "He's carrying a white T-shirt or flag."

Nick breathed a huge sigh of relief.

Nothing like eighteen armored Humvees to convince a bunch of guards that dying for a retired general is probably a really dumb idea, Nick thought.

CHAPTER THIRTY-SIX

The scene was a madhouse. Thirty-three guards, in various stages of dress from blue security uniform to boxer shorts, were sitting in two rows. Flexcuffed and searched, they were guarded by 3rd Squad while four Humvees pulled around to help box them in.

On the other side of the front yard, staff from inside the home were being processed. The retired general had butlers, house cleaners, and grounds keepers. All necessary to keep the multi-million-dollar home in top-notch shape.

The retired general had already been searched, cuffed, and whisked away by the Nigerian Army. They had even flown in a helicopter to get their hands on him quicker. The retired general was likely minutes away from brutal interrogation.

Tough shit, Nick thought. He could never feel any sympathy for a man who'd sell out his own country and the very men below him, who he had once led.

Nick glanced at his watch. He was exhausted from too little sleep. True, early morning raids like this caught a lot of the bad guys wearing nothing but their boxing shorts, but they were hell on a man in his mid-forties.

It wouldn't be much longer though. The Nigerian Army and federal investigative force were sending out a hundred men to process the scene. The investigators had a ton of work to do. They'd need to decide which of the guards to imprison and which to let go. They'd need to thoroughly search the house and the premises, including the woods around them. And finally, they'd need to run down any and all leads that came up from the questioning of the retired general.

Talk about sleep. There'd be a lot of Nigerian investigators who wouldn't be getting much sleep in the next three days or so.

Nick scanned the staff who had kept up the place. Thankfully, none of them had been injured in the firing from S3. At the first shot, all the staff had been ordered into the basement by the guards, who'd been preparing to put up a hell of a fight, a few had said.

But then they'd begun taking serious fire from the woods and watched the massive, armored Humvees rip up the yard as they swung into firing positions. At that point, they knew resistance was futile. They lacked any RPGs in the place, and none of their weapons would do any damage to the heavily armored vehicles.

Nick heard a man yelling along the first row of the guards and saw one of the S3 members trying to deal with him. He hustled over with Red, his heavy gear feeling even heavier with the drowsiness and fatigue.

"Shut up!" one of the members of 3rd Squad screamed, trying to get the situation under control.

It was always embarrassing when the boss and second-in-command had to come over to help you do your own job. Nick and Red drew up by the squad member, noticing that one of the guards scowled at them, hatred in his eyes.

"What's he jabbering about?" Nick asked.

"He won't shut up," the 3rd Squad member said.

Nick looked at the man. The man glowered at Nick, not an ounce of fear in his eyes. What the hell did that man know that Nick didn't?

The Nigerian Army Major walked up, and Nick pointed at the angry prisoner.

"Make sure someone does a good job checking this man out," Nick said. "He isn't your typical, low-level guard."

The Nigerian Army Major nodded, but the guard spit at Nick. The gob of spit landed about a foot short, which was a good thing for the prisoner's sake, Nick thought. Probably Nick's too.

"You are lucky you didn't come just five days ago," the guard said to Nick, an anger burning from his eyes. "We would have shot you up. And all of your men, too."

"You had your chance, hoss," Nick said, stepping

closer, "and you threw your weapon down like a little girl."

Nick knew calling the man a girl was particularly insulting in Nigeria.

The man cursed back at Nick in local dialect, some kind of gibberish that Nick couldn't understand. Nick considered stepping closer and knocking the man's teeth down his throat, but punching a handcuffed man was poor form. Instead, he walked away from the yelling and taunting man, saying to the 3rd Squad leader, "Duct tape that idiot's mouth shut. I'm tired of listening to him."

Nick headed over to the retired general's staff to apologize to them for the inconvenience of being seized as part of the raid. He also planned to let them know that they would be processed and released as quickly as possible. As he walked over, he took a deep breath and tried to calm down from the guard spitting and cursing at him. He had nearly put the raging lunatic's words out of his mind when he noticed one of the housekeeper's eyeing him.

She raised both her hands up, above her head, and flapped her hands. Her hands were flexcuffed together, but the staff's hands were flexcuffed in front of them instead of behind their backs, since they posed a lower risk than the guards.

"You, sir," she said, waving her arms even harder. "Are you in charge?"

"Yes, ma'am," Nick said, shifting his muzzle down and removing his helmet.

She was a big woman, probably in her fifties, but

with the kind of build that told you it wasn't all fat. And she had a look of toughness in her face that made Nick figure she could work all day without breaking a sweat. Hell, she could probably outwork him.

"Your mission was a failure," the lady said. "You came too late."

Nick furrowed his eyebrows. What the hell was she talking about? Had she not seen her boss, the retired general, ferried off in a helicopter?

Before Nick could say anything, the lady added, "You came for the missiles, right?"

Oh, shit, Nick thought.

"Come with me," he said, reaching to help her gain her feet.

CHAPTER THIRTY-SEVEN

Colonel Owan was happy. Not that he should be, had he given a shit about Boko Haram. But he'd never given a shit about Boko Haram. Not even after they helped spring him from prison.

As a hardcore criminal, Colonel Owan, who now thought of himself and called himself that name, had learned many years ago that you looked out for yourself first and foremost. He'd also learned early on that owing anyone was dangerous. When you owed someone, it was a good way to earn a bullet or a long prison sentence.

As such, Colonel Owan had never felt like he owed Boko Haram. In his mind, they broke him out of prison for their own interests – not because he wanted to be rescued. They stupidly thought he was a real colonel, who could help them. Tough shit for them that they'd been wrong.

But he'd gone along with the ruse for a while because they had access to loads of money and weapons. He'd helped them in the short term. But that time was coming to an end. Had come to an end, actually.

Owan didn't care that Boko Haram was getting hammered and in full retreat from the coordinated attacks by the coalition countries of Nigeria, Cameroon, Chad, and Niger. It didn't even matter to him how many members of Boko Haram were killed.

Most of those young men were fools for getting wrapped up so deeply in religion – a so-called religion that strangely allowed them to do the most terrible things to young women and defenseless men. The women, they raped and enslaved. The men, they executed with pleasure.

Besides the young fighters, who were far too devout for his liking, Owan was sick of the fanatical teachings and blatant acts of hypocrisy by Boko Haram's "leaders." He wasn't an expert on the Koran, but he knew enough of it to know the leaders of Boko Haram didn't follow it.

But none of that mattered to him. No way was he getting swept up in their silly caliphate dreams anyway. Even weeks ago, before the coalition armies had fired the first shots, he had seen the end in sight. And still, the idiot leaders of Boko Haram had predicted in speeches to their troops and on videos posted online that they would destroy each of the invading armies.

It was absurd beyond measure. Boko Haram had no effective way to destroy the tanks confronting them. They had no ability to stop the jets that would soon be bombing them. And they certainly lacked any tool to counter the long-reach artillery that would begin bombarding them without end. In fact, it was the artillery attacks that were the worst. The bombardments were relentless. It was as if each country had an unlimited supply of artillery shells with which to lob into the Boko Haram positions and camps.

Anyone with even a high school education should have seen how it would play out once the various countries unleashed their armies, but not the leadership of Boko Haram. They had seemed unfazed. The only thing worse than the military leaders and civilian administrators of the caliphate were the religious fools who had urged on their fighters, claiming they'd be back praying for their huge success.

Cowards, every one of them, Colonel Owan thought. But he had never said these words. No, a good criminal *never* allowed anyone to know what they were truly thinking. In fact, a good criminal never even showed anything on their face. A dead, unmoving face, which held eyes that stared impassively ahead, was the practiced appearance assumed by criminals.

Instead of telling them how idiotic their plans to attack actually were, he'd advised them from his standing as a "colonel" that their plans were perfect. With one minor exception. He suggested he could personally lead a top-secret, brilliant counterattack, which he couldn't share with them for fear of the information getting out.

They had foolishly agreed and with their approval, he had left camp with three of his best, hand-picked men. His most trusted men.

These men were *not* fanatical believers of the Koran. Fanatics were dangerous. Fanatics were delusional. Fanatics were impressionable by old men who quoted from silly religious books.

The men Owan picked were criminals, the kind of men he preferred to lead. They wouldn't kill you over some belief written in an old book, and you never had to guess their intentions. Criminals looked out for themselves and simply followed whoever was the toughest and most cunning man, and Owan had been that man since he was in his early twenties.

CHAPTER THIRTY-EIGHT

Before leaving on the "top-secret, brilliant counterattack," Colonel Owan had grabbed four Stinger missiles from one of the clandestine ammunition dumps Boko Haram had created. These were the only four Stinger missiles in the entire Boko Haram arsenal and had only recently been obtained.

Stinger missiles were the incredibly powerful American-made missiles that allowed ground troops to shoot down everything from attack helicopters to fighter jets streaking through the air. They were tightly controlled across the world, because every Western leader feared some terrorist group acquiring the missiles and using them against civilian airliners.

Boko Haram had only gotten their hands on the four missiles because the group had dropped millions from its rapidly disappearing cash reserves to pay the retired general for them. He had used his connections with some of the former officers he mentored during his career to attain the four missiles from an air defense battalion. With the loose inventory controls in place by the Nigerian Army, it might be three or four years before anyone realized they were missing. And then they'd never realize which officer during which year had allowed their theft.

The retired general paid six hundred thousand dollars for the four missiles, garnering him a great deal of money from the multi-million-dollar purchase from Boko Haram. He also knew the missiles took a lot of expertise and training to use correctly. More than likely, some dimwit fighter would waste all four on improperly attempted shots on jets screaming through the air.

The fact the Stinger missiles were so complicated were the very reason they hadn't been used yet. Colonel Owan had told the other Boko Haram leaders that he would refresh his memory on how to use them – meaning, he'd research online how to use them since he didn't have a clue – and train a couple of their men.

Boko Haram had sought out the missiles not because they planned to shoot down some civilian airliner but because they knew the air raids would soon begin in earnest from the coalition armies. In theory, the Stingers might limit the coalition's air power and cause them to reduce or halt their air strikes.

But Owan felt confident the fighter jets had electronic countermeasures that would counter the

Stingers. Plus, he'd come up with a better idea for them that didn't involve Boko Haram or their insane dreams to create an Islamic caliphate.

At the clandestine ammunition dump, he spoke to the two guards – both of whom looked to be about sixteen. This was all the proof you needed that Boko Haram was being quickly destroyed in a *very* one-sided fight. Something as valuable as a crucial important weapons cache merely had two sixteen-year-old boys guarding it. Clearly, Boko Haram had rushed even more of its fighters to the front line than Owan had been told.

Owan's men loaded up the four Stinger missiles in the back of a Toyota 4Runner that they were taking for their "mission." Each missile was stored in a padded aluminum transport case, the very ones they had shipped in from the United States. There was also a much smaller case that held the single launcher for the rockets.

Colonel Owan had a single plan for these missiles: he would sell them in Europe for several million dollars to some very bad people. Probably either ISIS or al Qaeda. Whichever terrorist group offered the most.

Owan didn't care which group bought them. Or even what they did with them. He was a criminal. He was in this for himself. And all he wanted was a nice stash of cash for him to get a new start in Europe.

As their white 4Runner moved south with its air conditioner blasting, Owan smiled from where he sat in the passenger seat. Compared to the miserable

Sambisa Forest or the dangerous prisons where he had spent the past couple of decades, he felt he was sitting pretty.

He had three brave, well-armed men with him. He had four missiles worth millions of dollars. And he'd soon be living on the beach somewhere in Europe.

Undoubtedly, his days as a lowly car thief, forced to steal clunkers in Nigeria, were over.

CHAPTER THIRTY-NINE

Nick, Red, and Allen sat in their office, frustrated beyond all belief as they tried to solve a nearly impossible riddle. The office was hazy, and Allen was smoking at least his fourth or fifth cigarette – Nick had lost count.

They'd been talking, arguing, and throwing out ideas for three hours, and each of them had brainstormed about as much as they could handle in a single setting. Nick was about ready to put on a pair of gloves and go for a few rounds with Truck, or else he was liable to put his fist through the wall.

Allen was leaning forward, his entire concentration seemingly focused on the burning end of his cigarette. Red was working his big Ka-Bar blade down the piece of wood, which was round now and no longer square. The Ka-Bar was too large for such a delicate endeavor as precise whittling, but Red kept his blade sharp enough to overcome the inappropriate use of the mammoth-sized blade.

Nick was leaning back in his chair, his legs propped up on the desk and his hands clasped behind his head. This was the part he hated. Solving some damn impossible riddle. It took everything he had not to pick up his rifle and go walk the lines. Or ask Truck to meet him in the ring for some friendly sparring.

The riddle in front of them was a complicated one. S3 knew some missiles of some type or other had been picked up from the retired general's residence, but that's about all they knew. The maid didn't know whether they were RPGs, massive anti-ship missiles, or some kind of skinny, Mach-3 missiles that could shoot down fighter jets.

The retired general that they had seized wasn't talking yet, and Mr. Smith was just as stumped as they were. He had no idea on how to move forward with their investigation of the missing missiles either.

"I still say," Allen said, "that we have to get the Nigerian Army to do an audit. See what kind of missiles they're missing. If the retired general had them before Boko Haram got their hands on them, then we know they came from the Nigerian Army. Who else would the retired general have gotten them from?"

Nick sighed.

"We've discussed this already," he snapped. "They can't possibly pull off an audit like you're describing. They have half a million men in their active forces, and more than three million in their reserves. And they have the worst records that you could possibly imagine. Most of which aren't even online or in computer databases. Hell, they're still using ledgers for most of the inventory of their hardware."

"And even if," Red added, still whittling and looking down, refusing to meet Allen's eyes as he delivered the final bad news, "they had decent records, it would take days and days – if not weeks – to discover what was missing."

"And by then," Allen said, nodding in agreement, "Colonel Owan is gone with them."

"Exactly," Red said. "We're basically fucked. Totally flying blind."

"There has to be a way," Nick said. "We're missing something here."

While they lacked all the facts, the information that they did know was incredibly disturbing. Satellite intercepts of radio communication from Boko Haram fighters on the battlefield indicated that Colonel Owan had fled the operating area. Several men, assumed to be mid-level leaders of Boko Haram, had been arguing over their radios about their once highly respected commander.

At first, they had been boasting about some kind of clever counterattack planned. But that had changed as the days of brutal losses mounted, and the men began openly bitching on the radio that Colonel Owan had fled like a coward.

With the news that the man they most needed to capture had fled south, Mr. Smith had gathered a huge team of intelligence folks to study satellite imagery from the days prior, looking for any vehicle that might have fled the fighting. But the intel experts had hit a wall immediately. With the all-out assault by the coalition of armies, the roads had been jam-packed with civilian vehicles. It wouldn't have been hard for Colonel Owan to hide his vehicle among the mass of fleeing vehicles.

A pic of Colonel Owan had been quickly distributed to police and Nigerian security forces all along the front. They had plenty of pics of Owan from when he had served his time in prison, and the Nigerian government had set up a ring of checkpoints all around the north.

The fear all along was Boko Haram would dissolve and flee the onslaught, escaping the trap and creating cells of terrorists through the country. With that in mind, the Nigerian police and military forces had been looking for young men of fighting age, looking especially hard for weapons.

But S3, as well as the Nigerian government, felt confident that Colonel Owan could have slipped past the checkpoints by using obscure back roads that might not have been monitored. Thus, the Nigerian government was in the process of also distributing Owan's photo across the rest of the country.

Bottom line, S3 had very little information, and it was hard to plan your next move with limited information. Besides the fact he had fled south, the only other thing S3 knew was he had a total of three other men with him. Four men, armed and dangerous.

Heading who knew where. And who knew for what purpose?

"We're fucked," Red said, slinging the whittling stick against the wall and placing his Ka-Bar in the sheath on his left hip. "If we're stuck in Nigeria until they dismantle Boko Haram's leadership structure, then that means we have to apprehend or kill Colonel Owan. And if we can't find him, that means we have to wait until he pulls off whatever crazy-ass mission he has in mind."

No one said anything, the silence and smoke filling the room until it felt oppressive.

The encrypted satellite phone, which sat on the desk, rang.

"Maybe this is something," Nick said, answering the phone and hitting the speaker button so all could hear.

"We're all here," Nick said when the phone connected. "Me, Red, and Allen, who probably wants you to send a couple more cartons of smokes at the rate he's going."

"He thinks best when he's smoking, so let him be," Mr. Smith said.

"It's not working tonight," Allen replied. "And I'm so stressed out about this that I'm about to switch to weed."

"Maybe this will help," Mr. Smith said. "We finally received some better intel that just came over. Listen to this."

Some papers rattled and he continued, "The NSA folks just broke this down from some satellite intercepts. Looks like the frontline fighters of Boko Haram are really bitching about all the air strikes against them."

"And not the artillery?" Red asked, knowing artillery fire almost always sucked worse, despite America's current obsession with laser guided bombs.

"That, too," Mr. Smith said, "but it's the complaints about the airstrikes that interest us."

No one in the room said anything to that, so Mr. Smith added, "The Boko Haram fighters are cursing the fact that Colonel Owan stole their Stinger missiles."

"Stinger missiles?" Nick asked, concern in his voice. He felt his heart rate increasing, probably doubling at the mere mention of those words.

"That's right," Mr. Smith said. "We now think Colonel Owan stole some number of Stinger missiles. We're not sure how many, obviously. And we need to confirm he in fact did steal them. We can't let those things into America, assuming he did. And if he did, then we'll need to alert the entire security apparatus from Homeland Security to Customs to Border Patrol to you name it. Everyone will need to be on high alert for them. It will even be suggested that the president increase the terror warning."

"Jesus," Allen muttered, his cigarette hanging from his mouth.

"It'll be bad enough," Mr. Smith said, "if they make it to Europe, but if they make it to America, I can't even imagine the panic of the people once the first airliner gets shot from the air."

"Or the hit on our economy," Nick said. "Remember how after 9/11, no planes were flying? Can you imagine that again?"

"I've got an idea," Allen said. He ground a half-smoked cigarette into the ashtray and said, "We could get photos of Stinger missiles, as well as their shipping containers, and show them to the maid. She could confirm whether the photos match what she saw being loaded."

"Great idea," Mr. Smith said. "Make it happen."

CHAPTER FORTY

By 10 a.m. the next day, Nick was back on the phone with Mr. Smith. Red and Allen sat around his desk, both anxious. Red was whittling again, while Allen smoked.

When Mr. Smith answered, Nick said, "We've got good news and bad news."

"Let's have it," Mr. Smith said.

"Allen and Red went out this morning and found the maid in her village no problem. They showed her the pictures of the Stinger missile cases, and she recognized them immediately."

"So our worst fears are a reality," Mr. Smith said. "Christ."

"We even," Allen added, "took photos of RPGs, AT4s, and several other missile types and their shipping containers just to make sure. She stayed firm. It's definitely Stinger missiles in Colonel Owan's possession."

Red spoke up. "One other thing. We showed her Owan's picture, and it was definitely him that took the missiles. She also confirmed there were three others with him."

"Shit," Mr. Smith said, sounding exhausted. "I'm going to have to go. I need to report this immediately, and I guarantee this is going to make it all the way to the President."

"We're going to track them down," Nick said, with more confidence than he felt. "Before you go, let me throw out something real quick."

"Make it quick," Mr. Smith said, his voice anxious and sharp.

"It's my belief, in talking with you and to Allen, that the Nigerian government isn't that focused on helping us track down Colonel Owan."

"Well, unofficially," Mr. Smith said, "that's my belief as well. But don't go screaming at some local officer in the Nigerian Army. These guys are just regaining their swagger after years of nasty losses. Our analysts even suspect they're not even that concerned with how many terrorists get away – either to other countries or outside the cordon that their forces are putting up. The Nigerian government figures tracking down terrorist cells after they regain all this territory is a whole lot easier, not to mention a whole lot less embarrassing internationally."

"I agree," Nick said. "My point is we should incentivize this. At the lowest level, even. My idea is we throw up a ten-million-dollar reward for information leading to Colonel Owan's arrest. We don't even mention the missiles he has with him, to prevent alarm. But we just get his face out there, because if we can find him, we'll find the missiles."

"And," Allen added, "we throw the Nigerian government a million dollars to get them to help us publicize the reward and his face through their contacts with all the local and national media."

"Eleven million dollars is beyond my range of authorization," Mr. Smith said, "and I don't have time to be trying to get that approved right now. As I said, I have to go."

"Make it happen," Nick snapped. "That amount of money isn't anything compared to some terrorist group buying these missiles and unleashing them on us back in the States. Authorize it now and ask for forgiveness later."

There was a pause, then Mr. Smith said, "I'm probably an idiot for saying this, but deal. I'm immediately approving a ten million-dollar reward, and a one million-dollar allocation to the Nigerian government to help us get the information out."

"And another million," Allen said, "for advertising. Ads, flyers, billboards, etc."

Mr. Smith sighed.

"Done. But we need Owan and we need those fucking missiles, or all of us will be out looking for new jobs soon."

CHAPTER FORTY-ONE

When Mr. Smith hung up, Nick stood. Allen ground out his cigarette, and Red sheathed his Ka-Bar.

"Allen, getting Colonel Owan's face out is all on you," Nick said. "Make it happen. Find a good pic of him, maybe from one of his recent stints in prison, and get it distributed."

Allen nodded.

"I'll need to get with some of my State Department contacts to get the Nigerian government moving," he said. "I'm going to be busy the next twenty-four hours or so, but we've got a good plan on getting this out to the public, and I'll make it happen."

"Red," Nick said, waving, "come with me."

The two walked out of the office and down the hall to the barracks area. Most of S3 was in the wide-open space, their homes either a cot or a wrought-iron bunk bed that was probably fifty years old. Gear, packs, and sea bags were strewn everywhere since all the footlockers and wall lockers had been removed years ago when the barracks first went into disuse.

Each squad had claimed its own small area, taking residence and ownership of it, no different than any other military unit would. As was so often the case, it was squad loyalty first, and squads hung together.

Nick and Red scanned the open squad bay, noticing that most of the men were resting or reading magazines and books. A few slept or scrubbed weapons that were already clean. All of them were dealing in their own way with the frustrating "wait" part of "hurry up and wait."

Nick and Red walked toward the corner where the Primary Strike Team stayed. Preacher was reading a well-worn Bible; Truck was drinking a can of Miller Lite (which was not permitted); Bennet was lying back on his bunk with a pair of shades on, either sleeping or meditating; and Lana was stretching, in the middle of a full split as they walked in.

"Listen up, guys," Nick said, as he and Red approached.

Bennet popped up immediately, removed his shades, and appeared wide awake. Truck didn't even try to hide the can of beer, tipping it back to finish it off. Lana stood and shook out her legs, while Preacher stowed his Bible.

Once everyone closed in around them, Nick announced, "We're going to be conducting an all-out media blitz, releasing tons of information about Colonel Owan to the public. He's our best shot at grabbing those missiles. And as tips come in, we need to be prepared to respond immediately. Our squad will be the primary responding squad, unless anyone wants to give it up and let one of the other squads take it."

"Hell no," Truck said. "We're bored out of our minds."

"Says the man holding a beer," Nick said.

"Hey, if we're not fighting, I'm drinking," Truck replied. "It's in my contract."

"Sure it is," Nick said, "except I think the part that mentions drinking says you have to keep it under control or you're off the team."

"It's under control," Truck said with a wink, lifting the empty can. "I haven't spilt a single drop of this one, or the one before it."

Red started to say something, but Nick lifted his hand to stop him.

"Let's keep this on track," he said. "Since the Primary Strike Team will be the squad on call, I want you all to have three sets of gear ready to go. Option one is a heavy loadout, with full assault vest, helmet, and Nigerian uniforms. If we go this route, we'll be rolling in armored Humvees. Option two is a paramilitary loadout with semi-civilian clothes, but with vests and long rifles. And finally, option three is completely undercover. I want you to have a set of civilian clothes ready to go, with nothing but pistols and extra mags. Understood?"

Everyone nodded.

"Then, make it happen and get your minds mentally prepared. Truck, go on the beers."

"Just hydrating a little bit," he said with a smile. "You know, three or fewer and I'm fine."

Nick shook his head and walked off with Red. They asked a few S3 troopers about Dean's whereabouts and soon found him outside with two men working on one of the armored Humvees.

"Hey, Dean," Nick said.

Dean slid out from under the Humvee, wiping his greasy hands off on a rag. He didn't have to be working with his men, being in a leadership position, but Nick sincerely appreciated the fact that he led from the front – no different than how Nick would do it if he were on the logistics side of things.

"Yeah, Boss," Dean said. "What do you need?"

"We're going to be broadcasting Colonel Owan's picture out to the public, and I'm placing the Primary Strike Team on high alert for when we get the call."

Dean nodded.

"I want a few different transportation set ups ready for us, depending on what kind of mission is necessary," Nick said.

"Makes sense," Dean replied.

"Get us a couple or three Humvees ready to go, gassed up, ammo'd up, et cetera," Nick said. "And I also want a couple of four-wheel drive SUVs in case we go paramilitary. Finally, nab a couple beaters, too, to serve as undercover vehicles. A station wagon, twenty-year-old Civic, stuff like that. Something that will fit in if we need to enter some city."

"Consider it done," Dean said, laying the rag on the Humvee to walk off.

"One other thing," Nick said, "and this one is the hardest. Nigeria is so big that vehicles may not get us there in time. So, find us a helicopter we can have on standby. I don't care if it's from the Nigerian Army or a civilian one. I just want us to be able to react and get somewhere quick. We may even need a plane, depending on where this asshole pops up at, but we'll cross that bridge when we get to. Just find us a helicopter to have on standby."

"Understood, Boss. I'll probably go ahead and hook the plane up, too. Better safe than sorry."

"You're a good man, Dean. Keep me updated as you get things arranged."

CHAPTER FORTY-TWO

The massive media campaign paid off quickly.

Everyone in S3 had underestimated the willingness with which the media would participate in broadcasting Colonel Owan's name and face. As soon as the Nigerian government asked for the media's help, each news station seemed to feel spurred into a competition with other outlets to see who could get the most coverage and come up with the best angles on Owan.

The newspapers went to even greater lengths.

It turned out that the media was as furious and angry as the Nigerian government about the nearly decade long war with Boko Haram. The reporters were outraged about the atrocities against innocent civilians and little girls, and the publishers knew that the terrorist group had cost the country – and consequently, their newspapers – an untold amount of money with foreign companies either packing up and leaving or declining to ever come.

Bottom line, once the media found out that Colonel Owan had been one of Boko Haram's leaders, they went ballistic and used their expansive reach to make the man more famous than he'd have ever desired. Social media from viewers magnified this impact.

This was the chance for the media to ride a patriotic furor as they wrapped themselves up in the effort. The country and its people had been beaten down and embarrassed for so long that it felt great to be winning again. And the media members, most of whom had never carried a rifle, fired the only rounds they could: launching long feature pieces on TV and spewing out in-depth articles in newsprint.

Besides the media itching to jump on board and push the information campaign, the massive reward helped it spread like wildfire. Ten million dollars is a lot of money by American standards. But in Nigeria, it might as well have been a billion dollars. A person who earned that reward could buy their entire family or street new homes, cars, and clothes, and still have enough for all of them to live off for the rest of their lives.

The largest lottery ever had come to Nigeria, and everyone wanted to buy a ticket and win. Packs of kids ran around streets with cut-out pictures of Owan, searching alleys and passing cars for the man. Police officers ignored other assigned duties while they patrolled their area, hoping to finally find a way out of their miserable jobs.

It took only thirty-six hours after Allen launched the campaign for the first snippet of success to arrive. Following a couple hundred inaccurate tips phoned in to a hastily set up call center by the government, the major from the Nigerian Army informed S3 they had finally found the trail of Colonel Owan.

The man, and his three hand-picked fighters, had robbed several jewelry stores in the capital city of Abuja – the same city where S3 had earlier apprehended the financier for Boko Haram. The city was both massive and opulent, and the major from the Nigerian Army said the four men had stolen millions of dollars of jewelry and diamonds. The total haul was estimated as high as five million, detectives in the city believed.

Nick's first instinct was to load up the Primary Strike Team and head to the capital city of Abuja as fast as they possibly could.

"Red, get everyone moving," Nick said.

But, before Red could dash out of the room, Allen stopped him.

"Wait a minute," Allen said. "What will we do there? The city's detectives are working the case, studying video and compiling information on what they're driving. If we go there, we're just going to be chasing their trail. Effectively running in circles as we respond to sightings. We may never catch them that way. But if we can anticipate where they're going, we can be waiting for them."

Nick hated to admit Allen was right, mainly because he was ready for some action. But the man had a point. Yet again the non-military, pencil-pushing writer was on the ball and way ahead of Nick.

"Red, bring the map," Nick said, waving him back into the office.

While Red grabbed a massive map of Nigeria, Nick called Mr. Smith to update him on the sighting and see if he had any additional information. It had taken several days of sitting around in boredom, but the real chase had finally begun.

CHAPTER FORTY-THREE

Nick quickly discovered that Mr. Smith had no additional information, but stated before ending the call, "We'll have our analysts hack into the city of Abuja servers so we can see what the detectives have. We'll study the video feeds they've seized, dissect their police reports, and keep you apprised of what they know."

"Sounds good," Nick said. "We're going to brainstorm where Colonel Owan and his men are heading and see if we can't arrange a surprise date."

After Mr. Smith hung up, Nick leaned over the map of Nigeria and began studying it with Allen and Red.

"So, where are they going?" he asked, as much to himself as anyone. "If memory serves me correctly, this country has 350,000 square miles."

"Yep," Allen said. "It's bigger than Texas."

"And," Red added, "it has some of the loosest, easiest-to-cross borders in the world."

"Thus we better be damn good at trying to figure out where they're going," Nick said, "or they'll slip away."

As the three of them stared at the map, hoping for some kind of epiphany that each knew would likely never come, Allen said, "Well, at least the coalition's offensive is going well. Boko Haram has lost control of all of its major population centers and only runs some of the smaller towns. Like, really small ones."

"But they still have operational bases inside Sambisa Forest," Red said.

"Guys," Nick said, a little sharper than he meant, "none of that matters. If Colonel Owan gets away with these four Stingers, we've got a serious situation on our hands. So let's focus here."

No one said anything for a moment, each keeping their eyes on the map. The silence sucked. It was uncomfortable, even for Nick. He never enjoyed disciplining his friends. It wasn't like Allen and Red were some of the regular guys under him.

Finally, after several minutes, Nick said, "All right, instead of focusing on towns and cities in Nigeria, let's begin from a broader perspective. Allen, grab your laptop and pull up a map of Africa.

Allen opened his laptop and almost instantly turned the screen toward Nick, revealing the map. Damn, that man was fast with a computer.

Nick pointed at the continent and said, "Here's

what I'm thinking. They can't really go east or west. There's nothing but oceans to either side."

"Agreed," Red said.

"That leaves north or south," Nick said. He pointed to the southern part of Nigeria. "And if they go south, they're going to have to go through Cameroon, Congo, Angola, and Botswana before they finally reach South Africa. From there, they could eventually fly out to Europe or America or really, anywhere."

"On the plus side," Red said, "each of those countries are remote and underdeveloped. They lack good police forces or secure borders. The trip south would be easy, but still take forever if they went by vehicle."

"It would be easy," Nick agreed, "but South Africa is probably the most modern and well-run country on the continent. Flying out would be very difficult, even if they buy some of the best fake passports and fake identifies around."

"Yep," Allen said, lighting up a cigarette and blowing out a cloud of smoke. "If it were me, I wouldn't want to try to fly out from South Africa. Very developed, with a modernized police force and security system at of their major airports that allow international flights."

"That's what I'm thinking," Nick said. "If I'm Colonel Owan, going south is out of the question. It's long and slow, and you end up at the most dangerous destination on the continent. But if you look at the map, it's quite the opposite if they go north."

Red ran his fingers from northern Nigeria, where Boko Haram had been establishing its caliphate, and said, "First of all, they leave from an area that they're already familiar with, and have been operating from for years. So the start of their journey is safer. Then they cross into Niger, a very underdeveloped country, and then hit either Algeria or Libya."

"Both of which have barely functioning governments," Allen noted.

"And," Nick added, "those two countries have probably two thousand miles of nearly wide-open coastline. Owan and his men can grab any kind of trawler or craft that they want, and cross the Mediterranean to Spain. Or France. Or Italy. Any of them would be easy trips."

"Or they go east or west to either Morocco or Egypt," Allen said. "Both of which would be easy to escape from if they wanted to avoid the coastlines of Algeria or Libya, since they may anticipate us expecting them to leave from there."

"Even scarier," Nick said, "is the fact that Libya may be their final destination for those Stinger missiles. ISIS has set up several bases there, so Owan could sell them the missiles and go on his merry way."

"He'd have close to ten million dollars by then," Red said, "and he skips across the Mediterranean to Europe and lives the rest of his life surrounded by money and wealth."

"And ISIS shoots down a bunch of airliners, either in Europe or America," Nick said.

"Most likely America," Allen said. "They have been dying to hit us as hard as they've hit Paris and Europe. I think they take the extra time and risk of hitting us in America. Especially with something as amazing and valuable as four Stinger missiles."

"I think you're right," Nick said. "They're coming for us. Not Europe."

"Plus, we're the big supporter of Israel," Red said. "Not France or Germany."

Allen shut his laptop and moved it away from the desk so they could see the map of Nigeria that lay under it.

"We just need to figure out Owan's course out of Nigeria and be waiting for him," Allen said.

"I'll call Mr. Smith to brief him on our conclusions," Nick said, grabbing the big encrypted phone and exiting the room.

CHAPTER FORTY-FOUR

The three leaders of S3 spent a couple of hours studying the northern part of Nigeria, looking at the roads and border checkpoints to determine the best place to cross the border. There were a multitude of options.

"Damn," Allen said. "Which one of all these options?"

"And we have to pick one assuming we're Owan and we're on the run and in a hurry, with a ten million-dollar reward on our head," Nick said.

No one replied to that, and they continued to study the map. With luck, they wanted to be waiting for Colonel Owan and his compadres when they made the crossing. Or possibly before, if they could pull it off.

After much study and discussion, the three finally decided that Owan would cross at either the towns of

Katsina, Daura, or Babura. These were smaller towns with well-built roads leading directly into the country of Niger, which would allow for rapid transit. Best of all, these three towns weren't major thoroughfares for those leaving Nigeria. As such, the checkpoints for each of them were lightly guarded. Even where checkpoints existed, several roundabout roads made it possible to cross the border with no problem.

If you wanted to sneak into Niger, you'd go through the towns of Katsina, Daura, or Babura.

"Damn it," Red said, leaning his head back and sighing. "It just hit me."

He paused and stretched, then said, "Even if we picked the right three route options, there are still a couple dozen roundabout roads that would need to be guarded."

No one said anything to that. Finally, Nick suggested, "We could put a single man or pair or men at each possible crossing? Give everyone a radio and have a small strike force on call."

"Or we could bring in drones?" Allen offered.

Nick stood. Damn it. Red was right. This was a long shot, and there were three or four other very viable towns that were also great options for crossing. There was Diru, Chirawa, Garema Maleri, and even Giri. In fact, these towns were actually controlled by Boko Haram, but the three S3 leaders had ruled them out because there'd be some danger for Owan if he picked them.

The three S3 leaders assumed Boko Haram might kill Colonel Owan. The man had, after all, abandoned the group and taken four of their best missiles that could have protected them from all of the devastating air raids.

"Are we back to square one?" Allen asked, reading Nick perfectly as usual.

The two had spent too much time together in their race to survive an out-of-control CIA unit that had gone off the reservation several years earlier.

"Probably," Nick said, "but we have to act. I say we cover the three cities we believe to be our best chances. What were they? Katsina, Daura, or Babura. And we just have to hope we catch a break."

"That's all we *can* do," Red said.

Nick, Red, and Allen got with the squad leaders and planned how best to cover the routes they expected Colonel Owan to use. Dean tackled the logistical nightmare of how to get fifty-plus shooters up to the border safely, while the troops began packing up their gear and mentally preparing.

The mission was going to be a long-shot and full of high risks, as some roads would only have two men covering them. It was a great way to get some good men killed on what was a dangerous border under normal circumstances, but no one saw a better way. And with four Stingers at risk of being delivered to ISIS, no one was going to duck their duty.

Thankfully, they caught a huge break before they ever stepped off.

CHAPTER FORTY-FIVE

Mr. Smith called with what he described as "huge news," so Nick told him to hang on while he pulled Red and Allen into the office.

Once everyone had gathered, Mr. Smith said, "We may have gotten the biggest break ever."

"There's going to be a few more S3 guys breathing tonight thanks to that," Nick said.

The mission had been a go for mere hours later and everyone felt they'd probably take casualties tonight, whether they caught up with Owan or not. The border had smugglers, drug runners, and diamond thieves, and there were still Boko Haram members rampaging throughout the area.

"Our biggest weapon in our fight against terrorism has paid huge dividends, I think," Mr. Smith said.

All three men around the table knew he was referring to satellite intercepts and radio eavesdropping. Technological prowess had always been one of America's biggest weapons against the terrorist groups they'd faced. Nick still believed that the American warrior and spirit was the biggest weapon, but intel weenies always ranked intercepts far above the fighting spirit and bravery of the men and women in harm's way.

"Our analysts," Mr. Smith continued, "have picked up a phone call into one of the Libyan ISIS base camps regarding Stinger missiles. When the supercomputer discerned the word 'Stinger,' the call was bumped up to a Category Five priority. It was declared an emergency transmission and studied and traced immediately."

"And they discovered that it emanated from Nigeria?" Nick asked.

"Exactly," Mr. Smith said. "We've got analysts studying the voice to confirm it's Colonel Owan, but unless there's more than one crazy guy who recently stole four Stinger missiles from the Nigerian Army, who's trying to flee the country and sell them, I'm pretty sure it's our guy."

"Tell me you have a location," Nick said, starting to stand.

"We do," Mr. Smith said. "The good news is we know where he's heading and we know he's riding in a Cessna of some kind with his men. The bad news is we don't know when he's leaving. Or if he's already left."

"That'll make it interesting," Red said.

Several hours later, a massive Marine Corps CH-53 Super Stallion helicopter roared through the night air, screaming across the countryside at more than 170 miles per hour. Inside, eight members of S3 rode, their weapons muzzle down.

The CH-53 Super Stallion is one of the largest helicopters in the world, and it could have transported almost all of S3 on this mission. That's how large they are. And while Nick wanted all fifty of his trigger pullers with him, the mission dictated something much smaller. He could only bring eight, so eight it was.

They'd make do.

The CH-53 Super Stallion was flying nap of the earth, staying under two hundred feet off the ground. This kept them under radar coverage.

The CH-53 Super Stallion had flown across Libya to Nigeria, departing from a U.S. Navy ship in the Mediterranean Sea. In Nigeria, it had been refueled and had picked up his eight team members to deliver them to an unmarked landing zone in a nasty part of Libya.

Their destination was a complete no man's land. The Libyan government didn't control it. ISIS didn't control it. A couple of local militias didn't control it. Instead, all three were fighting for the area, and S3 was about to plop down right in the middle of it.

Oh, this was going to be fun, Nick knew.

CHAPTER FORTY-SIX

A crew chief walked down the center of the helicopter and held up two fingers for Nick to see. Nick could just make him out with the aid of a few dim lights on the walls of the helicopter, which couldn't be seen from the outside. He acknowledged the signal and gave the man a thumbs up.

Nick yelled to Red and told him they had two minutes until they would land, and the signal was passed down the line to the other team members. Many of them made a last-second gear check, but that was nothing but last-minute jitters: their gear had been checked a dozen times already.

The CH-53 Super Stallion seemed to pick up even more speed, then suddenly flared up, slowed dramatically, and landed in the middle of a dusty, barren area. It was an aggressive landing, which told everyone the pilots knew they were in a dangerous area and wanted to get the hell out of there.

Nick and his seven shooters didn't need any encouragement to disembark. Flying in a helicopter in enemy territory is one of the most defenseless and terrifying feelings any combat veteran will ever face. With much relief, the eight members of S3 raced off the helicopter and sprinted down the ramp with all their gear, quickly dropping down into a perimeter.

They scanned their sectors of fire and listened to the helicopter as it roared out of the area. This was officially deep-water shit, Nick thought. There were no Cobra attack choppers circling the landing zone to help them if they came under fire. There were no artillery batteries to call for fire support. And there definitely were no quick reaction teams to come save them.

There wasn't even a way they could call the CH-53 Super Stallion back for a pickup. That flight would be recorded as nothing more than a routine training mission on some circular path across the ocean.

This was a no-shit, completely covert op. In Nigeria, had they been discovered, they could have claimed to be a paramilitary company advising and training the military. But here, they were on their own. America would deny any tie to them. Same as they would have done when Nick, Red, Truck, and Marcus had crossed the mountains into Pakistan.

The eight shooters of S3 continued to scan their sectors, looking for anything that didn't fit in. Given that the place was pretty barren, flat, and without vegetation, there wasn't anything for any enemy fighters to hide behind.

The team members wore local garb and had no form of American identification on them. They did, however, carry American weapons. The thinking behind this was ISIS had captured so many American weapons that it was pointless to carry AK's to fit in. Not to mention, even if they had wanted to switch out their weapons to Soviet-bloc weapons, there simply hadn't been time.

Colonel Owan and his three men were either heading this way with their four Stingers or they had already arrived. Nick also didn't know how many ISIS fighters were in the area. They had some satellite imagery, but that was from hours ago and it couldn't distinguish between fighters and civilians.

But Nick had insisted on immediate deployment. It was too dangerous to send snipers or recon into the area. Not for the snipers or recon element, but for the timeline. The reality was that the timeline was simply too tight, and they only had one opportunity to prevent these missiles from falling into enemy hands. And that was assuming that one opportunity still existed. Owan might have already landed, sold the missiles, and departed.

Nick pulled his night-vision goggles up and scanned the perimeter. He saw nothing, and for once in his life, that was a bad thing.

They were supposed to meet a local asset who would provide them with a truck. This truck was why Nick could only bring eight team members. There simply would have been no way to transport them, and stealing a second vehicle would have alerted locals that something sinister was going on in the area.

Nick had no idea if the CIA asset was a local or an American working undercover behind enemy lines. He really didn't care as long as the man did his job.

But if there was no truck, then this mission had jumped from "reckless, bordering on nearly impossible" to "apocalyptic, no one survives."

Red walked up and took a knee by Nick. Red wore a keffiyeh around his head, same as Nick and the rest of the members. The keffiyehs were traditional Middle Eastern scarves worn around the head by everyone from Arabs to Kurds.

"Tell me those pilots didn't drop us twenty miles away from where we were supposed to land," Nick whispered.

"I don't think so," Red mumbled back quietly. He pulled up a GPS and showed Nick the coordinates through the low-light screen.

Nick double-checked the numbers with a map he had, just to confirm Red was correct. The helicopter had dropped S3 precisely where it should have.

Nick said, "That asset better be here then."

"Well," Red replied, "if he doesn't show up, we're going to have a hell of a lot of fun. And ISIS is going to lose a couple hundred fighters. It'll be a shit-show, no doubt, at least for as long as it lasts."

"It'll last about twelve hours if we're lucky," Nick said, checking his watch. "It'll be daylight in three hours. Damn it, where's he at?"

“Fuck if I know,” Red said. “What do we do?”

“Let’s wait at least fifteen minutes,” Nick said. “If he doesn’t show by that time, then we’re going to be faced with some tough decisions.”

“None of them good,” Red said.

“No doubt about that,” Nick replied.

He scanned their perimeter and could just make out his members. For the mission, they had brought all their Primary Strike Team shooters (Truck, Preacher, Lana, and Bennet). In addition to Nick and Red, that left only two slots that could fit comfortably in the truck with all their gear.

After much discussion, they’d decided to bring Dr. Julia Clayton as one of their members. That would provide them with a doctor on hand to deal with any serious wounds. And they’d finally decided to bring Rider, as well. Rider was a sniper and the squad leader in charge of the sniper teams. He might be a tad older than the other snipers, but he shot nearly as well and had about ten times the experience.

In total, they were six men and two women, all incredibly experienced and among the best in the world at their jobs. But they were about thirty miles from the Libyan port city of Sirte, and it was estimated that within a ten-mile circle of where they lay, there were approximately two thousand ISIS fighters.

Nick certainly hoped they wouldn’t find out exactly how many ISIS fighters were around. Damn it, he thought, a nervousness growing in the pit of his stomach. Where is that guy at?

CHAPTER FORTY-SEVEN

Ten minutes later, two lights appeared in the distance, bouncing up and down across the desert as a vehicle approached them from an unpaved, unimproved road.

"What's he doing with his lights on?" Nick hissed, anger in his voice.

"Beats me," Red said. "It may not be our contact."

Nick gave hand and arm signals to the squad, and the eight-man circular perimeter changed into a linear line of shooters, facing the truck and prepared to light it up with maximum firepower. The truck approached at probably ten or fifteen miles per hour, though Nick wasn't sure if that was because of how rough the road was or because the driver wanted to approach something cautiously. At least the truck was far enough away that its lights were unable to pick up any of the S3 members as they moved into a linear formation.

Still, barren desert or not, the members crawled and dragged their packs to get into position, instead of rising up and bending over as they moved.

A very long sixty seconds later, the truck came within a hundred yards of them. Nick flicked his weapon off safe and heard several other members do the same.

He brought the Aimpoint red dot sight onto the windshield where the driver would be sitting and hoped his M4's bullets would cut through the glass and not ricochet up into the sky, should he have to fire. The truck stopped and cut off its lights. Whoever was driving it, though, kept the motor running.

"This has to be him," Nick said.

"I think so, too," Red said. "Maybe he's just keeping the truck running in case he has to haul balls out of here."

"I hope," Nick said. "Leave your pack, circle out wide, and go find out. Take Rider with you."

A very long five minutes later, the truck turned off its motor. Nick head a tsk, tsk on his radio, the signal for all clear.

Nick flicked his weapon off safe and stood.

"Everybody, grab your gear, and make sure to grab Red and Rider's packs, too," he said.

Nick slung his pack on and walked off to link up

with the truck alone, while the rest of the squad gathered all the team's gear.

Once he got close, Nick saw that the driver appeared to be a man in his fifties, who was clearly brown-skinned and probably Libyan. He was standing outside the vehicle, conversing with Red and Rider when Nick walked up.

"Why did he have his lights on?" Nick asked. "Is he trying to tell everyone within a two-mile area precisely where we are?"

The man raised his eyebrows at Nick with a stupid look on his face.

"He can barely understand English," Red said.

"That's just our luck," Nick said.

"As long as you talk really slow and use simple words," Red replied, "he's fine. I asked him about the lights and he said it would have been more suspicious for him to drive around at night without lights on than to have them off. He also says there are many ISIS fighters in the area, looking for spies and American Special Forces that may helicopter or parachute in."

"They know our playbook," Nick said.

"They ought to," Red said. "We've been kicking their ass with it from one end of Iraq to the other end of Syria."

The rest of the S3 members walked up, struggling to carry all the gear.

"Stage it here," Nick said, pointing to the ground. "And let's move fast."

Nick looked at Red. "Does he know where we're

going?"

Red laughed. "This man doesn't know anything. In one of the few words I was able to make out, he called us English troops. I think he believes we're British SAS."

"That's perfect," Nick said. "Tell him we're going south, and we'll be very careful tonight. Oh, and that we appreciate his assistance."

They were actually going north, but Nick wasn't telling such an amateur about their plans. Especially when he didn't trust the man's allegiance. He had accepted a bribe from the CIA, so nothing would stop him from taking one from ISIS. And worst case scenario, ISIS could torture him until he told the truth.

While Red gestured and spoke slowly to the man, Nick dropped the tailgate of the truck. The truck had a motorcycle in the back of it for the Libyan to ride away.

"Give me a hand," Nick said, and several S3 members walked up, breathing hard from carrying all the gear. Lana jumped in the bed, and Nick climbed up, as well. The two of them rolled the bike backward, where Bennet, Preacher, and Rider grabbed the rear of the bike. They lowered the back wheel to the ground and grabbed the front of the bike from Lana and Nick.

Once the bike was offloaded, Bennet popped out its kickstand and left it standing.

As the S3 members loaded their gear into the truck, Red finished his broken conversation with the Libyan.

The team had survived phase one of their mission: link up and acquire transportation.

Now if they could just keep up that good fortune.

CHAPTER FORTY-EIGHT

The CIA asset wasted no time in kicking the bike to a start and driving back the way he came in a hurry.

"We need to get as far away from here as we can before he gets wherever he's going," Nick said. "Just to be safe."

No one argued with that, and the eight S3 members loaded up. Truck took his seat at the steering wheel and checked the switches to get familiar with the vehicle. Nick sat in the passenger seat and pulled out his map to study it. The rest of the six members of the team took positions in the back.

The team had a good two-hour drive ahead of them, and Nick hoped they wouldn't run into any surprises along the way. He checked his watch, did some math in his head, and thought, "So far, so good.

We should arrive just in time to make our early-morning raid."

Nick's calculations proved correct and they arrived just before dawn to their final checkpoint. Truck parked the Toyota in a low dip. They were in a very rural area, so there wouldn't be a lot of people who could tip their location away to ISIS.

Their entire plan was based on two things: surprise and ferocity. They were counting on the ISIS folks to have their guard down, completely not expecting an attack this far within their controlled territory. Additionally, these ISIS folks had spent the better part of a year fighting militias and undertrained, underpaid Libyan soldiers.

That usually meant both sides fired a ton of rounds at each other, killed a few men with some lucky shots, and then one side would finally break and run. Or, they would end in a painless stalemate in their original positions, take a break, and repeat the same madness the next day.

This pattern the locals had been practicing wouldn't happen today. ISIS would learn what it was like when a professional NBA team dropped by to play ball with the local rec team players, who weren't even good enough to play on the high school junior varsity team. Unless something went drastically wrong, it'd practically be a massacre – much like the battle of Shewan in Afghanistan, when two hundred and fifty Taliban ambushed thirty Marines, using mortars, RPGs, and heavy machine guns. Unfortunately for them, they were up against Marines, and ended up failing to kill a single Marine, while losing more than one hundred and fifty of their own men.

Yet despite the training edge his team would have, Nick still wasn't sure how many ISIS fighters were at the small airfield. Nick would have liked to have had more time to plan some kind of attack. Any kind. But there simply hadn't been time. It was go as quickly as you could or risk missing Owan and losing the chance to grab the missiles back.

Nick told himself that American soldiers had fought across many a field and hill after they successfully landed at Normandy, and they hadn't had time to plan either those attacks out in detail either.

Sometimes, you just spread out in a line and push forward, determined to bust through whatever opposed you.

On the bright side, the target wasn't complicated. It was a rural airfield with an improved dirt runway. The airfield had a single office structure, which was a small mobile home. A single-wide, as they're called in the South. There was also a single hangar, large enough to hold two small planes.

It had doubtlessly been built a decade or more ago to protect a couple of crafts from the harsh winds that often blew in from the Mediterranean. These days, it hid small ISIS-owned planes from the onlooking eyes of U.S. satellites, analysts believed.

Sitting at the final checkpoint, with the truck in

the best low area around, the eight S3 members unloaded and quietly prepared their gear. Dawn was quickly approaching, so they needed to move fast.

"Radio check," Nick said into his lip mike.

Each of the members wore Peltor ear muffs under their keffiyehs. These ear muffs served three purposes. They served as radios, complete with lip mikes, so that the team could communicate. They also served as noise amplifiers of low-level sounds, giving the team almost animal-like, super-power hearing. And if the team started firing, the small intake microphones shut off all sound after eighty decibels were hit. That would protect their hearing from their powerful – and too loud – weapons.

Each member successfully checked in with Nick, proving that their luck had continued a bit longer. First with the link up with the CIA contact. Followed by the safe infiltration by truck, using the cover of night. Now, their gear continued to function as it should, which wasn't always the case on many missions.

Nick tapped his push-to-talk button and said, "Move out."

It was definitely on now.

CHAPTER FORTY-NINE

One thing the CIA hadn't known before departure was how many ISIS fighters would be on site. Analysts had done a quick estimate, looking at satellite images from the days prior and guessed eight to ten men.

But they had warned over and over that this was a low-percentage guess, and could be off the mark by a large magnitude. And, of course, there hadn't been time to do better recon or allow sniper teams to get eyes on the target beforehand, so this was where it would get tricky.

The squad spread out into a line, keeping fifteen yards between each person, and moved slowly away from the safety of their truck and toward the airfield. Sunrise was minutes away, according to Nick's watch, and already it was light enough to see your rifle sights without the requirement of night vision.

ISIS fighters would be waking soon to relieve themselves and feed their growling stomachs, so it was "go" time and Nick felt his adrenaline racing.

Julia was nearest him, but she only carried a pistol for protection. She was already carrying too much weight to go adding a rifle, six magazines, and extra ammunition. Her massive pack was crammed full of medical supplies, containing everything a doctor might need to keep a critically wounded patient alive until better medical care could be obtained. Part of Nick's job, besides overseeing the attack, was keeping Julia alive. She was easily the most critical member of the team. They couldn't lose her, no matter what.

The line of Americans kept moving forward, quietly advancing at a decent pace since the clock was working against them. The mist of dawn was already dissipating, and Nick could now see more than fifty yards over his M4 rifle.

They moved closer and closer, and could soon make out the start of the airfield. Someone had graded the ground, firming it up so it could safely accept small planes landing with no problem.

S3 planned to attack across the airfield so they'd have considerable, nearly-perfect shooting lanes into the small trailer and hanger. Americans specialized in accurate, long-range shooting and fighting. Barely trained terrorists with inaccurate, cheap AKs had little chance against precise, scope-mounted M4s, as long as S3 kept their distance. And they definitely planned to for as long as they could.

Nick strained his eyes, searching for either the hangar or office through the fog, which he knew to be just ahead.

Where is that damn thing, he wondered. The hangar would be to his front, while the office would be to his left. Unless they were off course, but that was nearly impossible given the two GPS's they carried on the team.

He kept walking, same as the rest of the team, the tension mounting. His heartbeat increased higher and higher. Soon, it would start.

He scanned with his Aimpoint scope, but still couldn't see the hangar.

And then he noticed something white. He took two steps further forward and realized it was a black truck, straight to his front. And before he could call a halt, he noticed two more parked near it.

S3's run of good luck had just run out, Nick knew. Those trucks weren't supposed to be here, and that meant there were going to be a hell of a lot more men here than a mere eight or ten. Of that, he was certain. But before he could call a halt and possibly change their plans, he heard over the radio, "I've got an individual to my twelve o'clock." It was Bennet's voice. "Forty yards ahead. He hasn't noticed me yet."

The two buildings were probably a hundred yards ahead, if Nick was estimating correctly, and they needed to be able to see them with their sights before making contact.

"Keep moving," he whispered into the lip mic. "We've got to get closer."

The line surged forward and Nick felt like his heart was going to explode out of his chest. He felt sweat bead up on his forehead and his palms felt slick with sweat. As he quickly walked forward, Nick took deep breaths to control his reflexes and hoped the others were, too. He glanced over at Julia, fearing she was probably the most panicked, but she appeared steady – her Beretta M9 pistol out and aimed at about forty-five degrees toward the ground.

He glanced up and down the line, the morning growing lighter and allowing him to see most of his squad. The line of shooters creeping through the mist looked truly fearsome to him, but that was probably because they looked like crazy jihadis with their head dress, native clothing, and clearly aggressive sweep forward.

Nick was getting closer to the first black vehicle, which had been his objective.

"Julia," he said into his radio, "move toward me and use this truck as cover."

He had to keep her alive, and nothing worked like an engine block to stop incoming bullets. Nick had no more finished his instructions to Julia when Bennet stated – incredibly calmly – "Contact front" through the radio.

Four shots rang out, and they were the sound of an American made M4. Nick felt certain the Delta Force man had dropped his target, killing their first ISIS fighter for the day. Bennet didn't miss. Period. He was that good.

With the silence broken, it was time to go. Nick

sprinted to the first truck, stopping by Julia and leaning across the hood to aim his M4. He could finally see the hangar straight ahead. Through his sight, he saw a man emerging from its darkness, rubbing his eyes and not fully awake. The man carried an AK in his left hand. The distance was probably sixty yards.

Nick centered the Aimpoint red dot on the target's chest and pulled the trigger twice. Before he could even judge the man's reaction, another ISIS fighter burst out of the hangar. He held some kind of bolt action rifle, which looked like it was some German Mauser from World War II. Nick dropped him with a headshot right to his face as the man paused to search for a target.

Never stop in the open, Nick thought.

Other shots were ringing out, up and down the line. So far, it was all outgoing from S3's line, but that would change soon once ISIS realized where the threat was coming from.

Julia slid in closer beside Nick, kneeling and placing her hand on his right shoulder. Nick ignored her, but was glad she was staying as close behind the engine block as possible.

More targets emerged from the hangar, but they were cut down by other S3 shooters before Nick could get his red dot on them.

"We've got enemy coming from the office," Red reported through the radio.

The office was still too far off to the left for Nick to see it, but he didn't have to. He knew where it was based on the satellite images he'd studied.

"Give me three people on the left covering the office," he ordered over the radio. "All others, keep an eye on the hangar. If you can't see targets, for God's sake crawl forward until you can and engage."

The firefight was getting heavier. Bullets pinged and slammed into the truck Nick knelt behind. He ducked momentarily, unable to force himself to stay up as bullets impacted into the truck or snapped past his head. He, as he'd done in dozens of firefights before, somehow willed himself to raise back up and reestablish his firing position.

An ISIS fighter, with a thick black beard, crawled forward out of the hangar, an RPG across his shoulder. Nick fired twice into the crown of his skull. He adjusted his aim and fired four more times into the man's back.

Another ISIS fighter screamed, "Allahu Akbar," and darted for the RPG. He made it to the fighter and was kneeling, reaching for the RPG before Nick could pour four rounds into his body.

Fast little bastard, he thought.

A bearded man wearing a black keffiyeh rushed up to the two men, reaching for the missile launcher. Nick aimed a bit better and sent a bullet into the man's cheek, then another into his temple and ear, which stopped the terrorist's jerky movement completely.

A mound of still bodies lay stacked by the RPG. Nick had been so focused on keeping the enemy away from the RPG that he didn't realize the fire had slackened greatly on the line.

He scanned the hangar's opening, but saw no

more targets. Seeing none, he said over the radio, “Keep the suppressive fire going. Sustained rate. Fire into the shadows.”

As the order was acknowledged, he aimed left into the far reaches of the hanger, keeping his point of aim at knee height into the shadows. Nick began firing, slowing on single shot as he swept from left to right. He tried to put a bullet every couple of feet.

More than likely, there were men back in the shadows that he couldn’t see, and he wanted to drop them while he could. He reached as far to the right as he could shoot without hitting the wall and re-traced his arc to the left, putting bullets into places he couldn’t see. His bolt locked to the rear about halfway back across, signaling his magazine was empty, and he reloaded.

With thirty rounds ready to go, he aimed at the thin, aluminum walls, assuming there might be fighters hiding behind them as well. Quite quickly, he ripped through the mag, walking thirty rounds across it. When the bolt locked to the rear again, he noticed there was little firing happening as he reloaded a fresh mag.

“Cease fire unless you have a target. Now, give me a sitrep, starting from the left,” Nick said, using the shorthand term for situation report.

CHAPTER FIFTY

Each member reported in, stating they hadn't been hit and their sectors were clear. No one from S3 moved. Experience had taught them that the silence following a firefight would often cause a foolish enemy fighter to show themselves, thinking it was all clear.

But that didn't work today. That meant they were all either dead or seriously wounded, or perhaps they were smarter than the typical band of terrorists.

Nick scanned the entire front again, one more time, just to be safe. No one moved or showed themselves. He stood a tad, showing just the smallest part of his body above the truck hood.

The first hints of sunlight had burned away most of the mist and Nick could now see the office easily. Four bodies lay fallen in the doorframe of the building, having tumbled forward on the ground.

They had bravely tried to exit the office and fight their attackers, but they paid the ultimate price. As Nick searched to the right, he counted more than twenty bodies lying either outside the hangar or inside what he could see of it. S3 had definitely caught a substantial number of ISIS fighters here. He wondered how many additional ISIS terrorists within the vicinity might have heard the fighting and be pushing toward their line.

"Give me," he said on the radio, "one man on each flank to watch our nine o'clock and three o'clock. Julia, watch our six o'clock."

Phase one of the op was complete. It had been a shooting gallery and the S3 members had proven all their time on the range had not been futile. Phase two would certainly be riskier.

"Rider, move up," Nick said on the radio. "Everyone else, keep a sharp eye."

Rider ran up to Nick's position, while the rest of the squad covered. Once there, Rider crawled under the truck and took up a prone position, covering the office to their left. He carried a larger caliber M-14 and the two-hundred-yard distance was nothing for the experienced sniper and his scoped rifle.

While Rider kept his sights on the office, Julia was ordered to stay and watch their rear. Nick didn't like leaving a medic with only a pistol to guard the rear, but at the same time he just couldn't afford letting their only doctor charge into the upcoming chaos.

With Rider and Julia set, Nick ordered the squad

to peel off in the radio. Each member ran up to the truck, working in pairs to cover each other.

Finally, the original six members of the Primary Strike Team were assembled at the truck, staying behind it as best they could. Nick didn't want to wait long. Bunched together, they were a vulnerable and tempting target.

"Lead the way, Red," he said. "And be quick about it."

Red jumped to his feet and ran forward with Lana and Truck. They sprinted fifteen yards and hit the deck, spreading out in a line and covering the hangar. Even with the sun working its magic against the mist, much of the hangar's interior remained dark, hidden in shadows.

Once Red, Lana, and Truck were set, Nick, Preacher, and Bennet rushed to the right of them and sprawled out as well.

Working in such a manner – one side covering while the other side moved – the two three-man teams bound forward until they were stacked on the right side of the hangar. There, they stayed out of sight of its opening.

The team waited, while Bennet ran to the back of the building to confirm no ISIS fighters were hiding behind the rear, where they wouldn't have been seen. He jogged back and reported all clear.

The six-man team tightened their stack and Nick whispered, "Red, go when you're ready."

Red took a deep breath and entered the hangar, the rest of the squad following and covering their various assigned sectors. When Nick looked around, there was nothing but bodies lying everywhere in pools of blood, none of them moving. Apparently, the remaining wounded ISIS fighters had bled out.

With none of their peers healthy, there had been no ISIS fighters able to help bandage or stop the bleeding and shock. As S3 worked its way through the hangar, covering each body in case some were playing possum, Nick saw that each and every man in the hangar had either run out or attempted to fight their attackers from within the shadows. Unfortunately for them, they had gone up against a professional force with great optics.

Two planes were sitting in the hangar, covered with blood spatters and bullet holes. S3 members searched them, but they were empty.

With the hangar clear, Nick ordered his Primary Strike Team to check each ISIS fighter's pulse and confirm that they all were dead. While they worked on that, Nick punched the transmit button on his radio.

"Rider, Julia, how's it looking out there?"

"All clear," reported Rider.

Julia responded, "Same."

"Roger," Nick said. "Rider, keep that office covered. We're about to push out of the hangar and clear it."

CHAPTER FIFTY-ONE

They hit the jackpot inside the office.

They tactically entered it, with Red leading again, fully expecting an ugly fight. But only a lone wounded ISIS fighter lay in the corner, holding his chest.

Most importantly, though, the four missiles and Stinger operating system were sitting against the wall on a table.

The wounded ISIS fighter had kicked his weapon away from him in clear surrender and to keep from taking any more shots. He held both hands against his wound tightly, clearly lacking any desire for resistance.

Perhaps paradise, even with all its promised rewards, didn't look so tempting once you started drawing close to its gates. Nick pressed his push-to-talk button. "Julia, get up here with your kit. We've got a prisoner I want you to patch up. Hopefully, we can keep him alive and get some information from him."

"Roger," she said. "On my way."

"Rider, come to the office as well," Nick added.

While they waited for Julia and Rider to jog the couple of hundred yards to them, Nick turned to Red, "Grab two people and use them along with Rider to set up a good perimeter, covering all four directions until we finish in here. Call me if you see any reinforcements heading our way."

"Roger that," Red said, motioning to Preacher and Truck before darting out the door with them. Julia entered and dropped her medical kit near the moaning and frightened man.

Most fundamentalist Muslims became quite antsy about having women near them, but this man was in so much pain that he didn't even appear to notice the presence of the offensive gender. He was pale and sweaty, and there was so much blood around him that Nick wasn't even sure how many shots he might have taken to the chest.

Blood was also oozing from his mouth, and he was probably struggling to keep from choking on it. In Nick's non-expert opinion, it looked as though death could claim him at any moment.

"Hurry up, Julia," Nick said, sharper than he really meant. But they needed to keep this guy alive. "Lana, tell him he's going to be fine. That we've got a helicopter on the way. Give him some hope, something to hang onto."

Lana rattled out something, which Nick assumed was Arabic. But she knew so many of the area and regional languages that even if he didn't speak Arabic, she'd be able to figure it out. She was an academic freak and had devoted herself to the mastering of the languages of the Middle East.

While Lana calmed him and Julia tended to his injuries, Nick stepped away to call Mr. Smith on the encrypted satellite phone.

"Good news," Nick said, once his CIA handler answered. "We've got the missiles and launcher."

"Excellent," Mr. Smith said. "Any casualties?"

"None so far," Nick said, "but we're still half-expecting a counterattack. We have no idea how many ISIS fighters might be in the area. Or if these guys at the airport succeeded in getting a call out to their command."

"Well, hang in there," he said. "I've got a platoon of Marines sitting on a flight deck off the coast, waiting to fly in. They'll help secure the area and we'll get you and those missiles out of there."

"Wait. What about Colonel Owan?" Nick asked.

"Hang on," Mr. Smith replied.

"John!" Mr. Smith yelled, holding the phone away from his face. "Call the National Security Council and the Chairman of the Joint Chiefs of Staff. Tell them we've secured the missiles and the launcher, and we need to immediately launch Operation Sea Rescue to get them out of there."

Nick overheard the man, "John" apparently, say something, but he couldn't make it out. Mr. Smith provided some additional instructions before saying into the phone, "I'm back. Get that perimeter set up and don't lose those missiles no matter what. The helicopter should be there in less than twenty minutes. They've moved the three support ships that were in the Med pretty close to the coast."

"We'll hold," Nick said. "You can count on that. But, what about Colonel Owan?"

"He's clearly gone, and he was never the priority," Mr. Smith said.

Nick didn't see it that way.

"The man led Boko Haram and is smart enough to have acquired missiles that would have killed a several hundred Americans, plus destroy our economy. You're telling me this man isn't pretty high up on our most wanted list?"

"Not even close," Mr. Smith said.

Nick was honestly a bit stunned, but he had his own priorities to focus on right now. "Well, we can argue about this later," Nick said. "I've got to check our perimeter."

CHAPTER FIFTY-TWO

"Red, how's it looking out there?" Nick asked over the radio.

"We're set," Red said. "Spread out nicely, each man completely hidden."

"We've got help on the way," Nick reported back. "There'll be a platoon of Marines here in approximately thirty minutes. Then we can all go home."

"Roger," Red said.

Nick looked back at the wounded ISIS fighter. He looked less pale and had stopped sweating.

"Will he make it?" Nick asked Julia. "He looks like he's coming out of shock."

"I think so. Especially if he's airborne in twenty minutes."

"He'll be a treasure trove of intel, so do whatever you have to do to keep him alive."

She nodded, pulling out another bag of blood expander to pump into his veins. Nick figured she'd been holding back a tad, preserving supplies for S3 in case ISIS showed up with serious numbers. But a twenty-minute extract was better than any of them had expected. Hell, Nick figured they'd be forced to transport the missiles by truck to the coast, assuming they were lucky enough to find them here.

Clearly, Mr. Smith had continued working while S3 flew into Libya and the target area.

"Ask him," Nick said to Lana, "when precisely Colonel Owan was here. As well as when he left. What he was driving. Et cetera. You know the deal."

Lana began talking with the man, asking sharp questions and practically screaming at him whenever he started to object. Nick couldn't make out a single word, but human expressions read loud enough, even if you couldn't understand a word.

Finally, it appeared that the man was willing to talk. Perhaps Lana had told him they'd withhold medical aid or simply leave him here. Nick didn't know, and he certainly didn't care. They needed the information.

Lana looked up.

"He says Owan left last night, headed for Sirte."

"That's not far," Nick said, pulling a map out of a pocket on his assault vest. "Does he know where?"

She asked the man and the two of them conversed some more. Nick quickly handed the map to Lana, who unfolded it for the ISIS fighter. He pointed at a place on the outskirts of Sirte, his finger trembling, but sure. The man babbled something and Lana nodded.

"Owan is hiding in a safehouse about a dozen miles from here," Lana translated. "He also stated there were three men with him, as well as a young girl. They didn't have transportation after flying in on the Cessna, so they bought an old burgundy Land Rover from the ISIS fighters here and were expected to drive to the safehouse."

"Wait," Nick said. "What's this about a girl?"

Lana's eyes flashed, a sudden rage sparking in them as she realized the reason for Nick's raised interest. She quickly laid into the man, fiercely drilling him for more information.

But the extra effort didn't appear to be necessary as the wounded man, who was now looking much more relaxed, was freely offering anything Lana asked for. When the man's speech began to slur, Nick worried that whatever he'd been given for the pain was about to knock him out. Nick looked at Julia.

"Don't worry," she replied, seeing his alarmed look. "This isn't my first rodeo. You've got plenty of time."

And though his speech remained garbled, the man continued to provide Lana and S3 more information.

"He's saying Owan and his men had the girl with them when they arrived yesterday, and that they took her with them."

"No girl was mentioned in the intercepts," Nick said, feeling a knot of panic tightening in his chest.

"He told me they were surprised to see the girl as well," Lana said. "But Owan told the ISIS fighters that they had been entrusted with her care."

Lana looked off, staring at the shot-out window of the office, visibly nauseated.

"Say it," Nick said.

She hesitated, clenching her jaw, but finally said, "He said that it appeared that the girl was being abused based on how she was acting. She kept her eyes downcast. Her clothing had been torn."

Nick balled his fists, tempted to punch the office walls down with his bare knuckles. Not another girl. Not with a guy like Owan.

"Did he say where their final destination was?" Nick asked.

"I already asked," Lana said. "He stated that Owan was being purposefully vague. Just said they were heading to a port to leave the continent and that he hoped the missiles would help ISIS in its fight against the West."

Nick cursed. There were fifty ports in a two-hundred-mile span of where he stood. Guessing the right port would be impossible.

Nick studied the spot the man had pointed at on the map. The supposed safehouse was about two miles from Sirte, the de facto North African capital for ISIS. Sirte overflowed with thousands of ISIS fighters, many of whom had fled from Syria and Iraq when the American air attacks had proven too much in those war zones.

"Ask him if he's sure that they're going to that specific safehouse," Nick said. "If he's willing to bet his life on it, because if we go, we're taking him with us. And if he's lied, we're removing those bandages and IV bags, and we'll be leaving him in a ditch."

Lana translated the words, and the man, despite growing disorientation, still managed to argue back and forth with her some. The overall effort had Nick believing he was being emphatically sincere.

Nick turned away and pressed the transmit button on his gear.

"Red, find someone to replace you on the perimeter and link up with me in the hangar. We need to talk."

"So we're defying orders again, just like in Afghanistan?" Julia asked, stopping Nick in his tracks.

He turned, hesitantly, bracing for an argument.

Even Lana looked uncomfortable, backing away from the wounded man and determined to look anywhere but at the doctor or the tense, old sniper.

"They have a girl, and we need to bag this asshole," he said defensively.

Julia was busy collecting wrappers and putting away her supplies, pausing only briefly to look up and address him.

"I agree," she said, matter-of-factly. "I just wanted to make sure I knew the plan."

And with that, she returned her focus on checking the area around her for debris, peeled off her black gloves, and closed her medical bag.

Nick stood there, pleasantly surprised, watching for a few breaths until his radio suddenly crackled.

"Hey. Where you at?" came Red's voice, shaking Nick back into action.

"On my way," he replied into the radio, quickly exiting the office.

CHAPTER FIFTY-THREE

Red and Nick were huddled inside the hangar, so they could talk privately as well as stay out of sight of any possible responding ISIS reinforcements. If ISIS fighters arrived, Nick wanted to allow them to get close and ambush them – not have his troops caught out in the open.

Nick passed along what he knew about Owan and the girl, then shoved the map toward Red. Nick had circled the supposed target home with a permanent marker. Red examined the map and used his finger to estimate the distance from where they currently waited for pickup.

"It's about twelve miles," Nick said, saving him the effort.

"Which by road," Red said, looking up, "is nothing."

"Assuming there's no checkpoints."

"True."

Red lowered the map and looked off to the side. Nick could tell he was thinking hard, considering the numerous variables involved. The potential for success. The hundreds of things that could go wrong. The counter moves they might have to institute while on the go.

"It's risky," Nick said.

Red nodded his head in his agreement.

Nick looked out the hangar at the dry, barren ground in the distance.

Honestly, it was more than risky. Eight S3 members, pushing closer to the de facto capital of ISIS with its hordes of gunmen. On paper, it was beyond crazy. But maybe that's what gave the mission a chance of success. It would never be expected, assuming ISIS even managed to learn of this raid before they made it to their target.

"Hmmm…" Red glanced at his watch. "We could be there in probably thirty minutes. Maybe fifteen or even ten, depending on the roads. Hit them while they're eating breakfast and still half out of it."

"Assuming we don't make contact on the way in."

"You know my vote," Red said, handing the map back. "Not even sure why you had to ask."

"I asked," Nick said, chuckling, "because someone has to keep me from doing something *too* stupid."

"Damn, boss," said Red. "I'm only one person."

"Good enough," Nick said. "Go check on Julia and the patient. I've got to call Mr. Smith."

Mr. Smith picked up the phone on the first ring, his voice sounded worried.

"How bad is it?" he asked. "Are you under attack?"

Nick then remembered that Mr. Smith hadn't been expecting another call.

"No," Nick said. "Calm down. Everything is fine here. But I have news."

"Can you confirm the missiles are secure? I've got people asking."

"Yes, of course they're secure," Nick replied. "Stop asking stupid questions."

Mr. Smith seemed more frazzled than normal. For a desk-trapped bureaucrat, he was an unusually plucky bastard. Nick had always wondered if, in fact, he'd originally worked as an operative in foreign countries before being promoted to a desk. Why else would he assume such a risk of trying to manage a gunslinger like Nick?

No typical bureaucrat would ever volunteer for such a job. It had career suicide written all over it.

But the four Stingers obviously unnerved him, and Nick couldn't really blame him. It was a terrifying thought to imagine the missiles in the hands of a radical group like ISIS.

"Then what is it?" Mr. Smith growled, attempting to reassert control.

Attaboy, thought Nick. And just like that, the old Mr. Smith was back, grinding his teeth, most likely, and trying to rein in his volatile problem child.

"Here's the situation," Nick explained. "We've

captured a wounded fighter who knows where Colonel Owan is. And best of all, it's only ten miles or so from here."

"Doesn't matter," Mr. Smith said. "He's not the priority. Never was, in fact. We've got the missiles and that was the primary point of this raid. Plus, Boko Haram is in tatters, running for their lives from the coalition. Owan can cower wherever he wants. We'll get to him another day. Or we won't. Regardless, he's insignificant in the grand scheme of things. Let's call this a big win for S3 and America and get you all back safely."

Nick took a deep breath, and said in a low voice, "He has a young girl with him."

Mr. Smith paused with that news.

"Nick," Mr. Smith sighed. "I'm not trying to be an asshole here, but it's one girl. Boko Haram probably kidnapped three hundred in the past five years. Hell, ISIS captured thousands of Yazidi girls in Iraq and Syria. Trust me, you can't save everyone in the world."

Nick watched from inside the hangar as a light wind blew dust across the shoddy runway. He really should have known Mr. Smith would react this way.

"If you won't let us do it for the girl, let us do it for Owan," Nick said. "He's nearby, he doesn't know we're coming, and he's probably exhausted from being on the run the past couple of days. This is our best chance. We can bag and tag this shithead and his motley crew. Wrap this whole operation up nice and clean."

Mr. Smith let out a slight groan.

Nick kept pushing. "Look, I'm tired of wars that don't feel like wins. I'm tired of being on the defense as a country, waiting to get hit again. I'm tired of having bad guys out there for years and years, studying how to kill as many of us as possible. We've got a chance to take this man down, and I want to take it."

"Enough," Mr. Smith curtly responded. "I've let you make your case and the answer is 'no.' You and the seven members with you are to load up and extract with the Marines back to ship. From there, you'll fly back to Nigeria, where you'll pack up the rest of S3 and return to Virginia. The mission is complete. No wild goose chases and no unnecessary risks."

Nick felt like he'd been backhanded.

"I've got to go," Nick said, clicking off the phone. He knew there was no point in arguing. Nick stowed the phone in his pack and issued a series of orders over the radio. Just stick with the plan, Nick told himself.

The squad jumped into gear, scouting and selecting a proper landing zone for the incoming helicopters. Red urged Nick to use part of the airfield near the three ISIS trucks, since those would allow a small place where the missiles and prisoner could be hidden. Nick checked it out and quickly agreed. It looked like a great spot to him.

The launcher and missiles were carried to the landing zone and placed alongside the trucks, on the inboard side of each vehicle. This would keep them hidden if any ISIS fighters scoped out the field with a pair of binoculars prior to an attack.

Once the missiles were safely staged, Red positioned S3 members into a good, wide perimeter, where they were hidden from view and could protect the helicopters once they arrived.

Nick confirmed the perimeter was as solid as possible, given how few men they had, then jogged up to the trucks, taking a knee next to one of them. There, sitting on the ground and leaning up against the truck's front tire, he found Dr. Clayton.

The patched-up ISIS fighter was precariously propped up against the truck's back tire. Though blindfolded, and lightly zip-tied, the man appeared to have finally succumbed to exhaustion and the painkillers. If it hadn't been for the slow rise and fall of his chest, Nick would have thought the man was dead. His slumped position looked extremely uncomfortable, his head lolling to the side and hovering inches above his shoulder.

Julia, on the other hand, was acting odd. She was sitting with her legs folded up loosely in front of her and trembling slightly. Her arms were out straight with each forearm braced on a knee. Spanning the space, each hand clutched an end of a long, ball chain necklace.

The doctor was staring at it blankly and restlessly flicking and snapping the chain, watching as a cylindrical metal pendant spun and tumbled over it in an endless blur. Julia seemed almost hypnotized by the flashing trinket. Enough so that she didn't even register Nick's sudden arrival.

Nick could only kneel, feeling awkward at unintentionally finding himself alone with her. Well, mostly alone, unless you counted the now drooling invalid as an active third party.

After an excessively uncomfortable number of seconds, Nick cleared his throat.

"You alright?" he asked.

Julia didn't respond. She remained fixated on the revolving metal.

"Julia?" he asked.

Her eyes then cleared, blinking several times before she looked over, meeting his concerned gaze. "Oh. Yeah," she finally replied, her wrists and the chain in her hands instantly going slack.

"Sorry," she said. "It's the adrenaline. Shit. I haven't felt like this since my first couple weeks as a surgical resident."

Nick simply nodded in acknowledgement. He knew all about that feeling. Adrenaline was a man's best friend in the heat of the moment. But once that moment was over, there was still the coming down. And while completely unpleasant, the effects could be a bit unsettling and leave a person feeling jittery and out of control.

At this point in his life, Nick was mostly numb to it himself, but he'd seen many men respond poorly to the ebbing off of adrenaline. He'd learned over time that distraction was the best way to push through it.

Nick looked around, tempted to radio Lana or Preacher to come and trade places with him so he could avoid the dreaded chore of chit-chat. Then after a few looming seconds, Nick gave an inward sigh and returned his focus back on the woman, who was again spinning the metal around its chain.

"So, uh," he stuttered, "what you got there?"

Her response was still slow, but came much sooner this time, as she again dropped her wrists and the pendant dropped mid-revolution. Her gaze remained on the object, but her eyes softened and a small smile hinted at the corner of her mouth as she beheld the treasured item.

"Engagement ring," she replied, bringing the chain closer to her face as the smile spread to the whole of her lips.

Nick felt like someone had punched him right in the gut at the news.

CHAPTER FIFTY-FOUR

Nick was still rattled.

And somewhere, deep in his brain, he could just make out his joints screaming for relief. He'd kept his kneeling position now for much too long.

His eyes scanned over the beautiful woman's face and then snapped to the silver piece now just swaying on the dipping chain. Now that he was finally able to get a better look at it, the reeling in Nick's head came to a screeching halt.

Nick gave into his bodily protests, sitting down against the truck. But he'd firmly locked his mouth shut to muffle any old-man groan liable to escape. Once he'd settled a mere foot or so away from her, Nick again looked over to investigate the curiously shaped item.

"But it's a turkey," he blurted incredulously, pointing at it.

"It's not a turkey," Julia snapped, but with slight amusement.

She straightened her legs out in front of her and tilted her hands to provide a better viewing angle.

"It's a peacock."

Nick squinted, looking it over again. He could confirm that it was, in fact, a ring. It had a thin silver band, topped with a flattened, fan-shaped plate of metal. The fan was then engraved with a series of loops and swirls that together portrayed an overall bird-like image. In totality, the piece wasn't cheap enough to have come out of a cereal box or gumball machine, but Nick guessed it hadn't cost much.

Even with how little he knew about such things, it certainly didn't look like the kind of thing a man would give to a woman when proposing marriage. Or at least not the kind of thing a smart man would give a woman.

Nick looked back to the woman's face, meeting her eyes with a look of confused disbelief.

"Look," she started at seeing his expression. "It's just a stand-in. Not that I can really wear jewelry while I'm working, anyway. But even if I could, I'm not going to bring a diamond engagement ring with me to some third-world country, am I?"

That stung a bit, Nick thought. But strangely the revelation that Julia was officially involved with someone else was turning into something more like relief rather than pain.

He didn't really understand why, but somehow this small offering of personal information had helped ease his anxieties about Julia. She was engaged, and that was that. So it didn't matter from here on out if he was into her, or whether she flirted (or didn't flirt) with him. In reality, she was taken.

I guess it's kind of like that closure thing, Nick thought. Whatever it was, it seemed to have set him free from awkward tension, and maybe now he could finally just be himself and talk to this woman like a normal person.

Nick found that he was even smiling a bit as the two of them sat in silence, staring off into the distance. Nick certainly wasn't uncomfortable about the silence anymore.

Out of the corner of his eye, Nick could see Julia looping the chain back around her neck, hooking it back together and lifting the neckline of her shirt to tuck the ring away.

And at least he'd help break her from the post-action adrenaline dump. She leaned her head back against the truck and closed her eyes.

Nick's mind, meanwhile, drifted back to the situation at hand. He glanced at his watch. Now all they could do was wait and hope ISIS didn't intend to retaliate.

Really though, he would have expected any backup forces to have arrived by now. But sitting here waiting, as it always did, gave Nick far too much time to imagine the worst. After all, it wasn't implausible that, given the delay, ISIS might be organizing an advanced response versus some impulsive, rapid reaction.

Then again, it was much more likely that there weren't any ISIS fighters close enough to have heard their strike on the airfield. The location was deep inside the enemy's territory, and therefore not likely to be attacked by enemy forces.

Intelligence stated that most of the ISIS fighters were reported to be on their frontlines, duking it out with other militias and pro-government Libyan forces.

The lack of a reaction suggested to Nick they were safer here than any had expected when they planned the mission. And with his anxieties about possible retaliation evaporating, Nick's mind turned to other worries. Worries about Colonel Owan and the innocent, young girl in his malicious grip. He glanced down at his watch again and did some quick calculating.

By his math, he had only about two minutes left to decide what he was going to do. Obviously Nick didn't have a big moral issue with blowing off orders. In fact, for Nick, the idea that he was even contemplating following orders for once was both bizarre and off putting.

Nick pulled a map of the area from his gear and sighed, staring at it absently. Everything in him was demanding he chase after Owan and capture the man. But the consequences worried him.

Because no matter how hard he tried, Nick couldn't shake the memory of Marcus. And he couldn't ignore the harsh reality of how his last all-out effort in Afghanistan had cost him one of the best men he'd ever known.

It was more than that, though, because not only had Marcus been a fucking outstanding Marine, Nick's own thoughtlessness had cost Nick a real, and true, friend.

Maybe Mr. Smith was right. Nick wondered, did his drive for justice make him too reckless as a leader? Did it make him too dangerous to be allowed to command? Was he somehow going to unwittingly get them all killed today?

CHAPTER FIFTY-FIVE

Nick sighed, much louder than he intended. These were complicated and deadly decisions. And with the loss of Marcus still fresh, Nick was struggling to pull himself together under a looming deadline that was seconds away.

"Hey," Julia said. "Penny for your thoughts? Or would you rather me just guess?"

Nick nearly jumped out of his skin. He had been so lost in his thinking and self-loathing that he'd forgotten she was even there. That she'd possibly been watching him in his unguarded moment.

"Really?" Nick asked defensively. "I've got less than two minutes to make a very difficult decision and you think you can just guess what I'm thinking?"

"Well," she started, shrugging innocently. "Is it really so hard to imagine that I might know?"

Nick grunted.

"I was there too, you know," she continued, keeping her voice soft and controlled. "In Afghanistan. And I also remember what happened. I remember it quite well, actually."

It was a good point, Nick thought, wincing inwardly. Of course she remembered, she'd been the one with Marcus when he'd…

And suddenly Nick was just angry that he had to be the one making these decisions. He was always having to make such decisions. And with having only a matter of seconds to make them in. Damn, he almost wished he hadn't heard about the girl from Lana.

Maybe he could have lived with himself if it was just about Owan's escaping. But the gut-wrenching news about the girl tipped the scales too heavily.

Nick spit on the ground, attempting to get the dusty, dry taste of desert out. He guzzled four big swallows of water from his CamelBak.

"The helicopters," he said, sticking to the practical side of things, "will be here at any moment. So if we decide to rescue the girl and nab Owan, we would need to do some quick planning over the radio with the team members."

"But that's not really anything new for you," she said point-of-fact. "No, I seriously doubt you're stressing over situational challenges. I'd say you're second guessing yourself based on past decisions, and because of what happened to Marcus."

Sometimes Nick really hated how easily women seemed to be able to read his mind. Julia hadn't needed to guess his thoughts. No. she had just flat out stated the absolute truth of the matter without asking a single damn question.

"I'm wondering," he began, though begrudgingly, "what one little girl's life is worth? Is it worth risking the lives of my entire team? What if something happens to Red this time? What would that mean for his wife, or for his two girls?"

Nick sighed heavily. He didn't know why he was sharing all of this with her, but he also didn't know how to stop himself now that the wounds were freshly ripped open.

"I just keep thinking that if it were only my life on the line, this decision wouldn't be so hard to make."

Julia simply nodded, looking ahead with a stoic expression on her face.

"I could even be putting your life at risk," he said, his mouth feeling uncomfortably dry again, although this time he doubted it was because of the dusty air.

It was, after all, a potentially stupid thing for him to say to, but there it was. And at least with the rest of the team all facing outboard, and the nearby prisoner all but dead to the world, there was minimal chance of anyone witnessing him in this vulnerable moment.

But if it bothered Julia, she certainly didn't offer any visible reaction to the statement; she didn't even look at Nick. Neither did she appear surprised or even upset that he had suggested such an idea.

"You forget," Julia said, "that I wasn't exactly in a safe place when we first met. I was in Afghanistan and had already spent more time there than most combat vets. That wasn't exactly the friendliest of places. And every day I knew, that literally at any moment, it could be all over for me."

"And don't forget." she went on, "that my job, has not only brought me face to face with death more times than I can count, but my job demands that I, under oath, fight that beast, head on for the sake of others. And that's on a daily basis and quite often with the shittiest of odds against me. So I know a life or death situation when I see one, Mr. Woods. And all of that has been my choice. So no matter what happens, I made the decision to be where I am."

Damn, Nick thought, feeling a bit dim for not having thought of any of that himself. And not knowing how to appropriately respond, Nick mindlessly lifted his wrist to glance at his watch. But there were no good answers there, only the horrifying realization that he only had a vomit-inducing forty-five seconds to make a decision.

"Nick," Julia said, startling him again, but this time it was because he couldn't remember her ever calling him by his first name. It had always been Mr. Woods.

He turned to look at her as she spoke, "There are always going to be risks, no matter what. Even inaction at times can lead to some unforeseeable consequence. But you know better than anyone that there are so few people even willing to face such unknowns. But still you show up and you do the job. Just like Marcus did. He chose to follow you then," she went on as a small encouraging smile lifted one corner of her mouth. "And I would bet my own turkey ring that he would choose to follow you now."

Nick could only sit there and let the words wash over him. He couldn't even respond to the easy target she'd waved at him regarding her fowl-themed ring.

"The bottom line here," she said slightly leaning toward him and forcing eye contact. "You are Nick Woods. This is what you do. And you do it because no one else is willing to do it. Marcus wouldn't want you to question that, and quite frankly neither do I. You lead, Mr. Woods, and the rest of us will follow."

It had been more of a speech than Nick might have preferred, but he had needed to hear it. He had needed to hear every single word. Medical prowess aside, Dr. Clayton had officially proven how immeasurably valuable she could be to S3, and to Nick as well. Was it possible that he hadn't just lost a friend in Afghanistan, but that he'd also gained one?

He smiled genuinely back at her, as a silent thank you for helping to bolster his resolve.

And with no time to waist, Nick pushed himself to his feet, ready to get back to work. But before he walked away, he turned back to face the doctor.

"Oh, Julia," he said.

"Hmm?"

"I don't think I'd bother with betting that ring," he teased. "I can't imagine you'd get much for it."

"Oh yeah?" she asked, her eyes wide in surprise at the sight of Nick Woods making a joke, of all things. "Well maybe, Mr. Woods, you should stop wasting your time trying to piss me off when you've got bad guy ass to kick."

Nick grinned turned halfway around before he remembered something.

"And, Julia," he said. "Call me Nick."

She smiled back. "You got it, Nick. Now go do your fucking job, before I make you look like our buddy over here," she said thumbing toward the drugged-out ISIS fighter?"

"Deal," Nick said, turning while he could and pushing the press-to-transmit button on his radio.

Using the radio, he quickly updated the S3 members about the fact that Colonel Owan was possibly waiting at a safehouse with three other men and a little girl. He then explained he and Red had decided to go against Mr. Smith's orders and were going to go after Owan and rescue said girl.

And with that, he outlined the plan.

The helicopters arrived just seconds later. Nick had no way to communicate with them, which definitely wasn't ideal. But Marines being Marines, they weren't afraid to answer the call and pick up a group of agents in a foreign country, even if they *did* lack communications with folks on the ground.

And, Marines being Marines, they brought the firepower. With no warning, two Cobra attack helicopters zipped across the airfield, flying so low you never heard them coming. They had no more than passed when two other Cobra attack helicopters screamed across from the other direction, just as low and fast.

Mere seconds later, four Harrier jets streaked across the sky, probably at two thousand feet if Nick had to guess. Soon, all eight attack aircraft were circling and watching for any enemy waiting to ambush the slow-moving, troop-carrying helicopters that were surely following.

Only then did two massive CH-53 choppers fly into the landing zone, quickly bringing their enormous frames to a rest on the ground despite their size. Marines in full assault gear poured from the helicopters, spreading out into a large, circular perimeter.

Nick tugged his keffiyeh off his head and tossed it to Julia.

"Stay here," he said, "and watch our friend."

He jogged up to a tall Marine who stood with his hands on his hips, no long rifle in sight. The man wore a pistol on his hip, but Nick couldn't tell if it was a Beretta M9 or something else since it had a canvass flap over the grip. A radioman stood near the officer, bent over by the weight of a heavy-looking pack that had an antenna sticking out of it.

Even new radios, with all their encryption and battery requirements, weighed a ton. Nick recognized captain bars on the man's collar.

"Didn't expect such a party," Nick said, tipping his head toward the jets and helicopters circling.

"Go big or go home," the captain said.

"Roger that," Nick replied. "By the way, warn your

Marines that my men are dressed as locals and wearing keffiyehs. We don't want any accidents."

The captain turned, grabbed the radio from his man, and yelled something into the horn. It was so loud from the CH-53s, which were sitting on the ground, that Nick couldn't hear him. Nick was surprised the birds hadn't lifted until things were situated on the ground.

Awfully inviting target.

When the captain turned back, Nick yelled over the rotor roar, "Two birds sitting on the ground and you don't seem in any hurry to get those missiles and get out of here? A bit surprising."

"We're hoping," the officer shouted to him, "that those ISIS bastards are stupid enough to come dance with us. We've been sitting on ship four months just praying for a chance to get off and expend some ammo downrange in the real deal. Hell, I bumped the platoon leader off the ground party so I could come."

Nick appreciated the captain's words, instantly respecting the man. Nick would have done the same thing, of course.

"It gets better," the captain continued. "The battalion commander has an entire infantry company – Delta Company – sitting on the ship waiting to fly in and reinforce us. I think the battalion commander is hoping we make contact, too. He's dying to defy the administration and send the whole battalion in. Says we could deal with this 'ISIS in Libya' situation in about three weeks."

"Probably could," Nick agreed.

A deployed battalion of Marines included more than a thousand men, supported by tanks, helicopters, and artillery. If they all landed, they'd indeed start rectifying the ISIS situation in a hurry.

Nick liked the captain, but also knew that sometimes you had to protect people like him from themselves.

"Let me get you those missiles," Nick shouted, "before you go and cause a national security incident."

The captain smiled.

"Probably a good idea," he laughed, pulling out a cigar slowly without the merest hint of worry or concern.

CHAPTER FIFTY-SIX

Nick called in his members of S3 and as they assembled around the missiles to load them, Nick asked the captain in which helicopter he wanted them loaded.

"Place them in that rear one," the captain said.

Working in pairs, the members of S3 carried the missiles and launcher toward the open bay of the rear helicopter.

"Hold up a sec," the captain said to Nick, lifting his arm to stop the S3 members before they reached the cargo hold.

"I have to personally inspect each case. None of us are leaving until all four missiles and the launcher are secured and in my control."

"Fair enough," Nick said.

The missiles were that big of a threat, for sure, and

Nick figured that had S3 *not* had the lethal weaponry, the captain and his men would have torn the shit out of every house on the horizon until they were found. Perhaps that was an additional reason for so much firepower flying overhead.

The plastic cases were unsnapped and the captain inspected each one before sending the S3 members forward to load up the helicopter.

Once all four missiles were inspected and loaded, as well as the launcher, the captain turned to Nick.

"Have your men grab the prisoner and their gear and load up. We'll keep my Marines on the perimeter until the last moment."

"We've had a change of plans," Nick said, hollering into the officer's ear. "We're not leaving with you all. Also, we'll be taking the prisoner with us."

"No one told me that," the captain said. "My boss said to bring your team, the prisoner, and the missiles and launcher back to ship. No ifs, ands, or buts."

Nick tried not to react. Clearly Mr. Smith had anticipated Nick's response to his orders and was using these Marines as a preemptive roadblock to his shenanigans, ensuring S3 returned safely to ship. Nick's quick-thinking skills didn't fail him for once, as he came up with an instant response.

"It just came down," Nick replied, pointing to his encrypted phone. "Straight from my boss while you all were flying in. I doubt he's even informed the ship captain or your boss yet. As you know, we don't work for the same people, and he wouldn't have any way to contact you while you're in the air."

The captain wasn't moved. He'd been around too long. He put his hands on his hips and a finger in Nick's face.

"We're not leaving without you," he said. "Those are my orders and I do what I'm told."

Nick restrained himself from breaking the captain's finger and beating his ass right then and there.

"Call your boss for clarification," Nick said. "My boss has probably contacted yours by now regarding this new development."

Unnoticed by the captain, the S3 members had drifted back to the three trucks after loading up the missiles on the helicopter. While the captain had his back turned, talking with his commander on the ship, two ISIS trucks pulled up next to Nick. He jumped in the passenger seat of the first one and slammed the door.

"See you, captain!" Nick yelled with a grin.

The captain screamed something, but Nick couldn't hear it over the helicopters' rotors.

And as the two trucks drove toward the perimeter, Nick smiled as he thought about the fact that the Marines lacked any vehicles to chase S3 down. Barring opening fire on the two trucks, the Marines couldn't stop them.

"Be ready for a couple of Marines to jump up and try to flag us down," Nick said to Truck. "You know how young and brave those guys can be. Just don't hit any of them."

But the captain must have lacked the time to call his squad leaders before the two trucks sped out of the perimeter. A few perplexed Marines watched the two trucks drive out of the perimeter, but they did nothing.

Young infantry Marines were used to being out of the loop and the last to know. This was probably nothing new to them, unless the Corps has seriously changed since Nick had served.

"I love it when a plan comes together," Nick said, laughing and using his best Hannibal Smith voice from the old *A-Team* television show.

Truck looked over disgusted.

"You need a cigar if you're going to say that. And he was much more handsome and cool."

"Shut up and drive," Nick said, as the wind blew through his hair. He wrapped his keffiyeh around his head again and felt a surge of confidence swell through his body. Their decision had been made and they were all in now.

Nick preferred acting to over-thinking, anyway.

CHAPTER FIFTY-SEVEN

The two trucks sped off toward Sirte, making it about a half mile down the road before they saw the two CH-53 helicopters pick up and leave.

Truck watched them in the rearview mirror.

"There goes our ride," he said.

"We're in our ride," Nick replied.

"And if they don't come back to pick us up in about an hour?"

"Then I guess we'll be looking for a gas station because I don't think we have enough fuel to drive to Nigeria."

"You know how to keep it interesting," Truck said.

"It's the only way to roll."

The two trucks drove down a rough road, which remained empty.

"Where the fuck is everyone?" Red asked over the

radio.

"If we're lucky," Nick replied into his lip mic, "those jets and helos convinced everyone it was in their best interest to stay indoors."

Truck checked his mirrors and said, "Wouldn't it suck if we got smoked by some drone?"

Nick looked over angrily.

"No, seriously," Truck said. "Some friendly fire incident made by some bored drone operator back in Nevada, who thinks he finally hit the jackpot as he watches two trucks full of ISIS fighters pass by on his screen."

The team members were prominently displaying their local attire again, wearing their keffiyehs on their head and keeping their weapons confidently displayed in the back of the truck. Truck had a point in that they *were* trying to look like a gang of local ragtags.

"Unless something has changed," Nick said, "they're only conducting drone strikes on high-value targets, which are approved pretty high up the chain of command. So, no drone operator can just blast us based on his own authority. But thanks for the pleasant thought. Can we now focus on thinking of all the ways this excursion might actually work?"

Truck nodded, looking appropriately stung. Nick hadn't meant to be such an asshole, but Truck's words hadn't caused him to imagine a friendly fire incident. But rather of being betrayed and sold out. After all, they had retrieved the missiles and eliminated Senator Ray Gooden.

If ever a time existed for Mr. Smith to start over with a clean slate, it was now. And if there was ever a place to do it, it was on the outskirts of Sirte, in the shithole of a country known as Libya on the maps. But more accurately depicted as no man's land between warring tribal leaders, militias, and ISIS. No way would any assets be flown in to investigate the incident this close to the main body of ISIS.

Nick's old paranoia was about to fully kick in when he recalled Marcus's words telling him time-after-time that he needed to chill the hell out with that stuff. Marcus had helped him with his paranoia immensely. The big prior Marine Drill Instructor hammered Nick over and over with the fact that Nick getting double-dealt was a single, isolated event. Something that almost never happened.

Nick relaxed the grip on his M4 and thanked his lucky stars he'd crossed paths with Marcus. The man was right – no betrayal was going to happen – and even if Marcus was wrong this time, it wasn't like S3 could do much to prevent a drone strike. If Mr. Smith wanted Nick or any of his men dead, it was as good as done.

Nick extinguished the thought of being betrayed once and for all, then pulled his map out of his cargo pocket and studied it while the trucks continued down the rough, paved road. Pot holes dotted the surface every thirty feet, and Truck swerved their vehicle back-and-forth to dodge them. The second vehicle, driven by Bennet, avoided them as well. The tires on the two trucks were almost worn bare, so hitting a hard pothole could spell disaster.

Did either of the trucks have spare tires? No one had even checked. Shit, Nick thought. Well, to start thinking of all the things that could go wrong on this little mission was not a road he wanted to go down.

The mission exceeded every conceivable safety parameter and there was little point in making a tally of the deficit.

"Take a right up here," Nick said. "We're going to get off this main road and take some back roads to the target house."

Nick and Red had originally planned to take the most direct route to the target home, but Nick had decided he'd rather make sure they avoided any locals, even though it'd take longer. His gut told him that with the helicopters and jets gone, ISIS would soon be sending fighters out to investigate whether the Americans had dropped off any troops.

For that reason, Nick didn't want S3 seen on the road driving away from the landing zone, even if it was in civilian trucks.

CHAPTER FIFTY-EIGHT

The eight members of S3 may have hit the airfield without getting eyes on the target, but Nick planned to follow the rules when they hit the safehouse. He wanted to do some recon and execute this raid by the book to limit the chances of any of them dying.

They stopped the trucks a quarter of a mile from the objective, parking them in a low wadi.

"Red," Nick said into his radio. "Get me some people on the perimeter."

While Red assigned shooters to cover the approaches to the low ground in which they sat, Nick exited the first truck and walked back to the second one, which was parked mere inches from the rear bumper of the first one. Bennet had positioned it as closely as possible so it would remain hidden in the low ground that had formed into a massive ditch due to erosion through the years.

Lana and Julia were in the back of the second truck with the prisoner. The man was still gagged and blindfolded, and, of course, his hands were bound behind his back.

"Lift him up and get that blindfold off him," Nick instructed.

Lana yanked him up and jerked the blindfold off him. Lana always handled prisoners roughly. She did it partly because she didn't want any men getting any ideas that they could make an escape attempt on her, since she was 5'7" and maybe a buck thirty. But she was even rougher with Islamic terrorists because she despised how such men treated their women.

She had explained this once to Nick, and Nick figured she was reflecting on how her mom had been routinely beaten and eventually forced to flee from Saudi Arabia with nothing but a few articles of clothing. Her mother hadn't even been allowed access to her husband's bank account.

The man seemed shocked by Lana's strength, as she had yanked the man's blindfold away so hard, that his nose began to bleed. It had practically been a punch to the bridge of the nose with her left hand, a sharp rip up, and a palm slam with the right hand to shove his head away. All of it with the speed and power of a well-trained martial artist.

"Turn him to face up the hill and point out that home you can just barely see," Nick said.

Lana yanked him around, and when he resisted, she kneed him in the balls with about half-power. As he slumped over in pain, she slammed his head against the cab of the truck simply hard enough to show him she was serious.

"Easy, Lana," Julia said. "The man's been shot."

"He must not be hurt too bad," she said, "or he wouldn't be resisting me."

It indeed *had* looked like he had tried to keep from turning, but maybe he hated having Lana's hands on him. It must be shocking for such a backward, Muslim male to be yanked around by an unknown female who was armed and had her face uncovered.

"We don't have time for this," Nick said. "Ask him to confirm that the house he's looking at is indeed the safehouse where Owan is supposed to be. And remind him that if he's lying, we're yanking his bandages off and tossing him in a ditch to bleed out. He can pray for Allah to rescue him as far as I'm concerned."

Lana removed his gag and rattled off a string of Arabic. He refused to face her, so she slapped his face and torqued his face around. He glanced at Nick, probably saw how little patience Nick had, and finally replied to Lana.

The two talked back and forth and moment, and she turned to Nick.

"It's the right place," she said.

"And he knows we'll drop him in the ditch if he's wrong?" Nick asked.

"Oh, he knows," she said.

"Good," he said. "I need to make a phone call. Julia, can you check the man's vital signs before Lana gets him bound and gagged again."

CHAPTER FIFTY-NINE

Nick directed Red and Bennet to conduct a recon of the home while he called Mr. Smith.

"Don't let them see you," Nick said. "No matter what. We have to keep the element of surprise on our side."

"Roger that," Bennet said.

As the former Delta Force man stepped away to grab some gear from his truck, Red stepped forward and whispered, "You say some of the most obvious shit sometimes."

Nick laughed.

"Hey, I'm about to get my ass chewed by Mr. Smith. Cut me some slack."

Red grinned and took the last few puffs off a cigarette.

"We'll get back quickly with some intel," he said.

"You still want to hit the house in daylight or wait for dark?"

"Depends what Mr. Smith says," Nick replied.

Bennet jogged up to them both and Nick said, "You two be safe."

Bennet wasn't much of a talker, but he nodded curtly and headed off with Red.

Nick turned his encrypted phone on and it vibrated immediately. He'd turned it off as they had driven away from the airfield, since there was no point in talking to Mr. Smith at that point. Mr. Smith would have ordered him back onto the helicopters and he would have been forced to disobey the order.

"Nick here," he chimed.

"What in the hell are you doing?" Mr. Smith yelled.

"Are you out of your fucking mind?"

"Great to hear from you, too," Nick said.

"This isn't some joke. How the hell do you plan on getting out of there, assuming you are lucky enough to survive?"

"I've got a top-notch commander who handles those kinds of details," Nick said, nary a hint of sarcasm in his voice. He actually believed it.

"Are you aware that U.S. Africa Command is all over my ass?" Mr. Smith shouted. "General Leventhal, who's a three-star general in case you forget, is asking what my guys are doing on his terrain on an unapproved mission. He wants to know where you're going and what you plan to do. Not to mention, the Joint Chiefs of Staff and the ship commander are blowing their tops wanting to know about how we're going to safely extract you. Where they'll need to go. When they'll need to go. How much warning will they have. It goes without saying but they're not thrilled to be flying more helos into Libya, pushing their luck again."

"Sorry I'm embarrassing you," Nick said, "but we need to take down Owan and rescue this girl. I'm just reacting to events on the ground."

There was silence for three long seconds, by Nick's count.

"You're not embarrassing me," Mr. Smith replied. "I'm taking full responsibility for this because the last thing I need is for them to believe we've got a rogue unit operating on its own. I've told everyone we've received new information on a high-value target that S3 is about to take down."

"You're going to get promoted when we bring Owan in," Nick said. "The man behind the four stingers; captured by the unit you oversee. Same as we made you look good in Kabul."

During their last mission, Nick had directly disobeyed government orders, which had come straight from the President of the United States. But that move by Nick and S3 had saved Afghanistan's government from falling to a ferocious, surprise attack from the Taliban.

"Let's talk about how we get you out of there," Mr. Smith said. "We can discuss your propensity to be a pain in the ass when you get back."

"What do you prefer?" Nick asked. "We're at the

objective. Red and Bennet doing a quick recon of the home as we speak. We can either hit it now or wait till nightfall. Whichever leads to an easier pickup."

"Let's hit them now," Mr. Smith said. "ISIS is gearing up and preparing to send loads of troops into your area. All that activity at the airfield probably kicked over a hornet's nest."

"Sounds good to me," Nick said. "Where's our exfil point and what's our timetable?"

"Looks like just a hundred yards from you is a good spot," Mr. Smith said.

"How do you know where we are?" Nick asked, glancing up in the sky.

"I've been following you with a drone from the moment your dumb ass made that stupid move. I knew you'd do it, so I pulled some strings to get a couple drones overhead to help cover you. By the way, they've got four Hellfire missiles on tap if you need them."

"See, I told you I had a top-notch commander," Nick said, actually pleased with Mr. Smith.

Mr. Smith didn't acknowledge the statement. "Once you're set to hit the house, we'll start the helos back in. They're being refueled as we speak."

"I love it when a plan comes together," Nick said.

"What's that?" Mr. Smith asked.

"Nothing," Nick replied. "A lame inside joke, apparently."

CHAPTER SIXTY

Bennet and Red returned to Nick with a solid description of the target home. After a couple of questions, Nick developed a plan, passed the word over the radio, and waited for the members on the perimeter to return to the trucks.

The team members made some quick gear adjustments, but there weren't any questions, and there was damn little that needed to be said. These were professional operatives who had trained most of their adult life for missions that veered off course like this.

Julia would be staying with the prisoner, who was bound and gagged in the bed of the truck. Nick didn't like leaving anyone alone, and though the Marine Corps and SEALs always stressed staying in pairs, he saw no other choice in this instance. He needed every gun he could get at the target objective. Nick knew they weren't going far, and Julia had a radio to call for help, as well as a pistol if worse came to worst. She also had the truck keys and could drive toward the house they were hitting.

"Keep your head down, Julia," Nick said. "We'll be back as fast as we can."

She nodded, not a hint of fear present in her big brown eyes.

"I'll be fine. Just try and come back in enough pieces that I can put you back together, alright?"

"Deal," Nick said. He nodded to her and walked back to his men.

After a quick brass check on his M4 and confirming the safety was on, he said, "Let's go."

The team stepped off in a single file, with Red in the lead on point. The home lay a mere quarter-mile away, but only its roof was barely visible from this direction. A small rise in the land would help shield the squad from being spotted for much of their approach. But that rise would end and give way to a flat piece of ground from which they wouldn't be able to hide.

The arid terrain provided shit for cover. As they weren't in the complete desert, there were a few small trees or shrubs here or there, but it still wasn't much. Sirte was a surprisingly dry location, especially considering its proximity to the coast. It clearly received only limited precipitation that blew in from time-to-time.

Nick hoped the need for cover wouldn't be a necessity. He also hoped that their local attire would help them blend in enough, so that if they were somehow spotted, any observer would at least hesitate before opening fire.

The team fit in with their civilian clothing and keffiyeh headwraps, which ranged in color from white to red to black. And though they wore tactical gear with magazine pouches, they didn't wear body armor. Besides, tactical gear was pretty common around here. From a distance, Nick felt confident that they looked like a ragtag group of ISIS fighters moving across the countryside.

This was Libya, a country Owan didn't know, and he was staying in a home provided by ISIS, resting under the safety of their protection. Owan believed he was deep in the heart of ISIS territory with nothing to fear. To him and his men, who were new to the Libyan branch of ISIS, the approaching group would mostly likely appear to be locals.

Furthermore, during the earlier recon, neither Bennet nor Red had seen any local support fighters around the house. As such, Nick presumed it was just Owan and his men in the house. Plus one potentially very scared little girl.

Red set an aggressive pace until they made it about halfway to the target.

"I can clearly see the objective now," Red said over the radio. "Slowing down my pace."

Red also brought his weapon from the ready position in his shoulder to the slung position, across his chest and aimed toward the ground. Each S3 member did the same.

Nick wanted the column to appear relaxed and calm, playing into the ruse that they were friendlies.

Nick could finally see the target home also. It sat alone, with no other structures in the vicinity. In addition, as Nick realized he could see more than a mile ahead, there were no nearby buildings in the distance from any direction. That was very good news. This location at least suggested that there should be few back-up options readily available to aid the cowering Colonel. In all likelihood, S3 should be able to strike fast and be well on their way out of the area before anyone would notice.

The small concrete home was a well-established look in Libya. Probably twelve hundred square feet, with a door at both the rear and front, according to Red and Bennet. It also had windows on all four sides, though they were small, as well.

It bore a flat roof and the majority of the concrete exterior had been bleached near white by the unimpaired and unrelenting sun. All of this, again, was so typical for the area that it was both disappointing and depressing to look at.

S3 continued their march, approaching from the rear, opposite from the driveway and road that lay beyond that. Their prey was literally out in no man's land, with a fierce predator stalking them from behind. And this was just the way Nick liked it.

CHAPTER SIXTY-ONE

Red, still at the front of the column, was only eighty yards from the home when tragedy struck.

The rear door popped open, and an African American male, in green camouflage pants and a blue tank top, stepped out. He wore a pistol of some kind on his hip – probably a 1911 – and hunched over to light a cigarette. He presumably felt pretty secure, so much so that he hadn't even bothered to glance around and check for any kind of danger.

The cigarette lit on his second attempt to draw out a flame from a Zippo lighter. Nick, watching the man's actions closely, whispered into his lip mike, "Everyone keep moving. Act as if nothing's wrong."

The man exhaled a cloud of smoke, squinting, as he lifted his head to take in the early-morning sun.

Instantly, he saw the approaching column. There was a visible flicker of panic in his body, but before he could burst back into the house, Red waved an arm and yelled, "Heyyyyy!" good-naturedly.

The smoker relaxed a moment and waved back warily, his eyes still watching with surprised suspicion.

"Keep walking," Nick whispered over the radio, sensing some hesitation among his members ahead of him.

The man studied the column of seven, their weapons casually held and their pace nice and easy. Red was within fifty yards when the man must have registered something that didn't sit right. He tossed his cigarette and turned, reaching for the handle and attempting to race inside.

"Take him," Nick said over the radio, raising his M4.

But before Nick could get the red Aimpoint dot on target, a series of shots went off behind him and the man stumbled and fell; the wall behind him splattered in blood. Nick glanced back to see that Bennet had stepped to the right of the column and dropped the man before Nick could get a round off.

Fucking Delta Force show-off, he thought, before screaming, "Go! Go!! GO!!! Immediate action, all-out assault!"

S3's plans had officially gone to shit. So much for a surprise raid on an unsuspecting enemy. They'd be lucky if no one got killed now.

But there wasn't time for analysis. Every second

counted. Every second wasted was an opportunity for someone inside to grab a weapon or move to a protected position.

The seven members of S3 sprinted as fast as they could for the rear door. There was nothing tactical about it. Just six men and one woman charging the scene. Thankfully, they weren't carrying the weight of helmets and heavy body armor, so they made good time.

Preacher and Rider were two of the faster sprinters on the squad, so they passed Nick and caught up with Red by the time he reached the door.

I'm not a spring chicken anymore, Nick thought, as he gasped and huffed, watching Red, Preacher, and Rider burst into the home with barely a pause.

CHAPTER SIXTY-TWO

The sound of gunfire rang out from the home almost immediately following the first three S3 shooters making entry. Nick hated not being at the front where he could see what was happening, but he had to trust that Red, Preacher, and Rider could handle their business.

"Lana," Nick said between gasps, "come with me."

The two turned from the rear door, which Bennet and Truck had entered to reinforce the first three S3 members. Shots continued reverberating inside.

Nick hoped none of his men were on the receiving end of any of those shots, as he and Lana sprinted around the back of the house and toward the front.

"Take point," Nick said, slowing up and reaching for the encrypted phone.

Lana rushed past him and turned the corner,

covering the front door. She held her position at the edge of the house so she could dart back for safety if necessary. Then with his back pressed to the concrete wall, Nick tried to call Mr. Smith. But his fingers were struggling to dial the small keys. It was as if his fingers were fumbling and barely functioning.

Fucking adrenaline, he thought. Maybe he wasn't as numb to the rush as he thought. Or maybe they needed to make the keys bigger on this stupid phone. He finally managed to get the number dialed as still more gunfire erupted behind the wall at his back.

"What do you see?" he asked Lana as the phone attempted to connect.

"Nothing," she replied. "All clear. Front door still closed."

The firing continued in the house, but with less ferocity.

The voice of Mr. Smith finally crackled against his ear, and Nick quickly announced, "Our breach is underway. Contact happened before we could set up. We've got fighting happening inside and should expect possible reinforcements to already be moving our way. Get those damn choppers headed our way."

And before Mr. Smith could reply, Nick ended the call. He stowed the phone and moved around the corner to join Lana, raising his rifle to help cover the front.

Suddenly there was yelling from inside, but it was muffled and Nick couldn't make out the words or voice. With great force, the front door was flung open and a tall African American backed out, dragging a young girl with him.

His left arm was tight around her neck, carelessly choking her without regard to her safety. His right arm yanked up and he fired a pistol back through the door. Once. Twice. Three times.

Nick acted. He shoved Lana aside and squared himself up, perpendicular to his target. The shot Nick intended to make was nearly impossible, and extremely risky. He'd have preferred to be prone with a sniper rifle if he was going to be shooting at a moving target with a young girl's life at stake.

But this asshole, who he now recognized through his Aimpoint sight to be Colonel Owan, was firing at S3 members. And Nick just couldn't allow that shit. Period.

He also couldn't allow Lana to take a shot that would probably kill a young girl. If that happened, Nick wanted it on his head. Not her's.

The red dot found Owan's head, its owner still oblivious to the threat at his flank, and Nick pulled the trigger. The red aiming point had been roughly on Owan's ear when Nick pulled the trigger, but the man had continued moving backward, attempting to fire again.

Who knew where the impact actually landed, but it had been effective. The man instantly dropped and the girl fell back in a tangle of legs and limbs before Nick could fire again.

Nick sprinted forward hoping to grab the girl before Owan could hurt her in some final, desperate act. Assuming Nick hadn't already shot her. The thought caused a flutter of fear in his chest.

But Nick couldn't allow the innocent blood on Lana's hands. She would have never attempted the highly dangerous shot herself, and for good reason. Not even one of the famed Delta Force shooters or SEAL Team Six operatives would have been comfortable making such a shot.

And Nick certainly wasn't either, but seeing Owan squeezing off round after round at his men had spurred him into taking desperate measures. He just hoped and prayed he hadn't hit the girl. That Owan hadn't yanked her up into the line of fire or somehow tripped before the bullet left the barrel.

Nick wanted to sigh in relief as the girl suddenly started screaming and squirming to unearth herself out from under the large, fallen man. Nick slowed, two feet away, his entire focus drifting back to Owan. His rifle remained up, covering what little he could see of the man.

Owan's face was covered in blood. The whimpering girl, now scrambling backward toward Nick and away from her captor, thankfully appeared to be unhurt by the shot. She gave a startled shriek when she nearly backed right into a man holding a gun. She was in such a state that her mind hadn't even registered Nick standing there.

Nick quickly grabbed the girl with his left hand, holding her upper arm tightly. The last thing he needed was for her to bolt and run from him, too.

He pulled her back, while keeping his sights trained on the fallen man before him. When the girl made no effort to fight him, Nick lightened his grip and guided her to stand behind him.

"House is clear, boss," Red's voice announced from behind him. Nick didn't turn. Instead, he kept his rifle aimed at Owan's lifeless body. By the amount of blood, Nick must have landed a great shot but he couldn't be sure.

Then off to his side, Lana suddenly yelled, "Here they come!"

"Red," Nick said. "Deploy everyone while I deal with Owan."

CHAPTER SIXTY-THREE

Nick risked taking his eyes off Owan and saw at least six or eight trucks barreling straight toward them. They were going to be in deep shit against that many fighters.

He reached down and placed his fingers on Owan's neck, discovering a surprisingly strong pulse. But that still didn't tell Nick how bad off the downed man was. Nick had, after all, attempted to put a bullet in the man's brain. So it was anyone's guess how long Owan might live, or if he would live at all. But the presence of a strong pulse at least carried a small glimmer of hope with it.

If they could get him back safely, the man would certainly be a treasure trove of intelligence on ISIS and the remainder of Boko Haram's terrorist network.

Nick released his rifle and allowed it to hang

across his chest as he grabbed the little girl's hand and pulled her toward the home. Red was yelling and pointing out positions as S3 readied themselves for the threat racing toward them. The trucks had closed to a thousand yards away.

Fuck, Nick thought.

Noting their blazing pace, Nick picked the girl up and ran her into the house. The floor was covered with dead men and blood decorated the walls. Some instinct, of unknown origin, reared up inside Nick, and he shielded the girl's eyes with his free hand. The two raced by the gore and into a room on the other side of the home. Just by the rear door, Nick managed to find a small room that had been miraculously spared of the surrounding horrors.

He placed the girl down, squatting to check her quickly for any pressing injuries. Part of her face was coated in dirt. Her hands, forearms, and knees bared a similar likeness, the result of sweaty skin making contact with loose earth.

Now that he was able to really look at her, Nick guessed that she couldn't have been more than ten years old. But as he twisted her and checked her back, he saw no wounds or blood that appeared to be coming from her. There was some of Owan's blood on the back of her shirt, but that was to be expected. Otherwise, she appeared fine.

Nick turned her back to face him and said, "You lay down. Just as low as you can. And don't move no matter what. I'll be back for you."

"Yes, sir," she replied.

Nick sighed in relief, thankful that Nigeria was rife with English-speaking people.

That settled, Nick ran back around the corner to grab Owan. He planned to drag the huge man in the home, then flexcuff him and bandage his wound.

But just as Nick hurried around the corner, a chair swung around and slammed into his face, knocking him completely off his feet and onto his back.

Motherfucker, he thought, as his head rang like a bell and blood poured from his nose and mouth. Nick's hands had been on his weapon, so he hadn't even gotten them up to block or slow the attack.

In his mouth, he tasted blood and felt loose teeth. And he knew his nose was shattered into who knew how many pieces.

Owan stood above him, laughing. Nick tried to get his hands behind him to stand, but his body would not respond. This was, without question, the mother of all concussions.

Owan wiped his sleeve across his forehead, where blood continued to pour from. That was when Nick realized that his shot had grazed deeply into the man's forehead. And considering the large quantity of blood, plus the fact that the shot had knocked Owan out temporarily, Nick guessed that the bullet had bit deep enough to hit bone, but then ricocheted right off the big man's skull.

Such things were known to happen, especially with the insanely high velocity of 5.56 rounds, but Nick still knew that Owan was one lucky bastard.

He had clearly come to his senses and made his

way into the home while Nick was at the back of the house and the rest of S3 was beyond him, facing the oncoming threat.

Then a roar of fire erupted outside and to the front of the home, the battle clearly underway. Nick again tried to get to his feet before this big bastard killed him, but his head was still swirling, his limbs heavy and uncooperative.

Owan bent down and removed Nick's pistol, slinging it across the room. The man then unsnapped Nick's M4 from its assault sling. It was like watching a scene in a movie. He could see what was happening, but felt utterly powerless to stop it.

Come on, he screamed to himself, finally forcing himself to make a reach for the rifle to stop his attacker. But Owan easily batted his clumsy hands away, as if he were a child, and punched him hard with another massive blow to the face. Nick's head slammed back into the ground, and he nearly blacked out from the pain.

Owan was turning the M4 around to aim it at Nick, but blood was pouring from the wound on Owan's forehead and into his eyes. He leaned his head to the side, trying to wipe his forehead again with his already blood-drenched sleeve.

He lifted the M4 and aimed it at Nick.

Nick kicked out at Owan's knee, but his legs lacked any real power. His boot connected, but failed to even make the man's knee wobble. Owan laughed and stepped back, lifting the rifle again.

Owan was out of kicking range now and Nick

knew he was fucked beyond measure. He had no pistol. He couldn't control his body, he couldn't hear or focus, and the pain from his nose and mouth screamed in a jarring protest, adding to the chaos in his brain.

He was going to die in this shithole of Libya, which was only marginally better than dying in the shithole that was Nigeria.

And he was going to die to the hands of a street thug, and by his own weapon.

CHAPTER SIXTY-FOUR

Owan lifted the M4 again. He aimed, placed his finger on the trigger, and pulled it.

The gun clicked, but didn't fire. Owan looked down, angry.

Of course, the weapon was on safe. Nick involuntarily switched it to safe every time that he wasn't engaging a target. Just an old Marine habit that had possibly saved countless lives through the years.

Owan tilted the weapon and glanced at the selector switch. He smiled, wiped more blood from his forehead so he could see, and clicked the weapon on semi fire. Nick had to do something, anything.

What could he do though? Owan was ten feet away and Nick's own limbs were reluctant to obey him.

Owan lifted the M4 and aimed again. And Nick

did the only thing he could think to do. He raised his right hand to stop Owan from firing, while remaining propped up slightly with his left arm. Owan paused a moment, looking at him curiously.

"You can't shoot me," Nick said. "My friends will hear you and come in here after you."

Owan also understood English as Nick watched him look down at the rifle and process what he had heard. There was still a tremendous amount of firing outside, but the M4 fired inside the house would resonate like a cannon in the sparsely furnished home, summoning S3 members to investigate.

Owan clearly came up with a better solution, as he stepped forward and lifted the barrel. His face went cold and his eyes appeared to darken, becoming wild and murderous. He quickly lifted the rifle over his head, its buttstock aimed right for Nick's head.

It looked as if he was about to thrust a heavy shovel into a particular piece of hard ground.

Nick's thoughts were still muddled, but he could see what was taking place. Owan would use the buttstock of the M4 to crack open Nick's skull. Some thought the M4's retracting stock was too fragile for such an act, but Nick had heard stories of it being done. And Nick was about to become one more piece of evidence backing up that possibility.

Nick could only watch his attacker's movements in horror. Time then seemed to slow, and Nick's mind blitzed through a series of memories, blurry snapshots of what few happy memories he had. But some bits were easier to make out. The faces of those he'd lost: his old spotter, Nolan Flynn; his loving wife, Anne; the quiet shooter from Puerto Rico, nicknamed "Lizard."

And then there was Marcus, whose still visage seemed to slowly come to life. And suddenly Nick was back at Bagram Airfield in Afghanistan. Marcus was laughing, falling all over himself, lost in joy and amusement as he regaled Nick with the tale of Red and the chair that had fought back.

In what was potentially his last moments on this Earth, Nick held tight to that memory, pausing it so he could burn every detail of it permanently into his brain.

And then the image began to move again. Marcus, or rather memory-Marcus, turned to face Nick, a smile still anchored in one corner of his mouth.

"This is how you're gonna go down, bro?" the memory-man asked teasingly, its smile growing larger. "To a chump like this guy? It took a damn tank to take my bad ass out! I thought you came to play, brother."

The vision began to fade and Nick bared his teeth at the challenge. He felt a growing and familiar rage rise up and lick furiously through his veins, like a match to gasoline. This devil dog was ready to fight. And as time resumed its unforgiving pace, the image of his friend gave way to reality.

His head now clearer, Nick braced himself for action, knowing that the stock was speeding toward his face and that it would kill him after the second or third blow.

Okay, Nick told himself, time to make this body move. Right. Fucking. Now.

Nick yanked his head to the left and the buttstock slammed into the home's solid wall, cracking it and sending pieces of old concrete flying. Owan lifted the rifle to strike again, but Nick's right arm snaked up and grabbed him between the legs. Nick felt what he was looking for and squeezed with all the muscle he could muster.

Owan yowled, but still managed to slam the rifle down. It caught Nick right in the chest, and it hurt like a bastard. Nick wasn't wearing body armor and he wondered if the strike had cracked his sternum.

He felt his strength falter with the blow, but Nick refused to release his grip.

Owan lifted the weapon higher to drive the stock down even harder. Nick wouldn't survive another blow. He knew it.

Desperation again took over and a fresh, though noticeably weaker, wave of adrenaline rushed through his body. Nick summoned his last bit of strength and raised up higher, wrapping his other hand around Owan's jewels. Nick squeezed with all his might, and with two hands, he felt he was finally getting somewhere.

The combined force of using two hands was more than Owan could take. He screamed and doubled over in pain, the M4 clattering to the ground.

Owan grabbed at Nick's wrists, wrenching apart the chokehold with little effort. Unfortunately for Owan, though, he missed the fact that Nick was already letting go.

Nick's free hands shot up toward Owan's exposed face, his thumbs driving into each eye socket of Owan. The man tried to pull back and stand up straight, but Nick held on tighter to the side of the man's head.

Nick pushed harder and harder with his thumbs into Owan's eyes. Screaming, Owan jerked back so hard that he lifted Nick to his feet, but Nick somehow retained his grip on Owan's head.

Nick's wobbly legs informed him that if he let go, he was a dead man. This brute wouldn't hesitate to kill him the next chance he got.

Suddenly, a small figured barreled through the open front door. It was Red.

Nick watched in his peripheral vision as Red ran forward and, before Owan could turn, kicked Owan in the side of the knee, dropping him with ease. Red elbowed the brute, applied a wrist lock, and flipped him to his back, applying a pair of flexcuffs to the man as if he were nothing more than a six-year-old kid.

Nick collapsed to the ground, shaken, and realized the firing outside had stopped.

"Fuck me," Red said. "You look like hell, Boss."

Nick felt his face gingerly and looked around for his M4. He remembered his pistol had been tossed, too, but his brain was back into the haze of the concussion. Where was the pistol? And what had happened outside?

"We stopped them," Red said, seemingly able to

read Nick's mind. Red stepped across Nick's legs and handed the rifle over.

Red snapped the M4 back into Nick's assault sling and said, not entirely joking, "You sure you can handle this?"

"Just make sure it's on safe," Nick mumbled through a bloody and mauled mouth. "And help me find my pistol."

CHAPTER SIXTY-FIVE

Nick barely remembered the next few days.

He was groggy and out of it when the Marine Corps helos arrived. Then he was drugged and semi-comatose when the medics conducted a partial facial reconstruction.

He had been told what hospital he was in, as well as what country, but with the drug-induced dreams and daytime hallucinations, he couldn't recall anything with much certainty. Had they said he was in Germany?

One thing he did remember was being alive enough to at least register an explosive string of curses and some concerned yet berating words from Dr. Clayton.

And while he couldn't be completely sure, Nick had a very strong suspicion that Red had once again seen to everything. From organizing the team's departure after the raid to getting everyone back to Virginia, minus their leader and the one wounded member from 1st Squad who'd taken a bullet in the shoulder.

Nick gingerly touched his nose and face, but it was covered with bandages and numb to the touch. The only way he was going to discover the full damage to his face would be via a mirror, and Nick wasn't ready to face that stark reality just yet.

Nick wanted to get up, but that drained, lethargic feeling was drawing him down, down, down. Just as his eyes were about to close again, the door to his room opened and in walked Julia.

"So the bloody nightmare is finally awake?" she said more joking than angry.

And despite the sharp sting he felt when the split in his lip reopened, all Nick could do was smile.

Julia clasped her hands around his.

"How you feeling?" she asked.

"Am I going to live?" he asked.

"For at least a little longer," she replied, smiling.

"Where's Red and the rest of S3?"

"Back in Virginia. He's taking care of everything."

Nick nodded. So he'd guessed right about Red stepping up.

"Owan?" he asked.

"Colonel Owan and the other ISIS prisoner both survived and are currently being interrogated. Owan took a while to crack, but from what I can gather, his information is going to be huge in helping the coalition nations finish off Boko Haram. And apparently that ISIS fighter had some useful details about the command structure of ISIS in Libya."

"They launching raids yet against them in Libya?" Nick asked.

"Well, I don't know for sure, and it's probably classified anyway, but my best guess would be yes," she said.

"How's Cooper?" he asked, referring to the other injured S3 member in 1st Squad.

"Recovering nicely. He's already flown back to the States. You and I are the only ones left in Germany."

Sleep continued to try and sweet-talk Nick back into its narcotic arms. But he still had more questions, so Nick pushed himself up into a straighter sitting position and took a couple of deep breaths to help him stay awake.

"What's my condition?" he asked.

"You're recovering from a *very* serious concussion. That chair did a number on you. We've kept you sedated so that you'd actually stay in bed. Do you remember how many times you tried to leave the hospital?"

"Uhh," he replied, feeling a bit alarmed. Nick really didn't like having that blank spot in his memory.

He lifted his left arm and gestured toward the IV tube in his arm, hoping to address his most pressing and present concern, while also avoiding any more revelations about his behavior while under the influence.

"I'm starving," he said. "Assuming this is all I've

been eating the past few days, do you think we could get a pizza up in here, and some Mountain Dew, as well?"

Julia grinned. "I think we might be able to pull something together," she said.

EPILOGUE

Nick traveled up the driveway and past the farmhouse at the top of the hill in his red Jeep Grand Cherokee. He waved to guards he knew would be watching his every move on a collage of monitors.

It was late. Nearly midnight. Nick had still been exhausted and used the majority of the flight back to try and sleep. But the few times he had been awake, Nick had enjoyed the new, relaxed, and friendly nature of his and Julia's relationship. He'd been surprised at how often she made him laugh, something, Nick admitted, wasn't all that easy to do.

So while some small part of him had probably been disappointed, maybe even a bit devastated, at the discovery of the doctor's engagement, a much larger part of him was feeling surprisingly grateful at the chance to simply get to know her without any games. It was a strange feeling, but it was one that Nick was determined, for once, to try and learn to embrace.

Nick felt lucky to be alive, and elated to be back in the States. But the sudden quiet of the rural scenery had his senses screaming. He felt paranoid driving down this dark road where potential ambush sites lay around every corner.

Nick was about to berate himself when he then began to imagine what Anne would have to say. He could see her smiling, telling him that everything was going to be alright.

Nick grinned at the thought and reminded himself that all he needed was time. And before long, he'd feel much more accepting of normal life and the safety it promised. Then, as it always seemed to do, his mind moved from Anne and back to Isabella, and without realizing it, he found himself thinking about Julia as well.

Well, he thought, you're back to square one in the love department. He doubted he'd really ever see Isabella again – Mexico was a long distance away – and Julia had that ring.

Wow. It had never really hit him before how few women Nick knew. And that realization, one that offered him so little hope for a possible future, left him feeling a bit lonely and listless.

Nick still felt a little melancholy as he headed toward his trailer at the end of the two rows. No cars were around, as everyone had gone home for the night many hours ago.

Note to self, Nick thought, try not to return from future missions all by yourself at nearly midnight. Otherwise, you might as well take depression up as a hobby.

Well, he had a bottle of Jack that might help keep him company. And another one if the first bottle wasn't enough. Maybe he'd drink himself silly. He'd earned another day off tomorrow. Besides, Red could handle things for another day.

But as he pulled up to his trailer, he saw two men smoking and recognized Red and Allen. He parked and climbed out, his spirit immediately lifted.

"About time," Allen said.

Before Nick could reply, Red shot out, "The things a man will do to get out of working."

Nick hugged them both a little more eagerly than he considered respectable, but damn, these were his friends, and this was his home.

And over a couple of celebratory drinks with the two, and many more laughs, he'd learn that Boko Haram was on the ropes, the FBI had no leads in the investigation into the shooting of Senator Ray Gooden, and Mr. Smith was already bitching, wondering when S3 would be ready to deploy again.

"Some things never change," Nick said, after Red mentioned the latter point.

But, truth be told, even with Mr. Smith's incessant harassment, Nick wouldn't change a thing. No, Nick wouldn't be needing the lone solace from the bottle of Jack tonight. Not when he had friends like these to share a drink with.

Nick was realizing that he was, in fact, home. And he knew as sure as he was standing there that Marcus, as well as all the others he had lost, would always be here with him.

S3 was his family now, and as long as he had that, he really didn't feel like he needed to worry about what or who he didn't have in his life.

After all, fate had brought him Allen, Red, and the rest of S3 without Nick really looking for any of them. So maybe it was a little bit shortsighted to believe that his future would be determined by his limited imagination.

The three men chatted on, when Nick thought to ask about the little girl.

"She's been returned to her family," Allen said, "after receiving some minor medical care. She'll be fine, though I'm sure she'll need some counseling. But the doctors say she's really tough, and they expect her to adjust without serious issue."

"I love it when a plan comes together," Nick said.

Red and Allen lifted their glasses to that, and the three spent the next couple of hours joking, laughing, and recounting the mission into Nigeria.

Nick could barely keep a smile off his face. It didn't matter where they were sent next, or how quickly. As long as Nick was with these guys, he'd be more than alright.

THE END

A REQUEST FROM THE AUTHOR

If you enjoyed "Nigerian Terror (Nick Woods, No.4)" please consider dropping a short review of it on Amazon. Reviews go miles and miles toward helping readers discover new authors, such as Mitchell.

BOOKS BY STAN R. MITCHELL

Sold Out (Nick Woods, No. 1)
Mexican Heat (Nick Woods, No. 2)
Afghan Storm (Nick Woods, No.3)
Nigerian Terror (Nick Woods, No.4)

Little Man, and the Dixon County War

Detective Danny Acuff, (Book 1)
Detective Danny Acuff, (Book 2)
Detective Danny Acuff, (Book 3)
Detective Danny Acuff, (Book 4)
Detective Danny Acuff, (Book 5)

Soldier On

Learn more about Stan R. Mitchell and his other works at http://stanrmitchell.com

ABOUT THE AUTHOR

Stan R. Mitchell, a prior infantry Marine, is best known for his rapid-paced writing style.

Mitchell learned to quickly hook the reader during his decade as a print journalist in the newspaper business. Faced with limited space requirements for nearly every article, he honed his skills at getting a story off the ground rapidly and bringing it to a speedy conclusion.

Mitchell is best known for his Nick Woods Marine Sniper series, which has remained in the Top 100 on Amazon for more than three years. The series has also been picked up by Audible.com for a multi-book audio deal.

Additional works include a Western thriller, detective series, and World War II story.

Mitchell cites James Patterson, Vince Flynn, and Stephen Hunter as his favorite authors and influences.

When Mitchell isn't writing, he's lifting, fishing, or practicing martial arts. His favorite styles are Isshin-Ryu Karate and Shaolin Kung Fu; though on some days, it's Krav Maga or Jeet Kune Do or Kajukenbo or Muay Thai. (He wholeheartedly confesses to being a martial arts addict.)

You can learn more about the author at http://stanrmitchell.com.